SPOOKY

The Spookiest Campfire Stories

Forty Frightening Tales Told by the Firelight

S. E. SCHLOSSER

ILLUSTRATED BY PAUL G. HOFFMAN

FALCONGUIDES

GUILFORD, CONNECTICUT
HELENA, MONTANA

FALCONGUIDES®

An imprint of The Rowman & Littlefield Publishing Group, Inc.
4501 Forbes Blvd., Ste. 200
Lanham, MD 20706
www.rowman.com

Falcon and FalconGuides are registered trademarks and Make Adventure Your Story is a trademark of The Rowman & Littlefield Publishing Group, Inc.

Distrubuted by NATIONAL BOOK NETWORK

Text © 2018 by S. E. Schlosser

Illustrations by Paul G. Hoffman © The Rowman & Littlefield Publishing Group, Inc.

The following stories were reprinted in accordance with public domain law in the USA:
The Masque of the Red Death. Poe, Edgar Allan, 1809–1849. *The Mask of the Red Death. A Fantasy.* (First printing). Philadelphia: Graham's Magazine, 1842, May (vol. XX, no. 5).
The Trial for Murder. Original title: *To Be Taken With a Grain of Salt.* Dickens, Charles, 1812–1870. *Charles Dickens's New Christmas Story: Dr. Marigold's Prescriptions.* (First printing) New York: Harper & Brothers, Publishers, 1866.
Dracula's Guest. Stoker, Bram, 1847–1912. *Dracula's Guest and other Weird Tales.* (First printing) London: George Routledge & Sons, 1914.
The Robber Bridegroom. English translation: Grimm, Jacob, 1785–1863 and Grimm, Wilhelm, 1786–1859. Translator: Hunt, Alfred William, Mrs., 1831–1912. *Grimm's household tales with the author's notes.* London: G. Bell, 1884. Translation first published in 1884.
The Legend of Sleepy Hollow. Irving, Washington, 1783–1859.
The *Sketch-Book of Geoffrey Crayon, Esq.* (First printing.) Paris: Baudry's European Library, 1836.

British Library Cataloguing-in-Publication Information available

Library of Congress Cataloging-in-Publication Data available

ISBN 978-1-4930-3268-6 (paperback)
ISBN 978-1-4930-3269-3 (e-book)

♾™ The paper used in this publication meets the minimum requirements of American National Standard for Information Sciences—Permanence of Paper for Printed Library Materials, ANSI/NISO Z39.48-1992.

Printed in the United States of America

Contents

PART THREE: S. E. SCHLOSSER'S FAVORITE CLASSIC
HORROR STORIES

Introduction

The flickering flames made strange patterns of shadow and light on the eager faces surrounding the campfire. Two guitarists sat on the rough logs dragged into the clearing to use as benches; tuning up while groups of people clustered around the fire roasting marshmallows. Those adept at outdoor cookery brought their toasty marshmallows to a nearby table filled with graham crackers and chocolate bars to make S'mores. Those whose eagerness outpaced their culinary skills used creative means to extinguish their flaming food before it ignited the woods around them.

I sat by the musicians with my feet near the crackling fire, rehearsing lines from the list of ghost stories I'd prepared for the Halloween outing. The teens from our youth group were already partially spooked by being out in the woods after dark. By the time I finished telling spooky tales, they'd be clamoring for a police escort to walk them across the darkened ball field to the parking lot!

Gradually the hubbub died as sated S'More eaters found seats in the flickering shadows and the music began. Campfire songs—old and new—filled the crisp air. I listened to the happy voices around me, saving my own for the storytelling, and sighed with contentment. There was no place in the world I'd rather be

1

than right here right now, I thought, fingering the list of spooky stories I planned to share after the singing.

The list of spooky stories that I composed for my Halloween outing that cool October night looked very similar to the Table of Contents in this collection of Spookiest Campfire Stories. Vengeful ghosts like Mary Whales and the Bell Ringer topped the rather ragged notebook paper clutched in my hands. Lurking dangers like the Wraith in the Creek and the Jack O'Lantern were right below; followed by tales of heart-catching suspense such as Initiation and Rubberoo.

The cast of characters ranged from jilted lovers to vampires; witches to werewolves; murderers to monsters. One poor fellow had every single hair plucked from his body by his brother's ghost. (Not a pretty sight.) And Bloody Mary also shows up in various forms. Two very different regional tales explain her origins (Bloody Mary and Mary Whales) while a third story gives a gentle nod to her influence in a modern tale of black magic. (Shattered)

Last but not least, my list contained five of my favorite classic tales of horror. The Headless Horseman of Sleepy Hollow, the towering Red Death, a stalking vampire and the cannibal bridegroom from the Brother's Grimm were all present and accounted for.

The biggest question I had: Where should I begin?

As the last notes of the last song died away, I folded the crumpled paper in my hand and stood up to face the wide-eyed youth group. I exchanged a mischievous look with the adult leaders lurking in the background and started with the first story on my list.

"There was something odd in the tone of the dispatcher's voice when he called to tell me a person needed picking up at Bramlett Road," I began, the firelight casting shadows across my face. The dark woods grew still and silent around us as I continued my tale. From the far side of the fire, someone whimpered softly and was promptly hushed by their neighbor.

Oh honey, you ain't heard nothing yet, I thought with a tiny smile.

Happy Hauntings!

Sandy (S. E.) Schlosser

PART ONE

Ghost Stories

Retold By S. E. Schlosser

1

Dispatched

There was something odd in the tone of the dispatcher's voice when he called to tell me a person needed picking up at Bramlett Road late one summer night in 1947. I shuddered when I heard the name of the street, and I glanced inadvertently at my watch. Nearly midnight. I did not want to go anywhere near that area at midnight. But I drove a Yellow Cab, and it was my job to pick up a call when it came. I swallowed and started the car with sweaty palms, heading toward Bramlett Road and the slaughter yards.

I'd been out of town when the incident happened. I call it an incident, but it was murder, plain and not so simple. The dispatcher told me the story when I got home, and he'd looked a little green when he spoke about what happened. One of the fellows who drove a cab with our company—name of Brown— was robbed and stabbed to death in his cab. That was bad. I knew Brown slightly, and I'd liked him. His death saddened me, and it worried me too. You spend a lot of time alone in your cab, and when you're not alone, it's because you are driving strangers around town. In my experience, not all of those strangers were nice; a fact Brown could attest too, had he lived.

Anyhow, the dispatcher said they caught the fellow that had done it. A man named Willie Earle was picked up by the police the very next day and put in jail. 'Course, his family stoutly denied

6

that he'd had anything to do with the murder. Said Willie had come home the previous day on the bus and hadn't used a cab at all. But there's no smoke without fire, the dispatcher said. Willie's family would say something like that, and the police around here were pretty good about finding the man who committed a crime.

I thought the story would end there, but the dispatcher kept on talking, and my heart sank as I listened to the rest of it. Apparently a bunch of hotheads who drove cabs for our company gathered together in the office, passing around a bottle of whiskey and talking about "getting" the fellow who'd stabbed Brown. One of the men went out and borrowed a shotgun, and a few minutes later a procession of cabs drove to the old jailhouse where Willie Earle was kept. Once the jailer saw the mob and the guns, he let them into the jail, and the mob grabbed Earle and threw him in the back of one of the cabs. They drove over to the slaughter yards, where they roughed him up a bit in the backseat. Then one man pulled a knife, and they dragged Earle forcibly from the back—had to pry his fingers loose from the seat. The men started hitting him with their fists and the stock of the shotgun, and the knife-wielder waded in and really made a mess. According to the dispatcher, Earle shouted: "Lord, you've killed me!" Then one of the cab drivers called for the shotgun and put a bullet in his head. They reloaded and shot him twice more. When they were sure he was dead, the mob climbed back into their separate cabs and fanned out, each heading back to Greenville by a different route.

The dispatcher started to give me the names of the men in the mob, but I made him shut up. I didn't want to know. Oh, I could probably guess without much difficulty. I'd been working in the company for years, and I knew the fellows pretty well by now. But it was better that I not know anything more than he'd told me, so I could deny any knowledge of the incident if I was questioned about it. Not that it did much good. Word got around soon enough, and thirty-one fellows were arrested for the crime. A few months later, they were all acquitted by a jury of their peers.

I was still thinking about dead Willie Earle as I drove along Bramlett Road, searching the area for my passenger, who'd told the dispatcher he'd be waiting on the side of the road near the slaughter yards. I slowed down to a crawl, glancing this way and that in the bright glow of the headlights. No one was there. Finally, I parked the cab on the side of the road and got out to have a quick smoke while I waited for my passenger to show up.

I stood in the darkness next to my car, the smoke from my cigarette helping to mask the stench from the slaughter yard. It was a cloudy night, and the wind ruffled my hair and swirled oddly in the tall grass at my feet. The only light came from the end of my cigarette as I smoked.

All at once, the temperature around me plummeted. It felt as if I were standing outside in midwinter. My breath came out as a puff of white steam in the red glow from the end of my cigarette. I froze in place, suddenly terrified, my heart thumping heavily against my ribs. Was that a groan I heard? Had my passenger been hurt?

The moan came again, and then I heard a voice crying: "I swear, it wasn't me. I don't know who did it!" A man began to scream. The sound tore through me like a razor blade, scraping my nerves raw. I dropped my cigarette and fumbled with the car door as the air around me grew colder. Now I could hear the unmistakable thud of hammering fists. The darkness of

the night was filled with swirling black silhouettes pounding on something . . . or someone. I caught a glint of metal—tinged with the red glow from the dying cigarette lying on the ground—as my hands closed on the icy-cold door handle. Then I heard the sound of fabric ripping, and I heard a man scream again in agony. The scream muted into terrible words: "Lord, you've killed me!" Another voice shouted for a gun, and I heard one shot, followed swiftly by two more.

I wrenched the door open with shaking hands and threw myself inside the cab. It took me two tries to get the engine started, and then I squealed the tires as I spun the cab around. Something was standing in the middle of the road, blocking my path. It was a tall, battered figure that glowed just enough for me to see its lolling head, the blood-stained, dead features, the knife-torn clothes. It reached toward the cab with bloody hands. I screamed and swerved to avoid it. Then I floored the gas pedal and sped from the gruesome place as fast as the cab would take me.

I slammed into the office a few moments later and told the dispatcher I was quitting. Then I grabbed my things and headed home. My missus had died a few years back and my kids were all grown and flown, so there was no need to stay here. I'd get a job in Columbia or maybe down in Charleston where my daughter lived. One thing was for sure: There was no way I was staying in this haunted town.

2

The Bell Ringer

"Honestly, that boy could get away with murder!"

His mother's oft-repeated complaint rang through the thief's mind as he drove his stiletto into the bell ringer's back, piercing the man's beating heart. The bell ringer slumped into the dirt of the deserted alleyway, blood pouring from the wound. The thief smiled grimly as he searched the man's pockets for the keys to the bell tower. Getting away with murder was the easy part, he reckoned. It was retrieving the stolen money that was proving difficult. His fingers closed around the keys, lying deep inside the man's waistcoat. At last! The thief hurried out of the alleyway, leaving the bell ringer behind in a congealing pool of blood.

It was a pity it had come to this. The bell ringer was a nice sort. But he was in the way, and the thief couldn't let a mere bell ringer stand between him and the small fortune he'd left in the bell tower of the church after the bank robbery.

If only the sheriff and his men had not been hard on his tail after the theft! But the constabulary had been everywhere, and the thief was forced to stash his stolen money in the first place he could find. Which happened to be the local bell tower, where ringers were practicing the Sunday carillon. The thief had hidden in the base of the tower until the last bell ringer left, then carried the currency-filled cardboard box upstairs and stashed it on a back shelf underneath a coil of rope.

The thief waited for three nights, until furor over the bank theft abated, before attempting to retrieve the stolen money. But when he visited the church, the door to the tower was locked. The thief swore several times. He didn't dare pound on the church doors and demand entry, for what explanation could he give for wanting in at midnight? He had no tools to break down the massive portal and no skill at picking locks.

Frustrated, the fuming thief hurried home. He had to get into the belfry tonight. He couldn't afford to wait for next week's bell practice. WANTED signs with his sketched likeness were posted all over town. His senses screamed at him to leave Atlanta, but the thief wasn't going anywhere without that box of money.

In the afternoon the thief visited the minister of the church, pretending interest in becoming a member. He spoke eloquently of his love for music in general and for church bells in particular. The obliging minister gave him the name of the director of the bell ringers, who would be delighted to have a new recruit.

Once he had a name, the thief tracked down the man with little difficulty and waited in a back alley while the man had drinks at an inn on the outskirts of town. When the bell ringer stepped outside for a breath of fresh air, the waiting thief attacked.

Leaving the dead bell ringer in the alleyway, the thief fled through the maze of streets toward the church. The bell tower loomed darkly against the night sky, silhouetted by the light of a waxing gibbous moon. He was almost to his destination when he saw a policeman sitting in a dilapidated old guardhouse that stood opposite the church. The thief swore and slid behind a tree to watch the man. No one had manned that guardhouse in years. Why now—tonight of all nights? The thief knew the answer. There was a bank robber loose in Atlanta. The sheriff had doubled the number of men on duty, and they grew more aggressive with each passing day.

The thief lurked in the shadows, hoping the policeman would head out on his beat. He only needed one chance to slip into the bell tower and get the box of money. Then he'd be out of town on the next train heading west. He waited for an hour, both anxious and bored. He still had his knife. After killing the bell ringer, it didn't seem such a stretch to kill the policeman as well to attain his goal. But the policeman was armed.

Out of options, the thief crept down the street toward the guardhouse and crouched beneath the back window, feeling for the sash. The policeman sat eating a sandwich and idly watching the street. Suddenly the policeman stood up and hurried to the front window. He stared at the church, feeling for his gun. The thief froze in place and then crept to the side of the building to look at the church, wondering what had caught the policeman's attention. At first glance the thief saw nothing in the street. Or did he? His heart started pounding when he spied a shadowy, cloaked figure in the moonlight. To his astonishment, the dark figure walked straight through the locked door of the bell tower and vanished. The thief rubbed his eyes. Strange.

He looked through the side window of the guardhouse and saw the policeman holding his gun cocked, eyes fixed on the belfry of the church. Above him the tower bells began to hum. The thief's gaze returned to the moon-silhouetted tower. Arms prickling with fear, he watched heavy dark bells swaying slightly against the silver light of the moon. A dark figure stood among the bells, running a skeletal finger around the massive rim of the bell closest to the window. Then the dark shape started ringing the bells with its hands, ignoring the pull ropes. The muffled, melancholy tune bit right through the thief crouched beside the guardhouse. With each note, the thief felt an agonizing pain strike through his back and into his beating heart with stiletto sharpness.

The dark figure stepped to the edge of the tower, bells swaying behind it, and pointed a skeletal finger at the crouching thief. The thief gazed upward in horror as the hood fell back, revealing the face of the murdered bell ringer. The man's eyes were two points of fire, his skin withered and blackened as if overwhelmed by a scorching fire that burned just beneath the surface.

The thief felt the knife in his hand go white-hot, like a burning coal. The thief dropped the stiletto in panic and stared incredulously at the raw knife shape burned into his palm. Inside his pocket, the stolen keys grew red hot. He yelped in pain and saw them burning through the heavy cloth of his coat, wisps of smoke rising from the beleaguered garment. Then his whole torso was ablaze, and fire ran down from his coat toward his boots.

The thief screamed, but the sound was as muffled as the ringing of the bells above. He rolled frantically in the dirt, crying out to the policeman to come save him. But his voice did not carry beyond his own ears, and the engulfing flames burned hotter and hotter, no matter how hard he rolled.

The thief flung himself frantically down a side street, searching for water. There must be a stream nearby or a water butt. Something! Anything! The burning thief spied a water trough for horses behind a local inn and plunged into it, body ablaze. To his horror, the thief realized that the flames still burned brightly underneath the water. His hair and face were on fire. In crucifying

agony, the thief heard his own skin sizzling, and the water in the trough began to boil.

Once again the thief heard his mother's voice in his head: "Honestly, that boy could get away with murder!" And he knew it wasn't true. Not then. Not now. Not ever again.

It was over in less than a minute. The water trough had boiled dry, and a small pile of ash lay at the bottom of a scorched, man-size hole. Back at the church the bells pealed loudly in triumph. Then they stopped ringing as abruptly as they started, and the dark figure in the tower vanished.

Inside the guardhouse, the policeman tore his eyes from the belfry and rubbed them with his free hand. Had he just seen what he thought he saw? How utterly bizarre.

A month after the murder of their beloved bell chief, the new head bell ringer brought a plain cardboard box to the minister. "I found this on a shelf in the belfry," he said. "It looks like someone made an anonymous donation to the church. Perhaps they want us to refurbish the bells?"

The minister's eyes widened in astonishment as he counted the cash inside the box. "How very generous!" he exclaimed. "I believe we have enough here to refurbish the lot, with some left over to buy a few more bells. Hallelujah!"

"Amen," said the head of the bell ringers.

3

Plucked

When Miz Mortimer got married, her family threw and wouldn't take her back after her man passed shortly after the war. Suddenly, she was all alone with two little boys to feed. The family was forced out of their home and ended up squatting in a remote old farm cabin, trying to scratch what living they could from the land.

All that hardship turned Miz Mortimer into a bitter, selfish, greedy woman. And she raised her sons to be just like her. By the time they reached their teens, all the Mortimer boys cared about was money. Lots of it. And they weren't too particular about how they got it. The boys built a still up in the holler and started running moonshine across the state line to earn a little cash. When they couldn't sell shine, they went to the local school to cheat their school chums out of their money. The brothers would set up card games, bully the other boys into playing, and then fleece their classmates of every penny. When the schoolboys protested, the eldest Mortimer made a great show of cleaning his gun while the younger Mortimer started sharpening his knife with a flint. The schoolboys got the hint and took off quick, leaving their money behind.

Drinking, hunting, quarreling, and swindling became a way of life for the Mortimer boys. So it shouldn't have come as a surprise when Miz Mortimer got her finger shot off one day when she interfered in a quarrel between her two lads. They were having a shouting match over $4 that the younger Mortimer had borrowed from the elder and couldn't pay back. The shouting got so loud that it gave the missus a headache. She marched out to the gate to give both her lads a licking. Unfortunately for her, that was the moment the elder Mortimer boy pulled out his gun. Unfortunately for him, the bullet meant to scare his brother into coughing up the cash not only took off his mama's middle finger but also entered the forehead of his baby brother, killing him instantly. But the judge was real understanding about it. After all, the younger Mortimer brother had pulled a knife on his brother. So the killing was ruled as self-defense.

"Served him right," the elder Mortimer muttered defensively to his mama, standing at the graveside of his younger brother. "He shouldn't a' borrowed the money if'n he couldn't pay it back."

What could the missus say to that? He was quoting the very words she'd used herself so many times, railing against the foolishness of her neighbors.

The elder Mortimer didn't want to admit that he missed his brother. Now there was no one to participate in his money-making schemes, no one to help with the still. Everyone in town was avoiding him, and the judge had told him straight out that if the elder Mortimer appeared in his courtroom again, he'd get twenty years in the slammer.

The night after the burial, the elder Mortimer boy had a strange dream. In his dream his younger brother came to him, white-faced and dead, with a red bullet hole in his forehead. He floated bonelessly up to the bed where the elder Mortimer lay, reached down with icy-cold fingers, and yanked a single strand from his brother's bushy red hair. It hurt like the dickens. The elder Mortimer let out a yell and woke himself up. His scalp was stinging where the ghost had touched it. When he rubbed it, a clump of hair fell out, plucked from his head by the roots.

"Maaa!" the elder Mortimer wailed in panic, rubbing at the bald spot on his head.

The missus came running, shocked to see her tough son wide-eyed as a frightened baby. She examined the small bald spot and firmly told him a mouse must have gotten into his bed and nibbled off his hair. The elder brother, shaking with cold, tried to believe her. But he couldn't figure out how a mouse could pluck hairs out by the roots.

The next night, almost as soon as he closed his eyes, the elder Mortimer boy saw his younger brother floating through the open window of the cabin. The dead boy's face was a hollow mask under the grotesque red hole in his forehead. His cheeks had withered overnight, collapsing inward like the cheeks of an ancient man, and his blue eyes were wide open and staring sightlessly at nothing. The elder Mortimer lay paralyzed with fright as the corpse drifted nearer, stretching out its hand toward his head. Cold fingers ran through his scalp and then yanked hard.

The elder Mortimer woke with a scream and sat up, huge chunks of hair scattering all over the bed and onto the floor—plucked out by the roots. The missus came running when she heard him, and she couldn't explain away the huge bald patch covering the right half of her boy's head, from his forehead all the way down to his neck.

"I'm being hainted," the elder boy wailed, wringing his hands like a tiny child. "Make it stop, Mama! Make it stop!"

"I'll get a preacher-man to come pray over the cabin," the missus said. "That'll frighten away any haints, don't you worry."

The elder Mortimer brother was comforted by this plan, but he still sat up the rest of the night feeding the fire to keep the cabin nice and bright. At dawn he went up to the holler and spent the day making moonshine while his mama called the preacher-man out to exorcise the haint. But he was tired out after his long, sleepless night. He lay down by the still to get some rest.

And dreamed of his younger brother. The dead boy's skin was rotting away from his face and hands, revealing bone underneath his eyes and allowing his sagging nose to collapse inward. The red bullet hole gaped in his forehead, and his dead head lolled against his shoulder. His white hands, bones poking through his fingertips, stretched out toward his brother's hair and pulled . . .

The elder Mortimer boy screamed himself awake, hair showering all around him, spilling over the boards of the still and across the dirt floor. He clutched at his head, which was plucked bald. With a long, wordless wail, he ran down the hill and burst into the cabin, where the preacher-man was standing with his holy book and a goblet of holy water. The boy fell to his knees in front of the preacher-man.

"Make it stop! Make it stop!" he sobbed, his bald head pressed against the man's shiny black shoes.

Behind him, the door was caught by a huge blast of frigid air. The wind slammed the door so hard that it splintered and sagged on its hinges. Filling the doorway was a rotting corpse, maggots writhing in and out of its eye sockets, bones gaping through withered gray skin, head lolling against bare shoulder bones. Its forehead was dominated by a huge, bloodstained bullet hole. It staggered forward on bony legs, its withered hands reaching toward the elder Mortimer boy.

The preacher screamed. The missus screamed.

The skeleton's fingers closed on the scraggly beard growing from the boy's chin . . . and yanked.

The elder Mortimer boy convulsed once against the preacher's shiny black shoes. Then he rolled onto his back, mouth agape, eyes staring sightlessly up at the holy book and goblet still held in the minister's hands. Every single hair had been plucked from his body—arms, legs, face, hands, and torso. Small red hairs were slowly raining down onto the dirt floor of the cabin, covering every surface and sprinkling the heads of the preacher-man and the missus. A few hairs landed in the holy goblet.

The missus screamed and ran. She ran out of the house, out of the yard, out of the town, and kept running. She was never seen again. The preacher, made of sterner material, wiped the hair off his holy book, said a prayer over the plucked corpse of the elder Mortimer boy, and carried him back to the churchyard to be buried.

After the deaths of the two Mortimer brothers, no one would go near the haunted cabin just outside town. In a few seasons it rotted away until only a few boards and a broken-down chimney were left to show where it once stood.

As for the old still . . . Well, they say a feller out hunting whistle pigs a month after the Mortimer boy's death stumbled across the old still and helped himself to a whole jug full of moonshine. When he awoke the next morning, he was completely bald. After that, no one went near the old still or the holler it sat in neither, just in case.

4

The Sausage Factory

My wife and I were introduced to Herr Mueller shortly after we moved to New Orleans. We quickly discovered that our families both hailed from the Black Forest region of Germany. In fact, we knew many of the same places and even had a few friends in common back in the old country. Eager to become better acquainted, Herr Mueller invited us to dinner in his home, and we were quick to accept his offer.

We met Mueller's wife over a meal of bratwurst and sauerkraut. Frau Miller was a sour-faced, bitter woman who—though only thirty-five—was wrinkled and old before her time. During the course of our dinner conversation, we learned that the couple owned a small sausage factory and that Frau Mueller's hard work had contributed not a little to their bottom-line income. Some people might think that Mueller was lucky to have such an industrious wife. Myself, I preferred my soft-spoken, pretty spouse and didn't care a whit how much she contributed to our bottom line. But each to his own.

A few months after we met the Muellers, the office in which I was employed as a bookkeeper burned to the ground. Herr Mueller generously offered me a job working in the office at the sausage factory. During the course of my new employment, I was able to witness up close the relationship between Herr Mueller and his Frau. It did not impress me. Frau Mueller was sharp-tongued and as hard as nails. Not an easy woman to live with. Or to work for, as I quickly discovered.

During my first month at the factory, Frau Mueller inspected my account books each night, down to the last penny. It was most disconcerting. She soon realized that I was an honest and ethical man who had no desire to cheat my employers. After the first month she left the bulk of the bookkeeping to me, merely inspecting the records once a week on payday. I took this as a high compliment from Frau Mueller. I could tell she liked me because she never complained of my work, and once she even gave me a compliment on my timeliness and the neat appearance of my office.

Frau Mueller was not so pleasant with the rest of the staff, and her treatment of Herr Mueller made my skin crawl. *Gott im Himmel* (God in Heaven), the woman never ceased complaining about her husband. And yet he bore the worst of her tongue-lashings with a smile on his face, as if he were deaf to her words. I could never understand it.

It was my wife who found out the truth. The greengrocer told my wife that Herr Mueller slipped out of his house each evening after Frau Mueller went to bed, to visit his plump girlfriend who lived a few doors down from the sausage factory. It was shocking behavior for a man who regularly went to church each Sunday. But it did explain how he could face his wife's bitter complaining with a smile on his face. Herr Mueller was cuckolding her. Frau Mueller did all the hard work at the factory and her husband used the hard-earned profits to shower his girlfriend with treats and take her to dinner.

Before I could decide what to do with this information, Herr Mueller came into the office to tell me his Frau had gone back East to visit her ailing mother. Mueller's cheeks were flushed, and he spoke rapidly, as if the news about his wife excited him. He was so chipper and jittery that morning that it made me nervous. Something didn't seem quite right to me. Perhaps he intended to divorce his wife while she was away? That would explain his nervous behavior. The negative press surrounding such a scandal would be dreadful, but Herr Mueller might think it worth the price of a lost reputation and customers to be rid of his Frau's complaints.

Mueller generously passed out bags of sausages to all his workers at the end of the day shift, something he would never have done if Frau Mueller were present. I took my heavy bag home and handed it to my lovely wife with a kiss. Dinner was already cooked, so she put the sausages in the cooler for another day. Over our meal, I told her about Frau Mueller's ailing mother and about Herr Mueller's strange behavior. "You may be right about the divorce," she said as she went to fetch a pot of coffee and dessert. "Poor Frau Mueller."

Throughout the following week, several of the factory workers dropped by my office to complain about Mueller's free sausages. "It was a terrible batch," the floor manager said one morning during his break. "No wonder Herr Mueller was giving them away. Did you eat any?"

"Not yet. To be honest, we put them in the cooler and forgot about them. My wife said she'd fry them up this evening for dinner," I replied.

"Tell her not to bother," the floor manager said. "The ones we ate had bits of bone in them and my daughter found blue threads in her sausage!"

My hand froze over the ledger, and I slowly set down my pen. The floor manager's daughter had found blue cloth in the sausages? That wasn't possible. Unless . . .

My body started trembling as suspicion blossomed in my mind. Frau Mueller wore a blue outfit to work every day. It was her favorite color. Oh, surely not. Surely Herr Mueller would never harm his own wife. It was a ridiculous notion. My thoughts were churning so hard that I barely heard the floor manager bid me a good morning as he returned to his duties.

I had a hard time acting normal when Herr Mueller popped into the office to discuss a few business particulars and assign me some extra duties. It was three days since his wife had left for the East Coast, and he was still acting jittery. His color was unnaturally high; his hands trembled when he gestured; and his voice was a touch too loud. *Gott im Himmel*, he was acting guilty. As if . . .

The extra work kept me busy until late that evening. There was almost no one left on the floor but Herr Mueller and myself when I finally finished my tasks. I was preparing to leave when I heard a "Thump! Thump! Thump!" sound coming from the main boiler vat. Alarmed by the noise, I rushed out onto the floor.

Herr Mueller was standing in the center of the room staring fixedly at the boiler, face snow-white and his body shaking. I followed his gaze and saw a greenish light approaching from the far side of the vat. The next moment, the glowing translucent figure of Frau Mueller appeared before us. Her head was crushed

to a pulp and lolled obscenely against her left shoulder. Her body was misshapen and bloody. She looked as if she had been ground to pieces and then stuffed into a human-size sausage skin. One of her eyes had popped out of its socket, and the other rolled back into her crushed skull. Her mouth was lopsided; one side leered upward while the other twisted down. Her teeth were sharp splinters that cut grotesquely through the flesh of her lips. "Mueller," she moaned. "Come with me, Mueller."

I doubled over and vomited on the floor as the apparition stretched forth skinless, broken hands and grabbed the lapels of Mueller's coat. With surprising strength for such a misshapen corpse, Frau Mueller dragged her husband toward the sausage grinder. Mueller screamed in terror and beat at the phantom with both fists until she released him. Then he rushed out of the back door into the alleyway, still screaming. When Herr Mueller vanished, so did his dead spouse.

I wiped my mouth with a trembling hand and staggered out the front door, wanting to get away from Mueller and his ghost wife as fast as my legs would carry me. I was going to have to call the police, but what could I say to them? I couldn't tell them that I'd seen the ghost of Frau Mueller haunting the sausage factory. They'd lock me up!

I tottered home on legs that would barely hold me, wondering what to tell my wife. How could I ask her to believe in a ghost when I barely believed in it myself? When I reached the house, I found a police sergeant in the kitchen with my wife, who was having hysterics. The room stank of vomit, grease, and fried sausages. As soon as she saw me, my wife flung herself weeping into my arms.

"What is going on?" I asked the sergeant, who was scraping the remains of my wife's dinner into a bag.

"I cooked up those sausages you brought home from the factory," my wife sobbed into my shoulder. "The first sausage tasted fine, but I almost cracked a tooth on something hard inside the second sausage. There was a wedding ring buried inside the sausage," my wife gasped. "I recognized it at once. It belonged to Frau Mueller. The police think Herr Mueller murdered her by pushing her into the sausage grinder. And I just *ate* one of those sausages!"

She tried to vomit again, but there was nothing left in her stomach. I held her during the dry heaves and then cradled her gently against my chest. I knew exactly how she felt.

"We've sent some men around to arrest Herr Mueller," the sergeant told me. "I'm sorry, ma'am, but you will probably have to testify in court."

My wife nodded weakly, clutching me tighter.

"I've got her statement right here," the sergeant told me. "You look after your missus, now. She's had a bad day, but she did her duty like a trooper. Credit where it's due." He nodded politely to us both and exited with his bag full of evidence.

We learned later that the police found Herr Mueller in the alley behind the factory, rolled into a ball and screaming like a maniac. He said he'd seen his wife's ghost rise out of the meat grinder. "She's trying to pull me inside the grinder, too. She wants to make me into sausage," he sobbed. "But I won't go." He ended up in an asylum for the mentally insane.

A wealthy man purchased the factory after Mueller was committed, and tried to continue the profitable sausage business.

But the ghost of Frau Mueller made so many gruesome appearances on the factory floor that the owner couldn't keep any worker longer than a week, and he was forced to close the shop forever.

As for me, I quit my job at the factory and found another position in a banking firm. And my wife and I never ate sausages again.

5

Forty-Nine Beaus

He was a fledgling reporter, just learning the trade, so naturally his editor never gave him the good assignments. But he was a handsome boy, with a charming manner and flashing smile that made girls dizzy, so he was frequently sent to cover the "human interest" angle. Ladies loved to talk with him, and even the gents unbent before his witty tongue.

Today's assignment was a piece of cake, the reporter reflected as he strolled toward his destination. The last scion of one of the original families was turning ninety-five, and she had graciously given the newspaper permission to conduct a personal interview. She was the daughter of one of the dons who came to the colony in 1770, shortly after France gave control of Louisiana to Spain to pay a war debt.

The reporter was composing interview questions when he rounded a corner and got his first look at the don's mansion. He stopped and stared, appalled by the dilapidated mess of grandeur fallen on hard times. Someone should pull the eyesore down, he thought, staring at the sagging roof, the rusting ironwork, the weed-stricken yard.

The reporter had to tussle with the ironwork gate. It reluctantly opened with a banshee's screech that raised every hair on his body. He shuddered past moldering piles of junk and clawing weeds and climbed unsupported up the rickety steps, afraid to touch the splintered rail for fear of catching a disease from the slime.

It took a long time for anyone to answer his knock. Finally the warped portal creaked open and a bent old servant peered cautiously out into the daylight. The servant looked the reporter over from one angle then shifted about a foot to the left and looked him over again. Then the wrinkled eyes peered blurrily over the reporter's broad shoulders. Finally the man whispered: "It looks like the coast is clear. You won't bring in any ghosts, will you, young Master?"

Ghosts, the reporter thought disbelievingly.

"No, sir, I won't bring in any ghosts," he told the old servant, tempted to pat the man reassuringly on the shoulder of his wilting, dusty uniform. The old servant tottered backward, swinging the door wide, and the reporter stepped into the gloom of glory long gone. The once-magnificent wallpaper and tiling was now coated with mildew and cobwebs. The servant's footprints could be seen in the dust on the floor. He'd evidently come from a room in the back, probably the kitchen, given the smell of cabbage and boiled meat wafting down the passage. The servant must be fixing the old lady's lunch.

The air in the house was frigid, unbelievably so, given that it was midsummer. The reporter shivered and wondered how they kept the house so cool as he followed the old man up a groaning flight of stairs. Surely they didn't have money to buy ice, given the decrepit state of the house and grounds. A chill breeze swirled around the reporter as he climbed. He shuddered, wishing he'd brought his winter coat.

The reporter sneezed three times as he entered a tawdry boudoir, his nostrils twitching at the smell of decay and dust and ancient perfume. The room looked as if it belonged in the red-light district, with its cheap decorations and lewd air of seduction. His eyes swept right past the heap of rags in the burgundy armchair, searching for the grand lady he'd come to interview. Then the servant announced his name, and the rags stirred. The reporter turned his gaze disbelievingly on the old woman who opened filmy dark eyes to look at him. The rags were actually a faded *quinceañera* dress covered in dust. The sparkle on her thinning scalp was a tarnished tiara, and the baubles in her ears and around her neck were probably priceless family jewels, though neglect had faded their elegance. There was a ring on every finger of her withered old hands, with string tied around the bands to keep them on her bony digits.

The old woman had no teeth and there was no beauty in her sucked-in cheeks and wrinkled skin. But a spark kindled in the old eyes, and the reporter saw that the bones of her face and body were slim and elegant. Hard to believe that this tiny woman that looked ready to fall apart was once a beauty, but the signs were there if you looked carefully.

The senorita cackled with delight when she laid eyes on the handsome young man. "Come in, come in, senor. Welcome to Casa Rosa. You are an appetizing specimen, I declare. I think I should have you for dinner tonight." She erupted with laughter, almost choking on her wit. Then just as swiftly, her mood shifted and she screamed at her servant to leave them alone and prepare for the grand supper that she was giving that night for all her beaus. "Including this new one you've brought me," she concluded, simpering at the reporter.

He masked his revulsion and took the chair the senorita offered, hiding behind his notebook until his face was back under his control. The room was stuffy and suffocatingly hot, as if all the summer warmth had been channeled into this one tawdry boudoir, leaving the rest of this sinister house cold and restless and unhappy. The reporter shook away the thought. He was not given to fanciful notions, but this place . . . and this ancient woman . . . disturbed him. Something about the old woman's eyes made him want to run from the room. But he had a job to do, and so he started asking questions of the withered creature in the burgundy armchair. When was she born? What was it like in the days under the Spanish rule? How had New Orleans changed since then?

It was uphill work. The senorita wanted to talk about her father the don, who was once an important man with money to burn. According to the reporter's preliminary research, the don died shortly after the senorita turned fifteen, but the ancient crone spoke of him as if he were still alive.

Then she talked about her Spanish beaus. Oh, how the men came courting her! She'd danced every dance at her quinceañera, and there'd been many more balls and grand suppers. And intimate dinners, too, she hinted with a simper and a flutter of filmy eyelashes.

"The gifts the men would bring me! Jewels and expensive cloth and fancy foods," she sighed. "They all wanted me. Half a hundred men. No. Only forty-nine men. I am just shy of fifty beaus, though we can fix that at dinner tonight, handsome man."

The reporter nodded with a pasted smile on his face, wondering what the senorita was talking about.

"Of course, none of my men ever left this house," the senorita continued, piercing dark eyes suddenly filling with a wicked red glow that made his heart pound heavily in his chest.

"Never left?" he croaked, hand shaking so badly that he almost dropped the pencil. "What do you mean, senorita? Your beaus never wanted to leave because you were so beautiful?"

"They never left," she crooned, stroking the rings on her fingers and rocking back and forth in the burgundy armchair. "I was the one they desired. My beauty enchanted them until they could talk of no one but me. Each time a man was overcome by desire for me, I invited him up to this very room to partake of my beauty. For them, there could never be another woman. Once they tasted my delights, how could anyone else measure up?" The sinister red light in her eyes grew more pronounced as she fixed her eyes on the reporter again. "No other woman could have one of my beaus. It would be . . . sacrilegious. So my beaus never left Casa Rosa. I made sure of that. They are—all of them—still here."

She stopped rocking suddenly and gazed at him thoughtfully. "I always wanted fifty beaus. Fifty is such a nice number. Half of a hundred. Forty-nine beaus were never quite enough. I didn't think another man would visit my boudoir at my time of life. But here you are, senor. Handsome and young and fit. You are worthy and should be allowed to partake of my beauty, just as the forty-nine who came before you. We will have dinner tonight, just you and me. And afterward . . ." She started to laugh again, and the light in her dark eyes grew stronger.

Suffocating waves of perfumed air washed over the reporter as she spoke. He felt dizzy in the heat of the room. Or was it the heat of her gaze? *She's mad*, the reporter thought, chills running all over his skin. *I must get out of here!*

The senorita shifted in her chair as if about to rise, and his heart leaped into his throat. What if she pulled a knife? She looked too decrepit to do him harm, but insanity lent strength to the smallest of people, or so he heard. Then her head flopped to one side and she was suddenly asleep. She snored once, twice.

The temperature in the room dropped precipitously, as if the heat were somehow fueled by the senorita in her dusty quinceañera dress. The reporter leaped to his feet, dripping with the sudden sweat of relief. He must get away at once, before the mad creature awoke. He raced for the door, but the handle wouldn't turn. The servant had locked him in! The reporter cursed and flung all of his weight against the door. He was afraid the sound might awaken the senorita; afraid of what she might do to him in her insanity. But he had to escape! He took a few steps back and kicked the door. His foot went through the wood near the handle. He thrust his hand into the gap and unlocked it from the outside.

As he raced into the hall, the reporter felt a wave of heat from the room behind him. A querulous voice called for her servant, for her father, for her beau. In his panic, the reporter turned the wrong way and nearly slammed into a shimmering figure clothed in the Spanish garb of yesteryear. The translucent young man had a sad face and luminous eyes.

Good God, there really was a ghost! The reporter felt himself gibbering in fear. The spirit grabbed the reporter's arm with ice-cold hands and tried to drag him down a slimy back staircase toward the rose garden at the back of the house.

"No," shouted the reporter, flinging himself backward. Ice-cold wind whipped around him, and for a moment he was

overwhelmed by the stench of rotting flesh and a vision of forty-nine white faces writhing around the hall, reaching for him with spirit hands. "Join us," they crooned.

Screaming, the reporter wrenched away from the specter and raced for the staircase, flinching at the blast of heat from the boudoir where the old lady still called for her servant. He whipped through the dust and the cobwebs and mildewed splendor of the decrepit mansion as the old servant doddered from the back kitchen to answer his mistress. The servant held a tray with two wineglasses and a decanter. *Probably full of poison wine*, the reporter thought with a hysterical laugh. He burst through the warped front door and ran down the littered path toward the gate. And skidded to a halt. A ghostly figure in full evening dress stood in his way. The ghost gave a mocking bow and swung the gate open for the reporter. Then it split in half as if cloven in two by an ax. Each half fell on either side of the open gate.

The reporter levitated off the ground and sped through the gate in two bounds. He was halfway across town before he realized he'd left his notebook at the old mansion. Never mind. He would buy another and would fabricate some kind of interview that would satisfy his editor. Great God in heaven, that was a narrow escape.

Shortly after this interview the reporter was asked if he wanted to cover the crime beat. He refused. A year afterward, the senorita died and her house was sold. When the new owners started renovating the mansion, they found numerous skeletons buried beside the north wall of the rose garden. All were male and all had died quite young. The forty-nine unfortunate beaus of the senorita of Casa Rosa.

6

The Mad Logger

Of course, we're not *supposed* to go to the abandoned logging camp. Our parents would read us the riot act if they knew. So Billy and I told them we were going camping in one of the state parks, and they accepted our story.

And we *were* going camping, after all. It just so happened that we were going camping at the old logging site. The one that had been destroyed by a forest fire. The one that was supposedly haunted.

Billy's already got his driver's license, so we went in his car. We packed a big tent and lots of food and everything into our knapsacks. We were just going for the weekend, but the way our sacks bulged as we locked up the car and staggered into them, you'd think we were hiking across America. We laughed as we set off on the trails leading up and into the forest.

'Course, we weren't laughing so much a few hours later. Those backpacks were heavy! But we didn't want to leave anything behind, so we trudged on. To take our minds off our load, we started discussing our destination in low tones, almost as if we were afraid of being overheard—which was ridiculous. After all, we were in the middle of one of the nation's gorgeous forests, surrounded by tall, mossy trees full of chirping birds and wildlife. But somehow, it was impossible to speak aloud about the mad logger.

Pieced together from the many rumors running around our school, the story went something like this. Once there was a thriving logging camp back in these mountains. Business was booming one hot summer in spite of an unusual dry spell that gripped the area, and the lumber camp was projected to have its best season ever. Then one day, several lumberjacks were out cutting trees, and one of them misjudged his angle so that the tree came tumbling down on another lumberjack. One of the thick branches gave him a fearful whack on the head as it went past, and the man slumped to the ground, unconscious. A couple of the men went running back to camp to get help while two others stayed behind.

The two fellows who remained sat talking worriedly as they kept watch over their injured comrade. Suddenly, the fallen man reared up as if pulled by a string. His eyes popped open and he leapt to his feet. The lumberjacks gave shouts of surprise that turned to yells of terror when they saw the maddened gleam in the man's eyes. They were glowing with a red sort of fire as he grabbed up his fallen axe and leapt toward them, swinging fiercely, his mighty muscles gleaming in the last rays of sunlight.

When the first two lumberjacks returned with help, they stumbled across a severed hand lying in the middle of the path. At first they couldn't believe what they were seeing. But as they drew near the bloody stump, they realized that the pine needles under their feet were soaked with a sticky red liquid and that other body parts surrounded them. A large toe, a shoulder blade, a severed head with eyes popped and mouth open in a silent scream. Several men retched, and even the physician they had brought in from a nearby town was sickened. They pieced the bodies together, finally, as best they could. That's when they realized that the pieces belonged to the two loggers keeping guard—and that the injured man was gone.

They headed back to camp and told everyone what had happened. A party of men was sent out to track the mad logger, but instead they walked right into a wall of fire that sent them running for their lives. Some careless hikers had left a campfire smoldering—a dangerous thing to do in the middle of a drought—and had set the underbrush ablaze. By the time the men made it back to the camp, the whole forest was on fire behind them, and the area had to be evacuated. The wind blew something fierce that night, and the fire raged out of control. Acres burned to the ground overnight.

Before the damage could get any worse, a huge, drought-ending rainstorm blew in from the sea. The hunt for the mad logger was called off; the police and the lumberjacks agreed that he must have been killed in the fire. But a couple out joyriding in the woods a few months later claimed that a man with body aflame and wielding an axe had come running out onto the lumber road after them and had slashed several holes in their trunk. Apparently, the fellow's car still bore the marks of the axe, as well as some large scorch marks where the flaming ghost had burned the paint right off. After that, folks never went back into the burned-out woods—not on foot, and not in cars.

All this happened forty years ago or more, and though occasionally you'd still hear stories about foolish kids who went to the haunted lumber camp and never came back, Billy and

I didn't believe 'em. We decided the old logging camp would be a great, creepy place to camp out. And if we could tell our friends that we saw the "ghost" . . . all the better.

It was dusk when we reached the rotting remains of a few burned-down buildings in the middle of a thicket of spruce and fir.

"This is it!" Billy said gleefully. I nodded dubiously. This place was really spooky, with strange, dark shadows surrounding the remains of the dead buildings and an air of menace oozing from the looming trees. I caught sight of a pale white shape. For a moment I took it for a severed hand and jumped backward with a gasp. Then I realized it was just a fallen branch. Billy laughed heartily, and I reluctantly joined in, pulse still pounding madly in my wrist and throat.

We put up the tent in the shelter of the tallest ruin, made a small campfire, and cooked some hot dogs and baked beans. Our merry voices were the only sounds in that dark place. I kept straining my ears to hear crickets or owls or any sort of night creatures, but the only sound I could hear was the soughing of the wind in the firs and the quiet swishing of a nearby stream. Outside the light of the fire, the night seemed very, very dark.

I hate to admit it, but I was real glad to turn in. We carefully put out the fire with stream-water, joking the whole time that we didn't want a repeat of the fire that killed the mad lumberjack. Then we crawled into the tent.

About midnight, a blaze of bright light surrounding our tent tore both Billy and me out of our sleep. I could hear the crackle of flames and the crashing sound of a tree falling nearby.

"Forest fire!" Billy shrieked, jumping up and hitting his head on the top of the tent. "Al, I thought you put the fire out!"

"I did! I did!" I shouted, struggling out of my sleeping bag.

"We've got to get out of here," Billy cried, rushing through the tent flap. I was caught in a tangle of blankets and sleeping bag and couldn't follow. Finally, I ripped the bag apart in desperation. I was crawling to the door of the tent when I heard Billy give a desperate scream that ended in a gurgle and a thump. Peering through the mosquito netting of the door, I saw the lumber camp as it once must have looked. The buildings and surrounding trees—much taller than the ones we'd seen—were all overlaid with flickering, half-seen flames. Standing in the center of it all was a tall, heavily muscled man. He was wrapped in flames, and in his hands was an axe.

Lying slumped at his feet was a dark figure that I recognized at once as Billy. Only he seemed shorter than usual. That's when I realized that he had no head. My eyes popped in horror, and I scanned the ground around the flaming man until I saw Billy's severed head, face permanently frozen in a ghastly look of terror, lying a yard away from the tent flap.

I wanted to scream, but instinct kept me silent. Maybe the ghostly lumberjack hadn't seen me; maybe he didn't know I was there. I crept back into the tent as silently as I could, hoping the ghostly flames in the trees around me weren't highlighting my every move. I fumbled with the back flap, got it open, and then was running through the ghostly forest fire, running faster than I ever had in my life. *Away*, was all I could think: *I have to get away.* Around me, the flames started dying out, and I soon found myself running in total darkness. I banged right into a tree and staggered back, my eyes blazing with stars. And then I was enveloped in a huge, ghostly ball of flame. A figure towered over me, and the white dots of light in front of my eyes seemed

insignificant compared to the blaze of fire crowning that massive form. I ducked frantically as an axe came swinging toward me. It swooshed just a fraction of an inch over my head. I leapt backward, dodging this way and that as the blazing figure pursued me. And then I fell over a tree stump, and my head slammed so hard against the ground that my eyes filled with tears of pain. So I never got a clear glimpse of the axe as it swung toward my neck. All I saw was flame.

7

Sifty-Sifty-San

There was once a beautiful old house right on the edge of a lake, surrounded by lovely woods about ten miles outside of Wallis. The house was set so far back from the road it couldn't be seen. It was considered prime real estate in those parts, but no one wanted to live there because the house had the reputation of being haunted. In fact, no one had ever spent a single night in that house, because a spirit calling itself Sifty-Sifty-San drove everyone away long before midnight.

Now the owner of that house was tired of paying taxes year after year on the home when he couldn't get anyone to rent it for more than one night. He was anxious to prove that the house was livable, and he offered a very large reward for anyone who would spend a whole night there. Several cowboys and even a few Texas Rangers took him up on the offer, only to flee screaming just before midnight at the coming of Sifty-Sifty-San. The owner of the house raised the amount of the reward, but such was the reputation of the haunted house that no one was willing to take him up on his offer, no matter how much money was offered.

In desperation, the owner of the house went to the big city, looking for a man or woman who had some experience with ghosts, figuring such a person would be able to banish the spirit of Sifty-Sifty-San once and for all. He was in luck. The first night in town, he came across a man named Sam who had spent much of his life banishing ghosts from haunted properties all over the West. When the owner of the haunted house had explained his predicament, the ghost-buster at once agreed to come to Wallis and spend a night in the haunted house. The owner was so happy he went right out and bought Sam as many groceries as he could carry, so Sam would have plenty of grub to eat while he waited for the ghost.

At dusk the next evening, Sam started down the long drive leading to the haunted house with a big bag full of potatoes, bacon, cornmeal, and red beans in his hand.

He whistled cheerfully to himself, happy to have such an easy assignment. Who could be afraid of a silly ghost when the sun was shining and the colors of the sunset were glowing across the waters of the lake? With the prospect of a good meal in his belly, a good night's sleep in a fancy house, and a big wad of money in his pocket come the morning, Sam was a happy man.

If he heard the ominous creaking of the big pine trees or saw the way the water at the center of the lake began to swirl madly like a whirlpool, Sam gave no sign of it. He just waltzed through the fancy front door and settled himself down by the fireplace in the large kitchen to cook up a wonderful meal.

Darkness came swiftly to the grand house by the lake, and with it came a sinister hissing sound in the forest around the lake. Sifty-sifty, the wind whistled in the treetops. Saaaannnn, the little waves lapping the shore agreed. Sifty-sifty, the crickets chirped restlessly. Saaaannnn, the old owl hooted mournfully.

Sam shivered a little next to the little fire as he fed it a log, suddenly aware of the isolation of this particular house. There were no other homes on the lake, and this one was set so far

back from the road that he couldn't hear the hoofbeats of passing riders or the rattle of carriages traveling by. It was just him alone in a huge, drafty house in a menacing, dark forest beside the deep, threatening lake. He shook himself to stop his anxious thoughts and threw another log on the fire. Outside, the wind picked up and the tree branches lashed together. A huge gust of wind shook the house and howled down the chimney, making the fire flicker wildly. Sam threw on another log and nursed the blaze until the fire regained its former strength.

The wind settled down a bit, and Sam could once again hear the tiny sounds of night through the open window. The frogs were croaking softly to themselves in the reeds by the water. Sifty-sifty, the little ones croaked. Saaannn, belched the biggest of the bullfrogs. The sound of the waves grew louder, as if something—or someone—were stirring up the lake. As the bacon began to sizzle and crisp in the frying pan, Sam heard a huge thud-thud-thud sound coming from the forest on the opposite end of the lake. The sound rattled the furniture in the kitchen and made him jump and his arms break out with goose bumps. He hopped up and ran frantically around the house, making sure all the windows and doors were locked—all save for the back window in the kitchen, which he kept open a crack as a possible escape route, should Sifty-Sifty-San come to get him.

Then he settled down by the fire to watch his red beans cooking in a little pot while the bacon sizzled and spat in the pan. He put the bacon on his plate and tossed the potatoes in the bacon grease to fry, all the time listening for another thumping noise from the forest. He heard nothing but the soft hiss of the wind in the treetops.

And then there came a soft cry from the far side of the lake. It was a faint mewling cry, like that of a small kitten, but it raised the hairs on the back of Sam's neck. The frying pan shook in his grip, and he hastily put it back on the fire, wondering if he should close and lock the window. But if he did, his final escape route would be cut off!

"Don't be silly, Sam," he said aloud, trying to remember the prayers and spells his grandmamma had taught him for conjuring a ghost. But he couldn't remember a one, not even when he pulled a Bible out of his pack and tried to pray.

The mewling cry came again, louder. It didn't sound like a kitten this time, but like some sort of large cat stalking its victim. Sam shuddered at the thought, forgetting to stir his potatoes or check the boiling pot of red beans.

A gust of air blew through the small opening of the window, bringing with it a strange musty smell, like the dust in a graveyard. And out on the lake, Sam heard a soft voice chanting: "I am Sifty-Sifty-San. I'm here on the lake, but where is the man?"

Sam froze in place like a rabbit confronted by a coyote. What was that? The wind picked up again, pummeling the house like a huge fist and howling down the large chimney until the fire flickered wildly and the frying pan toppled over.

"I am Sifty-Sifty-San," a sinister voice hissed from the shore of the lake. "I'm here on the shore, but where is the man?"

The broth from the beans bubbled over and the fire hissed and sparked as the water hit the burning logs. Sam dropped his Bible in his fright and scrambled frantically for his bag. He had some goofer dust somewhere inside. And a few other supplies his grandmamma had given him to banish ghosts. But he couldn't seem to find any of them. His hands were shaking too much to grip anything, and the dusty, decaying smell coming through the window seemed to dull his thoughts and numb his body.

The broth overflowed again, putting out a section of the fire, making the kitchen seem darker and more menacing.

"I am Sifty-Sifty-San," a terrible, howling voice called from the front of the house. "I'm here on the porch, but where is the man?"

Abandoning food, Bible, bag, and sanity, Sam wrestled desperately with the suddenly stubborn back window, trying to open it wide enough to climb through. He heard the fancy front doors slam open with a bang that made the whole house shudder, and down the passageway came the thud-thud-thudding of footsteps. Then the kitchen door slammed inward, and a huge shadow with burning yellow eyes appeared in the frame.

"I am Sifty-Sifty-San," a horrible, blood-chilling voice bellowed, a dusty-decaying smell cutting right through the smell of burning potatoes and bubbling beans. "I'm here in the house with the trespassing man!"

"No you ain't, on account of I'm gone," shouted Sam, springing through the recalcitrant window, glass, wood frame, and all. He moved so fast that he barely got cut by the breaking glass, and he hightailed it back to town faster than a jackrabbit.

And that was the last time anybody went near the old house on the lake. If it hasn't fallen to pieces by now, then Sifty-Sifty-San may be there still.

8

Get Out!

The old woman had no idea, when they sold her the house, that it was haunted. It didn't come up in any of the Realtor's conversations about the place. But of course, it wouldn't. Why jinx a sale? So the ghost—when it first manifested itself—came as a bit of a shock.

It happened the second night that she stayed in her new house. Just as she was drifting off to sleep, she heard a child's voice say: "Get out of my house!" The words were spoken right in her ear, and she jerked awake, pulse pounding wildly.

She was not a young woman, and she didn't recover quickly from surprises. She lay gasping for a few minutes, trying to convince herself that she'd imagined the whole thing. Then she went downstairs and warmed up some milk to calm herself. Surely it was just a dream? She drank the milk and went back to her bedroom. The air was chillier here, and she walked through a cold spot near the closet that made her wince. But at last she relaxed under the covers and felt sleep settling down around her. Later, she decided she had imagined the horse's whinny she'd heard as she drifted off.

A week later, she was mounting the stairs with a vase of flowers in her hands when a paper-thin, two-dimensional apparition of a little girl appeared at the top of the steps. She looked more like an upright black-and-white playing card than a person, and she was slightly out of focus.

"Get out of my house!" the apparition cried, shaking arms as thin as paper at her. The old woman dropped the vase, spilling flowers and water all down the staircase.

"L . . . look what you made me do," she scolded the ghost in a high-pitched, trembling voice.

"Get out of my house," the ghost girl repeated. Then she started twirling around in a dizzying circle that got smaller and smaller until she disappeared.

The old woman sat down abruptly on the steps, shaking. There was no doubt in her mind that she'd seen a ghost. But who was she? And why was she so angry? It took nearly ten minutes to calm herself, and another ten to clean up the mess. Really, this came as quite a shock!

About a month later, the old lady opened her front door to find a horse grazing in the yard. It was coal black and beautiful. It was also floating a good foot above the ground. The old lady let out a shriek, leapt back inside the house, and slammed the door. She leaned against it, panting, and distinctly heard the nasty snickering of a cruel child who liked to play practical jokes. "Get out of my house," the girl's voice said from the window overlooking the front yard.

"No," the old lady said in her firmest voice. "You get out."

A snort of rage came from the empty air. And a moment later, the back door slammed expressively.

The old lady turned the handle of the front door, opened it slowly, and peeked outside. The horse was gone.

"I've had about enough of this," she told herself. Time to find out what was going on. She went to the local newspaper office and went through the archives, searching for information about the death of a little girl and—as an afterthought—a black horse. It took a while for her to locate the story. It had happened nearly fifteen years ago. A little girl and her horse were struck by a drunk driver one evening on their way home. It was dark, and the horse was black, and the driver just didn't see them in time. Animal and child were both killed. The child's home address was the same as the old lady's. So this was her ghost.

The old lady also found a reference, just last year, to the death of first one and then another of the child's parents. Apparently, the house had gone to a distant family member, who had sold it—with its resident ghost—to her.

The old lady sat thoughtfully at the desk after she'd finished her research. The child was probably missing her parents and was angry that a stranger lived in her house. But short of selling the house and moving away, there was nothing the old lady could do. Hopefully, the little ghost would become reconciled to the new owner and would rest in peace at last.

But that was not to be. The appearances of the little apparition became more frequent. The two-dimensional figure would leap out at the old woman from behind doors. She would shout in the old lady's ear while she was holding fragile objects. The horse appeared in the house—chewing on the curtains in the parlor, swishing its tail over the quilt on her bed, crowding into the kitchen with a paper-thin rider on its back.

But the old lady was just as stubborn as the ghost. Whenever the ghost shouted: "Get out of my house," the old lady shouted back: "No!"

One evening in late summer, the old lady entered the kitchen holding a basket of tomatoes, and the ghost attacked her with a

knife. The old lady just managed to parry with the basket, and the knife flew out of the ghost's hands and clattered to the floor. Her whole body shaking in terror, the old lady realized the ghost had attacked her with the cleaver she used for cutting meat.

"Get out of my house!" the shimmering, black-and-white, paper-thin ghost screamed at her. Behind her, she felt the cold whoosh of a ghost horse's breath on her neck. "GET OUT!"

The old lady flushed a brilliant red and threw the basket of tomatoes at the shimmering ghost-girl.

"NO!" she screamed. And felt a horrible pain rip through her left arm, fill her chest, smash through her mind. The world turned searing white, and she felt her body tumbling to the floor amidst the rolling red tomatoes.

A visiting neighbor found the body and called the police. The doctor said the woman had died of a massive heart attack, and the matter ended there. None of the visitors to the house heard the rude, high-pitched laughter coming from the front parlor, and the doctor walked right through the body of the coal-black horse grazing in the vegetable garden by the back door.

No one else bought the house after the old lady died. The people who came to view it were frightened off by slamming doors, cool breezes, and a sense of menace. The house fell into disrepair, and the town eventually had it torn down.

But they say that on moonless nights, people driving down the road where the house once stood sometimes see a black horse trotting beside them. On its back is the shimmering, black-and-white figure of a little girl, who waves paper-thin arms and shouts: "Get out!"

9

One Last Head

Folks hereabouts were never too fond of the Quick family. Old Man Quick had moved to Michigan territory with his son Billy shortly after the death of his wife. He built a house out back in the woods a long way from the settlement and eked out a living by hunting and trapping. Folks tried to be friendly with Old Man Quick and his boy when they first came to the settlement to sell 'coon skins and buy supplies for the winter. But the hunter and his son weren't much on socializing, and their taciturn ways and rough speech soon turned people against them.

When young Bill turned eighteen, things changed a bit. The lad started coming to some of the town socials, and he even cracked a few jokes with the fellows playing checkers in the mercantile. Then he started courting a nice young lady from a good family. Bill soon won her heart and her hand, and they settled down with Old Man Quick out in the backwoods. Surprisingly enough, the marriage was a happy one, though the girl's parents disapproved of Bill and were upset that their only daughter lived so far away. When the girl died in childbirth, her parents swept down upon the grieving father and took their little grandson away with them before he knew what had happened.

After the death of his wife, Bill grew as taciturn as his father and stopped coming in to town. He rarely saw his son and didn't interfere in his upbringing in any way. Things went on like this for years. Then one day Bill came home to find his father dead on the cabin floor. Old Man Quick had been tomahawked to death and partially scalped by an Indian war party that had raided the lonely cabin while Bill was out checking his traps.

Well, Bill just about went mad with grief and fury. And in the years that followed, Bill became even more reclusive. He came to town only once a year for winter supplies, and he rarely communicated with his son, young Tom Quick, who still lived with his in-laws. Bill Quick's cabin became more and more decrepit. The smell coming from it got to be so bad that passing hunters took to avoiding that patch of the woods altogether, opting to make the long trek to town rather than bunking with Bill for the night.

It was during this period that the relationship between the settlement and the local Pottawatomie and Wyandot tribes became strained. No one knew for sure why the tribesmen became so wary of their white neighbors, or why they stopped trading with the people in town. Eventually they withdrew completely, staying close to their tribal lands and avoiding the white men altogether. Things stayed this way for a long time. As the years passed, the townsfolk almost forgot that the settlement had ever traded with the local tribes.

Tom Quick grew into an easygoing young man who was nothing like his taciturn, reclusive father. He'd been much indulged by his maternal grandmother, and he took to drink and cards rather than hard work and religion. Still, folks preferred him to his father. Bill Quick behaved more and more like a wild man during his infrequent visits to town. There was something about him that frightened even the toughest frontiersmen, and something in his eyes that terrified the womenfolk. They claimed time and again that his pupils gleamed red like those of a maddened beast.

One day, a local hunter passing near Bill Quick's cabin heard a heart-rending wail coming from inside. He went to investigate and found Bill Quick lying on a cot in the main room. Quick begged the hunter to send his son Tom to him before he died, and the compassionate man hurried into town to do as Bill bade him.

Tom was surprised and touched by the summons. He had almost reconciled himself to his father's complete indifference toward him, though he secretly wished that his father would love him, if only a little. He hurried through the woods toward the Quick cabin, hoping to get there before Bill died.

As he entered the clearing where the cabin stood, he was overwhelmed by the stench of rotting meat. Tom gasped and reeled backward, retching and fighting to control his stomach. The smell was far worse than the hunters in town had described. Tom no longer wondered that they avoided the place. He wanted to turn and run—but his father was dying inside that cabin, so he forced himself forward.

He called out to Bill as he knocked on the door, and his father answered from a cot by the closed door in the far wall. The smell was even worse inside the cabin, but Tom steeled himself and stepped into the room. Bill's emaciated, fever-stricken form lay on the bed. His rough face was flushed with fever, and he was picking restlessly at the tattered cover that lay over him. He snapped at his son to come over where he could see him, and Tom walked slowly to his side. The smell was so bad now that he had to concentrate on controlling his stomach. It seemed to be pulsing out from behind the closed door beside his father's cot.

"I'm dying, curse it," Bill began abruptly when Tom reached the bed, "and I won't be able to finish my life's work. So you're going to have to do it."

"What life's work?" Tom asked. This was the first time the old man had ever spoken of such a thing.

"My revenge!" his father shouted, his pupils gleaming red with madness. "My collection!" Bill gestured toward the closed door and told his son to go into the next room.

Trying to breathe only through his mouth, Tom opened the latch and stepped through the door. He was met by a blast of foul air, and he paused in horror as his eyes took in shelf upon shelf of human heads lining every wall of the room. Some were merely skulls; others were half-rotten and crawling with worms and beetles. At least one was nearly fresh, and Tom could still see the look of shock on the face of the Pottawatomie tribesman to whom it had once belonged. There was only one empty space left in the room, at the center of the back wall; a gap just big enough to fit one more head.

"Dear God in heaven!" Tom cried. He backed out of the door, wanting to run but unable to tear his eyes from the grotesque collection.

"Father, what have you done?" he cried, whirling at last to face the dying old man on the cot.

"I have avenged your grandfather," Bill Quick said. "On the day he died, I swore to take the heads of one hundred Indians in exchange for the scalp they took from my father."

As Tom struggled to listen, Bill described how he tracked down his prey, waiting until he found a tribesman hunting alone and then shooting him through the heart. He never needed more

than one bullet for each man, he told his son proudly. And he removed each man's head for his grisly collection.

At first, it had been easy to find individual hunters, but the Pottawatomie and Wyandot tribes had become wary as the death toll mounted, and soon none of the men went out hunting alone. But Bill had continued his hunt, stalking his victims ever more carefully, and had continued to add to his terrible collection until this fever had laid him low.

"Ninety-nine heads line my walls," he told his son. "You must kill the last Indian and fulfill my oath to your grandfather."

Fighting to control his revulsion, Tom glared at the figure on the bed and told him that he would have nothing to do with his terrible oath. Bill Quick rose up from his pillow, his eyes red with rage. Tom backed away in horror, afraid that he would become his father's next victim.

"Give me one last head," Bill Quick howled, his voice that of a madman. "One last head!"

Tom ran for the door as fast as his shaking legs would carry him. He fumbled with the latch, hearing the cot creak as his insane father tried to rise. His sweaty palms kept slipping off the metal latch, but finally he got the door open and threw himself into the yard.

The voice of his father followed him as he fled from the Quick cabin: "Fulfill my oath or my spirit will return from the grave to seek you out! One last head!"

Tom ran as far and as fast as he could. When he could run no longer, he flung himself down upon the leaf-strewn dirt and sobbed in fear and rage and revulsion. Time passed; how long, he didn't know. Finally, when all traces of tears and sickness were gone, he went back to the settlement and straight to the pub to drown his sorrow in whisky.

It took several days and many drinks to ease the horror of Tom's meeting with his father. One evening, the hunter who had brought Tom his father's deathbed message came and told him that the old man had died. He'd checked on him that day and found him dead in his cot. The longer he talked, the harder Tom found it to control his countenance as he visualized every sordid corner of the cabin.

"Don't feel bad that he was alone when he passed, son," the hunter said gruffly, reading only grief in Tom's expression. "Ol' Bill preferred it that way."

Tom nodded wordlessly, and the hunter took himself off, privately touched by the depth of feeling Tom had for his crazy old father.

That night, Tom was awakened by the sound of the wind howling outside his window. He sat up in bed and saw a glow coming from the treetops outside. It formed into the face of his father, his eyes glowing red with insanity, his open mouth a fathomless black hole. "One last head!" the apparition shrieked.

Tom screamed in terror and hid underneath his covers until the ghastly face disappeared. Then he jumped out of bed and ran into the main room to get a bottle of whisky, which he speedily emptied. He spent the rest of the night by the fire, his back to the window, refusing to look up from the flames.

Everywhere he turned the next day, Tom saw his dead father. A pair of red eyes watched as he rode away from the farm toward town. An emaciated form appeared on the roof of the mercantile, glaring down on him as he tied his horse to the hitching post.

The wind howled through the main street, whipping around him and shrieking "one last head" into his ear. Tom ended up in the tavern, seeking courage in a bottle, and was so drunk by the day's end that he spent the night in the lock-up.

Tom spent more and more of his time that way, since it seemed the only way to avoid the ghost of his father. But drink only muted the terror he felt when he saw his father's specter lurking in the shadows, or felt malevolent red eyes watching him. And soon, even the voices of other people could not tune out his father's shrieking. "One last head! One last head!"

One night, he told the bartender the whole story, and it became a joke among the townspeople. Every time someone mentioned seeing a Pottawatomie or Wyandot warrior in Tom's presence, folks would nudge one another knowingly. "Here's your chance, Tom," they would say. "Better go get him now, before your father's ghost returns!" Tom's life became one of sheer misery. He couldn't hold a job because of his drinking, and he was teased and tormented constantly by the wags in town over his father's curse.

Just when Tom thought things couldn't get any worse, he was visited at midnight by the rotting corpse of his father. Bill Quick stood in the doorway, his maggot-ridden skeleton and shredding skin clear as day in the bright moonlight. The specter held a hunting rifle in one hand and a knife in the other. Pointing the rifle at his cowering son, Bill Quick made his demand. "Ninety-nine heads line my walls! You must kill one last Indian and fulfill my oath to your grandfather!"

Tom was so terrified he couldn't speak. He backed away until his shoulders hit the wall behind him. His body was shaking uncontrollably. He wanted to flee, but he stood frozen in place, unable to take his eyes off the demented figure in the doorway.

"One last head!" the corpse shrieked, a piece of its lip dropping off as it howled. "I need one last head. You have until midnight, or the spirit of your murdered grandfather will return with me, and you will answer to him."

Tom's courage broke, and with it went his mind. With a shriek every bit as horrible as that of his father, he dove out the window and ran toward the settlement. His screams of terror woke the whole town. He leapt from house to house, pounding on the wooden doors until they buckled, babbling insanely about his father's specter, and begging someone, anyone, to take him in. The good people of the town barred their doors, and the townsmen ran him off with rifles, fearing that the drunken madman might harm their women and children.

Tom was last seen plunging into the woods in the direction of his father's cabin. When the townsmen went to check on him the next day, they found his house empty. Taking their rifles, they started a careful search, not sure what would happen when they found the poor, insane drunk. They followed his trail easily through the woods, but the tracks disappeared just inside the clearing where the Quick cabin stood.

The air still reeked of rotting flesh. To the right of the cabin, Bill Quick's grave lay undisturbed in the flickering afternoon light. The searchers approached the cabin reluctantly, covering their noses before they entered. The main room was empty and showed signs of long abandonment. The dirt floor showed no new tracks, but there was still the back room to check.

One man crossed to the door and pulled it open. The stench of rotten flesh bellowed out into the room. Gagging desperately, the man stepped through the door and gave a cry of terror that brought the other searchers running. They were instantly overwhelmed by the grisly sight of rotting human heads lining the shelves in the room. But it was the bulging eyes and agony-twisted face of the latest victim that held their attention. Filling the one hundredth space at the center of the back wall was the head of Tom Quick. The rest of his body was never found.

10

The Miner

He was aching, tired, and covered in smelly mud when he saw the little house on the outskirts of town on a rainy evening in early spring 1827. He'd spent months searching for gold, and he was ready to abandon his search when he'd found placer gold in the foothills. He had a pretty darn good idea where to find the mother lode, but first he needed to stock up on supplies and buy better tools using the gold nuggets he found. The miner was heading toward the nearest town when the thunderstorm hit, frightening his mule so much the creature had bolted, throwing him off the wagon into the mud, where he'd lain in a daze, watching his wagon disappear into the distance. The fall had injured his head, and he staggered slowly down the road, hoping to find help somewhere.

When he saw lantern light in the window of the little house deep in the woods, he staggered in at the gate, hoping the occupants would have pity on him and take him in. He pounded on the door, and a moment later it opened and a middle-aged woman peered out cautiously. Behind her, a voice called: "Sister, who is it?"

Before she could answer, the miner collapsed on the stoop, done in from his fall and subsequent long trek through the woods. The sisters clucked at each other and brought him inside. They tucked him into a blanket and when he awoke, they fed him soup and brought him warm water so that he could wash the mud off. They even found him some dry clothes left in the house by their deceased brother. The miner was grateful for the attention, and he didn't say no when they insisted he take a drink of their homemade remedy, which was mostly made up of moonshine.

It was the moonshine that did him in. Literally. He got roaring drunk and told the sisters all about the gold he discovered. He was still rambling when the younger sister hurried into the kitchen to take the kettle off the stove and returned with a sharp carving knife in her hand. He was shocked into silence when the knife was thrust into his heart. He stared at the handle in his chest for what seemed an eternity, and then fell over and died without another word. The sisters searched his dirty clothes and found a small pocketbook full of gold nuggets. They smiled at each other in satisfaction, and the elder sister went outside to dig a hole in the vegetable garden for their permanent guest.

A month passed while the sisters debated what to do with their newfound fortune. They couldn't spend it in town. People would talk. Finally, they decided they would walk to Spartanburg and hire a coach to take them north to Asheville, where their cousin— a notorious moonshiner—could advise them. Of course, he would make them split the gold with him, but it couldn't be helped.

The next afternoon, they tied on their bonnets and began the long walk toward town. It was a grim day with clouds so low they almost brushed the tops of the trees. The light was dim and uneven, and the sisters hurried along the road, hoping that a farmer might drive past and offer them a lift. An hour passed, and a light rain began to fall. The sisters were still alone on the road to town.

"Walk carefully, sister," said the elder. "This path will soon turn to mud."

"Carry your skirts higher, sister," advised the younger. "We don't want to look untidy when we get to town."

At that moment, they heard the jingle of a harness and the clip-clop of hooves behind them. The sisters turned, peering out from under their bonnets through the gray light. A wagon was coming toward them, pulled by a mule. It appeared to be full of digging and panning equipment, and the man driving the mule had the rough appearance of a miner.

The sisters exchanged sly glances. Here was another lonely miner. They might get lucky twice. The elder sister glanced at her sister's handbag, which held the kitchen knife they always carried with them when they walked to town, for fear of robbers. The younger sister smiled and patted the handbag. Then she waved at the approaching wagon and drawled prettily: "Sir, can you give us a ride to town?"

The man on the wagon seat had a face that was mostly beard, just like the first miner. In fact, he resembled the first miner so much that the elder sister felt a pang in her chest. Surely this was not his brother, come searching for him? The miner stopped the wagon and beckoned for the sisters to join him. The younger sister sprang daintily aboard, and the elder sister pushed aside her misgivings and climbed up on the far side of the wagon.

The sisters sat on either side of the miner, and he continued his journey without a word spoken to either of them. The sisters politely said nothing about the stench rising off the miner, though they were both overwhelmed by it. *Really,* thought the elder, *he must not have bathed in months.* His clothes held the sickly sweet smell of decay, as if he'd rolled in a compost heap and

then perfumed himself with the meat of a long-dead deer. How vulgar. The elder sister put her handkerchief daintily to her nose and tried to breathe through it, to calm her roiling stomach.

On the far side of the driver, her younger sister gave a sigh as if she wanted to speak but couldn't. Glancing toward her, the elder sister's eye was caught by the gaunt cheekbones pushing through the man's skin. Really, the man could almost be a skeleton, he was so thin. And his bulging eyes stared straight ahead, like those of a dead fish. The elder sister shuddered and turned away.

The man's stench filled her nostrils and seemed to enter her bloodstream and move like poison through her whole body. The smell seemed to burn her under her skin. Then it turned to ice, and she shuddered in the seat. She wanted to get up and throw herself out of the wagon, but her body was heavy. So heavy.

The younger sister sighed again, as if in pain, and the elder sister glanced toward her. But the miner was still in the way, bulging eyes staring out at the misty rain without blinking. The skin of his face appeared grayer now, and—the elder sister swallowed suddenly—it looked gooier. It reminded her of the damp decay that curled along the edges of leaves of uneaten lettuce. *His skin was melting away,* she thought, burying her face in her handkerchief.

The man's stench no longer bothered her but his metamorphosis did. Once again, she tried to move her body, to jump off the wagon full of mining tools. But her legs felt brittle and frail, as if they could not hold her. As if her bones were rotting from the inside out. But how could bones rot? She glanced down at her long skirts, as if she might see through the thick covering to her agonized limbs. They were throbbing hot, cold, hot. So were her hands under the long gloves she wore. The elder sister pulled off a glove and gazed in horror at her hand. It was gray, and the skin looked gooey, as if it were rotting off her throbbing bones.

On the far side of the wagon, her sister sighed a third time. The elder turned in panic toward the sound, only to encounter the skeletal face of the miner, reduced now to a few ragged patches of skin with maggots writhing just behind the bones. The elder sister clapped her bare hand to her mouth, and felt the gray skin of her hand burn the flesh of her lips. She forced her eyes passed the dead miner toward her sister and saw a skeleton wearing a bonnet tied under its jawbone. Bones peaked through her dainty walking dress, an hour before held so carefully above the mud by the gloved hand that was now tatters of damp cloth over withered gray skin and sharp splinters of finger bone. The skeleton turned toward the elder sister and said: "Sister, I do not feel well." Then it burst into flames, beginning with the too-clean hem of the walking dress and rapidly boiling upward with a smell of brimstone and sulfur. Moments later, the blackened bones of the skeleton rattled to the floor of the wagon.

The elder sister opened her mouth to scream, but there was nothing left to scream with. Her tongue and throat had rotted away. Her skin was melting off her bones in a gooey, smelly trickle. She smelled of rot and decay, and her eyes were beginning to burn from the inside out. She turned her head as her vision faded and stared at the miner driving the cart. A skeleton grinned back at her in triumph. Bony hands urged the glowing, translucent mule to walk faster as the elder sister's skirts began to burn.

11

Heartbeat

Something was going on. Jason felt it in his bones. Polly was too happy, too cheerful all the time. No woman could be that upbeat and still be faithful to her husband; of this he was morally certain.

It maddened Jason that he could never catch Polly flirting with another man, or even talking with one on the phone. She stayed near him at parties and local charity events, and they sat together holding hands each Sunday morning at church. All their friends and neighbors thought they were completely devoted to one another. But he knew better!

Polly had married beneath her class, of course. Her parents had always hated him. They still joked about how she gave up marrying her high school sweetheart—who became a lawyer—to marry him. Polly thought they were kidding, but Jason knew they weren't. He'd seen the sideways glances they threw at him when she wasn't looking, and they still had Polly's prom photo— *with the other man*—up on the living room wall.

Jason sat down to a delicious, warm meal every night—that couldn't be right—and Polly sang to herself as she washed up afterward. What kind of woman could be cheerful doing dishes, unless she was sure that in the near future she would never wash a plate again? As Jason read the newspaper after dinner, he would listen to her chatting on the phone with her mother or one of the church ladies. Strain as he might, Jason never heard anything that hinted of a secret romance. It drove him crazy. Life was not this perfect. It couldn't be. There was a flaw somewhere, and he was determined to find it.

Maybe Polly was seeing the milkman, or the greengrocer. Jason started getting up early in order to see who it was that delivered the milk. Much to his disappointment, the fellow that creaked up to their front door looked as if he'd been born several centuries ago and had kept living out of sheer stubbornness. The remains of his white hair were thin and greasy, he had so many wrinkles it was hard to tell where his eyes were, and he stooped over so low that he had to drop his hand only a few inches to place the bottles on the doorstep. Just in case, he asked the old man his name. Joe Smith. Ha! Obviously an alias. Still, he looked a bit too creaky to be courting a beautiful, classy lady like Polly.

Jason started doing the food shopping, and checked out every single male employee in the local grocery store. They were either antediluvian relicts—like the milkman—or still in diapers. None seemed the type to sweep his wife off her feet. Jason grumbled to himself as he stomped home. Polly met him at the door with a kiss, and she'd made a plate full of his favorite cookies while he was gone, just to thank him for doing the shopping. Yes, there was definitely something going on!

In mid-September, his father-in-law called and jovially asked if Jason would like to help fix up his old car. He agreed at once, rather pleased the old man thought so well of his abilities. They joked around as they poked and prodded at the old car, sliding under it skillfully like a couple of grease monkeys.

Jason was working underneath the car when he heard his father-in-law call: "Hiya, Hank!"

Hank was the name of Polly's high-school boyfriend. Jason rolled out from under the car and quickly stood up.

"Hello, Mr. Parker." A tall, handsome young man had come to the entrance of the driveway to shake hands.

Jason's father-in-law beamed. "It's nice to see you! How are Helen and the kids?"

"Fine, just fine," Hank said with a smile.

"Say, have you met my son-in-law? This is Polly's husband, Jason. They just got married about this time last year, isn't that right, son?" his father-in-law said, pulling him forward and introducing the two men. Jason gripped Hank's hand so hard the lawyer blanched a bit, and massaged it behind his back once they dropped the clinch.

"Hank and his family just moved back to town," his father-in-law continued, oblivious to the rage shaking his son-in-law. "You joined Ted Mallory's firm, right?"

Hank nodded and elaborated on the topic for several minutes before continuing on his way. Jason kept his cool and went back to working on the car as if there were nothing wrong. But inside he was triumphant. Now he knew! He knew why Polly was so happy all the time. Her parents must have told her that Hank was coming home, and she was planning on running off with him. Jason disregarded the notion that Hank would remain faithful to his wife and children after meeting Polly again. Why would he want someone else if he could have Polly?

Enraged with jealousy, he was waiting in the kitchen when Polly got back from her church meeting and began roaring out his anger as soon as she shut the door.

"What are you talking about?" Polly yelled when he paused for breath. "Why would I want to be with anyone else but you? I love you!"

But Jason was beyond reason. He snatched up a newly sharpened steak knife, howling: "You've cut out my heart, now I'll cut out yours!" He leapt around the table toward his cowering wife and ripped her still-beating heart out of her chest with the knife. Blood streaming everywhere, he sailed out the back door into the dark night and flung her heart, still thumping warmly against his hand, over the side of the bridge that spanned the creek next to their home and into the swirling water beneath.

He cleaned up the blood-stained house with extreme care and buried Polly's body deep in the woods outside of town. Then he wrote several letters, carefully mimicking Polly's handwriting, and mailed them to himself and her parents. Within a few days, everyone in town believed that Polly had been secretly seeing a man from the next town that she'd met through her charity work, and that they had run away together. Polly's parents were heartbroken and apologized again and again to Jason for their daughter's cruelty. Jason was careful to play the role of a grieved and betrayed husband. And he *had* been betrayed—he was convinced of it in his soul. He knew that Polly had decided to get back together with that lawyer, even though it hadn't actually happened yet.

He went out to the bridge later that evening and watched the dark water swirling around in satisfaction.

Polly had gotten what she deserved, he thought. As he breathed in the night air, he became aware of a vibration under his feet.

Da-dum. Da-dum. Da-dum.

The sound was so faint that Jason could barely hear it at first. It floated softly through the air, a rhythmic thudding that trapped everything else in its beat.

Da-dum. Da-dum. Da-dum.

Jason's hands began to tingle as he recognized the soft thudding sound. It was the same beat he had felt when he held Polly's bleeding heart in his hands as he ran from their house to this bridge.

Da-dum. Da-dum. Da-dum.

The heartbeat grew louder as he stood frozen beside the railing of the bridge.

Da-dum. Da-dum. Da-dum.

The heartbeat rang in his ears, thundering so loud that he was afraid it would wake the neighbors.

"No!" Jason shouted. "No, Polly! No!"

He clapped his hands over his ears and ran back to the house, slamming the door against the terrible, relentless beat that pulsed from underneath the bridge. He couldn't hear the sound in the kitchen, but the floorboards seemed to vibrate slightly under his feet to a slow, steady rhythm. He fled into the living room and picked up the newspaper, trying to regain some semblance of normalcy by returning to his nightly routine.

Da-dum. Da-dum. Da-dum.

He gradually became aware that the words in the article he was reading were following a faint, rhythmic pattern that ebbed and flowed around a soft, steady beat.

Da-dum. Da-dum. Da-dum.

It sounded like a heartbeat.

Da-dum. Da-dum. Da-dum.

Polly's heartbeat.

Da-dum. Da-dum. Da-dum.

Jason screamed in terror and flung himself out of the house, running toward the bridge as the heartbeat grew louder and louder in his ears.

"Curse you, Polly! Curse you," he shouted dementedly.

Lights went on in the neighboring houses as Jason leaned over the railing where he had flung Polly's beating heart.

"Curse you!" he shouted, as his next-door neighbor tried to pull him off the rail. Jason yanked away from him impatiently, intent on reaching the heart—that horrible, betraying heart—and silencing it forever. He could hear nothing of his neighbors' frantic cries or the women screaming. Nothing save the dreadful heartbeat.

Da-dum. Da-dum. Da-dum.

With a wild shriek, Jason flung himself headfirst off the bridge like a diver. The neighbors all heard the very final crunching sound of his head hitting the rocks below, and the snap of a breaking neck.

There was a stunned silence. Then, the gathered neighbors became aware of a very faint vibration coming up through the soles of their feet: *Da-dum. Da-dum. Da-dum.*

It felt like the slow, steady beat of a human heart.

12

Barn Dance

As I drove down the seemingly endless dark road, I cursed myself for ever having listened to my friends. "It will be fun," they said. "A quaint little bar in the middle of nowhere," they said. "Great beer on tap. Gotta try it." Right. Sure.

About the only thing they'd gotten right, as far as I could make out, was that the location of the bar was the middle of nowhere. They'd hit that one bang on the nose. The bar was so far out in the middle of nowhere that I'd become completely and utterly lost trying to find it. I was pretty sure I would die of old age before I ever made my way out of this endless labyrinth of dark woods, dark fields, and ruined buildings. There was not one blessed sign of civilization anywhere to be seen.

Surely there must be a farmhouse somewhere on this benighted, twisty road where I could ask for directions back to Madison. Assuming I was still in Wisconsin, that is. I'd driven long enough by now to be in California. What a wretched, wretched night this had turned out to be.

It was at this juncture in my whining that the sound of music drifted through the open car window. I slowed down, listening. Then I caught a glimpse of a lighted building down a road that branched off from the one I was traveling. I turned at once, heading toward the lights and music. Civilization at last!

I slowed down after a moment when the road turned into a dirt lane. My headlights caught a number of wagons, carriages, buckboards and buggies parked beside a huge round barn. I whistled at the scene. Some rich folks had really gone to town for this party, I thought, parking near a fancy carriage with a horse hitched to the front. The bay horse blinked placidly at me as I got out of the car and headed for the lighted building.

The party was in full swing as I stepped through the large double doors. The building had obviously been converted long ago from a working barn to a dance hall. The center of the barn was filled with singing, swirling dancers in merry outfits that spanned every color of the rainbow. The dancers were all dressed in the costumes of yesteryear, reinforcing my impression that the people attending this party had gone to a great deal of trouble to recreate an authentic nineteenth-century barn dance.

I stood in the doorway admiring the huge, converted barn around me. The horse and cow stalls to my right had been replaced by a large alcove lined with tables full of good things to eat. The stalls to the left now contained benches filled with laughing, chatting folk, and a pot-belly stove had been installed near the door. Above our heads, the hay lofts remained in place but were filled with playing children and giggling teenagers sweethearting in the semidarkness. At the far end of the huge dance floor, a makeshift stage stood under the hayloft. An old-time band was sawing away at fiddle, guitar, jug, banjo, and so forth while a man with a shock of white hair and a large handlebar mustache called out the figures to the swirling dancers on the floor.

A large bearded chap clapped me on the shoulder in greeting and handed me a mug of beer. I took a sip and then gulped it

down eagerly. It was the best beer I'd ever tasted. I was sure the quaint little nonexistent bar in the middle of nowhere had nothing to touch it. I'd landed on my feet, alright. My feeling of goodwill was enhanced when a dark-eyed beauty grabbed me by the hand and pulled me out onto the dance floor to make up a square with her and her friends. I hadn't square-danced since primary school, but it all came flooding back during that magical evening. I swung my partner and do-si-doed and even managed to do a star at the center with the other fellows. I was flying high, dancing and drinking, and singing along whenever the band played one of the old-time songs I'd learned as a little fellow at school. I forgot all about asking for directions and meeting my friends at the bar.

It wasn't until midnight, when the band took a break and I stood with my new acquaintances before a table lined with drinks, that I remembered to ask where I was.

"At the barn dance, silly," giggled my inebriated beauty. "Give us a toast to the night," she added, thrusting another beer at me. I cuddled her close to my side and raised my mug.

"To a delightful night," I said, loudly enough for everyone in the vicinity of the table to hear me. "And to a delightful party. Good fortune and long life to everyone present."

The crowd went silent when they heard my words. The stillness grew, flowing outward from me like a wave, until you could have heard a pin drop. As I glanced uneasily about me, wondering why my words had caused such a dramatic reaction, I saw the skin slowly peeling away from the merry faces, until all that remained were bone, rotting skin, and staring eye holes. A few faces had the withered gray skin of a mummy, with maggots writhing grotesquely under cheek and chin. And the girl in my arms was nothing but a skeleton in a moldy blue dress. With a gasp of horror, I dropped my mug and leapt away from the skeleton. The mug hit the floor with a loud bang. It was completely empty now, although just moments earlier it had been foaming with beer.

There came a long sigh from the foul corpses in the barn. And then the lights went out. I screamed in terror and stumbled backward, slamming into a damp, foul-smelling pile of hay in the absolute darkness. Next I ran into a post and then got tangled up in some old rope as I frantically tried to find my way to the door without the use of my eyes. I kept expecting withered, bony hands to grab me, or the skeleton in the blue dress to reach out for a kiss. I couldn't see a thing as I slammed into the open door of a stall. It knocked the wind right out of me and made me pause long enough to realize that moonlight was streaming through a small hole in the ceiling. I used it to orient myself, spotting the barn doors a moment later. I rushed toward them, my feet crashing again and again through the rotten floorboards. In my panic I thought I'd never escape the old round barn. Then I was out in the moonlight and running to my car, which was parked beside a rotting wagon that had lost its wheels eons ago.

I leapt into the car and backed down the lane as fast as I could go, screeching my tires as I turned the car. My headlights caught the barn, which only had half of its roof and was sagging sadly to one side. Vines grew up and over the gloomy remains. Obviously, it hadn't been used in a very long time. I slammed the car into gear and drove as fast as I could away from the horrible, rotting barn with its dancing corpses.

Somehow, I found the highway and made my way, trembling, back to my home in Madison to spend the remainder of that restless night sleeping with the light on in my bedroom.

To this day, I have no idea where I was or how I managed to stumble across the ghostly barn dance in the middle of nowhere. Truthfully, I don't want to know. I heard later that folks in Vernon County sometimes hear strange music drifting over the hills at night, though no one can identify its source. And in my mind, I can see again the bright lights spilling out into the lane, and the bright happy faces of the ghostly farmers dancing the night away in a rotting old barn.

13

Dark Presence

They wanted the house as soon as they saw it. Her husband loved the wide-open spaces of the West and the stories of Buffalo Bill. She loved the proximity of Yellowstone National Park. Their son happily eyed the pretty daughter of the next-door neighbor. It was a perfect place to live. The realtor told them that the stone circles near the property were traces left from a tipi encampment long ago. The circles add a wonderful Western touch to this lovely home. Or so she thought at the time.

The family moved in right away and their son transferred to the local high school. On weekends, the couple cheered their son on at his sporting events, took scenic drives, and visited Yellowstone.

Time passed swiftly, and the son graduated from high school and college, then moved away from home. Empty-nesters now, the husband spent most weekends riding his motorcycle while the wife stayed home and baked.

She was baking blueberry muffins when the hospital called and told her to come at once. Her husband had been in a serious accident on his motorcycle. She was out the door in two minutes and raced recklessly to the hospital, hoping to get there in time to say goodbye to her husband.

Someone was waiting for her at the entrance to the emergency room, and she was rushed to her husband's side. There was barely time for him to squeeze her hand and smile into her tear-filled eyes. "Love you, beautiful," he said, and died. It was the worst moment of her life.

Her son arrived soon afterward and drove her home. He took over the funeral arrangements while she wept and finished making the blueberry muffins—her husband's favorite.

The next few days went by in a haze. The house felt empty without her husband, in spite of the friends and family that filled it. And the dog seemed to go mad. He barked and growled whenever anyone opened the door to the cellar, and he refused to go into the den where the family kept his bed.

Soon—too soon—her husband was laid to rest in the local graveyard. Everyone left, including her son, who was packing up his apartment so he could live with her until she grew accustomed to widowhood.

The moment she walked into the empty house, she knew something was wrong. She stood frozen in the living room doorway as the dog came up to her, tail wagging. The dog stopped abruptly and stared into the empty living room, growling softly. His eyes followed the path of . . . something evil . . . that was moving across the floor. Boards creaked under invisible pressure as the . . . something evil . . . entered the den. She watched in terror as the door to the den swung shut of its own volition. The dog barked once, low and fierce, hair spiked up along its back. She shrieked and ran to her bedroom, dog at her heels.

Inside the bedroom, the feeling of malice abated. She knew at once that the Dark Presence could not enter this room. When her eyes fell on the icon of Mary and Baby Jesus hanging on the wall, she understood why: The holy object was generations old, and it glowed faintly in the dimness, its goodness actively pushing back evil.

She sat on the bed and tried to think, the scary scene replaying itself in her mind. Her dog refused to enter the den after her husband's death. Why? *Because it overlooked the tipi ruins.* The thought lodged in her head out of nowhere. She wondered if this house was built on some native burial ground. If so, why hadn't they felt the evil spirit when they first bought the house? Had her husband's presence kept it at bay? Or had it been sleeping until aroused by her terrible grief? She had no answer to these questions.

She kept the dog with her that night. He slept at the foot of the bed, and she was grateful for his snoring presence.

Daylight woke her. She lay sleepily in bed, trying to decide if she should rise. Then she remembered the strange presence in the house last night and sat bolt upright, body cold with fear. "I'm being ridiculous," she told the dog, who was dancing impatiently at the door.

They entered the hall together, and at once she knew she hadn't imagined the Dark Presence. The house seethed with malice. She hurried into the kitchen, where the sense of menace seemed weaker in the dancing sunlight, and let the dog outside to do his business.

As she drank her coffee, her eye fell on the cellar door. The dog had barked and growled whenever someone opened it. Was the Dark Presence in the cellar too? Her hand shook suddenly, splashing coffee on the table, when she remembered that she had a load of laundry in the dryer. She would have to go down in the

basement to remove it. She took a deep breath. There was *no way* she was going into the cellar alone.

When the dog finished eating, she put on his leash. He started growling when she opened the cellar door. A flood of cold air rushed over them both. The dog barked sharply as she snapped on the cellar light and gazed down the empty staircase.

"We have to get the laundry," she said, grabbing his collar as she placed her foot on the first step. The dog growled again and showed all his teeth. He backed away, pulling her away with him, and she followed with relief. She sensed a wall of evil at the bottom of the steps, and she did not want to cross it. Better to buy new clothes than go down into that cellar.

She hurried to her room to shower and dress. She wasn't going to spend any more time in this empty house than was strictly necessary. The dog padded into the living room and jumped on the sofa, which she took as a sign that the Dark Presence wasn't in there at the moment. Thank God.

She went to the store to get groceries, then spent the afternoon with a friend who was a grief counselor. She heard the dog barking as soon as she pulled into the driveway at supper time. The dog scraped frantically at the front door as she turned the key and shot into the yard when she opened the door, tail between his legs. He circled the yard several times before he calmed down enough to do his business. She waited for the dog on the doorstep, and they went into the house side by side. She took one shuddering look into the dark living room and swerved into the bright kitchen.

A radio tuned to a Christian station kept the darkness at bay through dinner. As she ate dessert, she reflected that her son would arrive tomorrow afternoon. He would know what to do about the Dark Presence. In the meantime, the dog would stay in her room tonight, and she would take him with her tomorrow.

As she washed dishes, the air in the room chilled noticeably, and she heard a scratching sound at the cellar door. The dog growled, and she hastily dried the last cup and hurried to her room. The scratching sound ceased when she shut her bedroom door, and the icon glowed reassuringly on the wall.

It was easier to ignore the Dark Presence the second morning. She dressed hastily and opted to eat out rather than cook breakfast. The dog leapt eagerly into the car when she opened the door, delighted to ride with her as she did errands.

They were taking a stroll at the local park that afternoon when her son called to say he'd reached Cody. She asked him to remove the laundry from the dryer, and he agreed with a laugh. "Putting me to work already?" he teased.

"That's what moms do," she said.

The dog entered the house without hesitation that evening, barking joyfully and jumping all over her son. "I'm happy to see you too," he said, rubbing behind its ears.

She'd decided not to mention the Dark Presence. She didn't want her son to think she was crazy.

Later, over dinner, her son said, "I folded the laundry and put it on your bed. It smelled a little musty. You may want to wash it again."

"Thanks, son," she said, serving herself more pasta.

"That cellar is real creepy," her son continued. "It felt like someone was staring at me the whole time I was down there. Gave me goose bumps!" He laughed uneasily. "But that's stupid, right?"

A huge BANG from the den cut off his last word. Mother and son stared at each other, aghast. Her son leapt through the door, switching on lights as he raced toward the den. The dog stayed on his heels until they reached the den. It stopped in the doorway and growled. The mother stood behind the dog and stared at the huge encyclopedia lying on the floor. Normally, the book stood in the middle of the desk between two bookends.

"That's weird," her son said, picking up the encyclopedia and returning it to its place on the desk. "I wonder how that fell." He glanced around uneasily and then hurried her back to the kitchen, closing the den door firmly behind them.

They finished dinner in silence, and then she retreated to her room to read while her son watched TV with the dog. He stopped by her room to stay goodnight, and the dog jumped on the bed. Her son laughed incredulously. "I thought the dog wasn't allowed on the bed!"

"That was your father's rule," she said, rubbing the dog's ears fondly. She kissed her son goodnight and turned out the light.

She woke in the middle of the night, heart pounding in fear, but was unable to say why she'd awoken. The dog was growling, and the holy icon on the wall glowed brightly as it kept darkness at bay. Then she heard a terrible scream from her son's bedroom. She realized it was the second scream she'd heard. It was his first cry that had woken her. She leapt out of bed, motherly instinct overriding her fear. She grabbed the icon off the wall and charged into the hallway, just as her son bolted out of his room.

"In there! In there," he screamed, pointing toward the door. "A dark shadow, hovering at the foot of my bed!"

Chilled, she watched the bedroom door swing open. A looming shadow floated into the hallway and hovered between them and the rest of the house. She held up the glowing icon, body shaking with fear. "Leave my son alone," she shouted. The dog growled and pressed against her legs as she recited the words of the Lord's Prayer.

Slowly, the Dark Presence fell back toward the living room, forced away by the powerful icon. She pressed forward one step, then two. She could hear something scratching on the cellar door as the black shadow fled toward the den.

"Pack your bag. Right now," she told her son. She stood in the hallway dressed only in a nightgown, icon held high to ward off danger as he raced to obey her. Then he held the icon as she threw her belongings into a bag.

They fled past the scratching cellar door and burst through the front door with cries of relief. She drove them to the nearest hotel that accepted dogs and booked rooms for several days. In the morning, she called the local realtor and put her house on the market. Then her son made some calls and located a house they could rent down in Jackson. They hired a moving company to pack up the house and then left Cody, never to return.

Mother and son never spoke of the Dark Presence to each other or anyone else. But they hung the holy icon on the wall of her bedroom as soon as they moved into their new home, and purchased a second holy icon soon after for her son's room. Just in case.

14

Pray

He was a jolly, round little man with a cherry-red face and a button for a nose. His mouth was all smiles, and he loved to make puns and tell funny jokes to every person who passed by. He sat every day in the front window of his house with a bottle of whiskey at his side. He would beckon folks over to the windowsill, put up the pane of glass, and tell them his latest riddle or story.

Folks in town shook their heads over little Simeon, but they liked him. He would tell the children strange and wonderful stories about faraway places and magical beings. Everyone wondered how he knew such tales, for they never saw him reading or writing or doing anything except sitting in his chair. He never did a lick of work, as a matter of fact. Folks in town said he'd ruined his health in the mines long ago, and his heart was too weak for him to do anything but sit around and watch the world go by.

Simeon's wife, on the other hand, was tall and spare and dour. She wore gray on weekdays and black on Sundays, and a large crucifix hung around her neck. And she was as hard-working and critical as Simeon was lazy and kind. She despised her husband's indolence. Every day, before she left to clean at the mansion house in the city, she would stop in front of her husband's chair, glare at her rosy-cheeked spouse, and say sternly: "Pray, Simeon. Pray for your soul. If you cannot work, then pray!"

Simeon beamed at her and said: "Yes, Constance." But no one ever saw him pray. Not once. Nor would he go to church on Sunday or on high holidays. Even on the coldest day of winter, Constance would bundle herself up against the fierce winter winds and march stolidly downtown to church, where she would pray for hours on her hands and knees before marching home again. But jolly, round Simeon just sat in the window and smiled as the world passed by.

"Pray, Simeon," Constance would thunder at him as she marched to and from the church. "Pray!" But Simeon refused to pray.

Simeon told the local minister once that he'd lost his faith down in the mine, when the shaft had caved in on him and he'd lain for hours in the darkness, hallucinating as the air grew more and more poisoned. "God abandoned me down there," said Simeon. "I prayed all day and all night for him to send an angel to rescue me, and the angel never came. If my shaft supervisor hadn't come a-looking for me, I'd have been dead. And he didn't get there in time to save me heart and me lungs. They were wounded s'bad I couldn't ever work again. After that, I cursed God and the angels. They'd abandoned me, so I abandoned them."

It seemed wrong somehow, to see such a happy, jolly fellow so solemn and stern. The local minister didn't know quite what to say. He wanted to point out that the shaft supervisor might be considered, by some, to be an angel sent by God. But something in little round Simeon's eyes defeated this idea before he could form it into words. It would have been easier to defend his faith if Simeon had been passionately angry or bitter. But such matter-of-fact heresy was impossible for the minister to combat. So he didn't try. He just told Simeon he would pray for him.

When he heard that familiar word, Simeon's jolly face twisted as if he'd bitten into a lemon. For a moment, he looked strangely like his cross and dour wife. "Pray!" he spat out the word. "That's what Constance says. She says my disability was caused by my lack of faith. Me, who went to church faithful every Sunday since I was a lad! Don't pray for me, minister. I'm done praying!"

The local minister went away, shaking a little at the depth of bitterness in jolly, round Simeon. Who could ever guess such darkness lay at the heart of the happy relater of riddles and jokes, the wonderful storyteller whom all the schoolchildren adored?

And always, looming in the background, grimly cleaning the house and scolding him night and day, was dour, gray Constance. "Pray, Simeon! Pray, you sinner," she'd cry out so loud that the neighbors on both sides could hear her. "Get on your knees, and pray!" But Simeon never prayed. He never did anything but sit in the window and watch the world go by.

Never once did anyone hear him raise his voice to Constance, though she made his life a misery with her scolding and her dire predictions. He rose above it, smiling at her and nodding in agreement with every scornful sentiment. But he rarely left his chair, and he never went to church, and he drank deeply of the whiskey in the bottle, for—had she but known it—the drink helped to mask the pain that grew worse day by day.

Simeon was telling his latest riddle to a group of businessmen on their way home from work one evening when he gave a sudden gasp, right before the punch line. The whiskey bottle slipped from his grasp and smashed on the floor. And little round Simeon dropped dead, just like that, slumping forward until his forehead lay across the open windowsill.

They shouted for Constance, and one man ran for the doctor, but they all knew it was too late. Simeon had gone to meet his Maker, happy of nature and bitter of soul. All Constance could say, when she saw him lying in the window was: "Pray, all of you. Pray that this doesn't happen to you. Pray!"

The men backed away from the little round body of Simeon, unnerved by the grim, gray presence towering behind him like a vengeful spirit. Constance's eyes were sparkling with manic fervor, and the men were grateful to turn her and poor, dead Simeon over to the doctor and walk away.

Everyone in town was stunned by Simeon's death. They'd heard that he was poorly, but he'd never shown it. Only the doctor had known the true state of things. Had known that Simeon's poor, injured heart was slowly losing ground. Had put strong medication in his whiskey to help him with the pain. Not even his dour and grim wife had realized that Simeon's laziness stemmed from true illness. Not until it was too late.

The children, especially, were devastated at his death. They'd come every day to the window to listen to his stories, to hear his jokes. He was "Uncle Simeon" to every boy and girl in town. And they were heartbroken to lose him.

Everyone in town came to the church when the huge bell tolled on the day of the funeral. There wasn't a dry eye in the place when the minister gave the eulogy, standing beside the closed casket. Then he asked Constance to speak. Constance stood up beside her seat, black veil quivering with her intensity, and spoke only one word: "Pray!"

The word echoed and reechoed around the great hall. It seemed to grow louder with each echo. One by one, the candles around the altar blew out, until there was only a shadowy darkness behind the casket. Outside, the sunlight was dimmed by dark storm clouds until the interior of the church took on a ghastly, greenish tinge and quivered with the electric intensity of an approaching storm.

And a voice from nowhere repeated Constance's message from the air above the altar. "Pray," it whispered. "Pray!" And then it thundered the word: "Pray!"

A ball of light appeared above the minister's head and grew larger and larger until it formed into the round figure of Simeon. His red face was twisted with pain and anger, and his eyes were fixed on the black-veiled figure of Constance.

"You gave guilt when you should have given compassion," he cried, his round body slowly elongating and twisting into a huge, foul parody of a man. The shadows in the hall darkened, and the children whimpered in fear and clutched at their frozen parents. Simeon's ghost shone with an eerie light that made every face in the watching congregation appear grim and hollow-cheeked. Towering taller and taller above the altar, his round form began pulsing from dark gray to blinding white in a way that stung the eyes and made people's skin crawl.

"You gave scorn instead of understanding," he boomed, raising one arm slowly and pointing a finger at his wife. "And hatred instead of love." The light within Simeon's massive form wriggled and writhed as if a thousand maggots were eating his spirit flesh.

Constance gasped and shrank back from the terrible, pulsating figure. Every eye in the church was fixed upon him in horror as he leaned closer and still closer to his wife, his massive face pressing into hers.

"Pray, Constance," Simeon said, and his voice was suddenly happy and gentle. "Pray for your soul." Then his twisted figure shot suddenly upward until it reached the arched ceiling far above. *"Pray!"* Simeon howled, his voice rising until stained-glass windows started shattering. Everyone in the congregation bolted out of the doors and windows into the biting wind and thunderous rain, their hands clapped over their ears. A bolt of lightning lashed forth from the heavens and crashed into the large oak tree in the center of the graveyard adjoining the church. And then Simeon's wailing voice ceased as suddenly as it had started. The congregation stared at one another in consternation, wondering what was going on inside the sanctuary. For a moment, they stood still as the rain pelted down upon them. Then, one by one, dreading what they would see, they crept back into the sanctuary.

Inside, the candles had flickered back into life, and the air was once more warm and sweet with incense, the atmosphere gentle and sorrowful and kind. And slumped on her knees in front of the altar beside the closed casket, her hands clasped in an attitude of prayer, was the stiff and still figure of Constance. Her forehead touched the floor, and her wide-open eyes were fixed in an expression of fear and dread. Blood trickled slowly from both her ears. She was dead.

15

I Know Moonrise

Mama told me I should never to walk along the marsh shortcut that led from our plantation to the town of Brunswick. She said it was dangerous and I'd get myself killed if I didn't listen to her. At first this restriction didn't bother me none. I had plenty of work to do in the forge helping Pa, who was the plantation blacksmith. My tasks kept me on the plantation most of the time. But when I grew older, the fellers started laughing at me, saying I was a baby because my folks wouldn't let me take the marsh shortcut. I got so mad I told Mama to her face that I wasn't listening to her no more. She gave me a terrible scold and sent me to bed without supper. I was so mad over the whole thing I could have spit nails! She treated me like a baby and I was thirteen years old!

It was Pa, still smelling of charcoal and smoke from the forge, who came and told me why Mama was so scared of the marsh path. "We thought it best to wait until you had grown some afore telling you the story of the marsh path," Pa said. "Yer mama's little sister disappeared in the marsh a long time ago. She was taking the shortcut to the old pond to gather some firewood, and she never came back. They found her straw hat floating in the stagnant water, but they never found her body."

"I ain't gonna fall into the water like Mama's sister what passed," I protested. "I'm thirteen. Big enough to walk alone in the marsh."

"That ain't it, son," Pa said. "I know you're big enough to walk the marsh path without falling in. It's . . ." He rubbed his face with a sweaty palm, eyes troubled. Chills ran up my arms. I'd never seen Pa at a loss for words before. "It's the spirit of yer little aunt," Pa said finally. "She comes to the marsh path some evenings and she . . . she sings."

Color drained from my face and my arms grew goosefleshed. "She's a ghost?" I gasped, clutching the blanket with tense fingers.

"Not just a ghost, son," Pa said. "You heard about the Jack Ma Lantern?"

" 'Course, Pa," I said. "It's an evil spirit that tries to drown you in the marsh. You can see his lantern flashing sometimes at night. That's why all the fellers wear their jackets inside out when they walk through the marsh."

"That's right," said Pa. "Yer little aunt, she's kind of like the Jack Ma Lantern. After she drowned, her ghost started floating over the marsh at night, singing softly of death and the grave.

She's lonesome and wants her family to join her, so she lures them into the water with her song." Pa swallowed hard and continued: "It's safe fer your buddies to walk that path 'cause *they ain't family*. But if you go there, the ghost will come fer you."

I pulled the covers up around my eyes, and my whole body turned to shivers as Pa described the little girl in the swamp.

Pa continued, "The ghost almost got yer mama, back in our courtin' days. If I hadn't been with her, yer mama would have drowned. She was waist deep in the water, following that singing

voice afore I realized she'd left my side. I hauled her out of the mud and threw her over my shoulder, dripping gunk and weed all over my new shirt. Yer mama kicked and hollered something terrible, trying to get away from me so she could follow her little sister's ghost. The spirit floated beside me as I jogged down that trail with yer mama over my shoulder, singing 'I Know Moonlight' in a sweet voice that made my body shake all over. Yer mama screamed at me, wanting to go to her little sister, but I held on tight. As soon as I stepped off the marsh path, the ghost vanished and yer mama went limp. Fer a moment I thought she was dead, but she'd just fainted when the ghost disappeared. That was the last time anyone in yer family ever walked the marsh path."

I blinked. He was right. I couldn't remember seeing anyone in my family on the marsh path. Grandpa, Grandma, my aunts and uncles and grown-up cousins, they all used the road. Pa saw realization dawn on my face and rubbed the top of my head.

"You stay away from the marsh, son," he said.

I should have listened to Pa. But it was easy to forget the ghost in the long days of summer as the fellers and I rambled around the countryside after the day's work was done. I sure wasn't thinking about it the day Jimmy and I were caught in Brunswick after sunset. "My pa's going to be sore at me if I miss dinner," Jimmy said. "We better hurry." We raced down the road toward the plantation. Suddenly Jimmy swerved toward the marsh, and I realized he meant to take the shortcut.

I stared after my buddy, torn between speed and safety. I should take the road. But Jimmy was there, so chances were good that the ghost wouldn't come 'cause he weren't family. Besides, I reasoned, the little aunt never met me, so why would she want me to join her on the other side? Jimmy's head appeared around a tussocky bend in the path. "Come on," he called impatiently. I whipped off my jacket and turned it inside out to keep Jack Ma Lantern (and my aunt) away. Then I raced down the marsh path after Jimmy.

It was getting real dark, and phantom lights were popping up in the distance while the sky was still turning from gray to black. The wind swished through the marsh grasses, all whisper-whisper-whisper. Jimmy hugged his arms around his body. He didn't like the sound of that wind.

We were walking single file along the path with Jimmy in the lead when a bullfrog bellowed beside us. We shouted in fear, nearly toppling into the water beside the path. Then we laughed nervously, clutching at each other to steady ourselves.

"I thought that frog was the Jack Ma Lantern!" Jimmy exclaimed. With a grin he shook me off and headed down the path. I paused for a moment to admire the moon, which was rising over the treetops, making a glittering path across the still water.

As I turned to follow Jimmy, the air around me grew cold till my whole body shook with chills. Out of the silvery moon-sparkle there came a childlike figure that danced and floated above the dark water like a will-o'-the-wisp. I gasped, my throat tight with fear. I called to Jimmy, just a yard in front of me, but he didn't hear me, and I knew he couldn't see the spirit floating toward us across the marsh. My legs shook so bad that I couldn't walk. The silvery will-o'-the-wisp shimmered and grew until I saw a shining little girl in a straw hat. My mouth opened and shut like a dying fish. Puffs of freezing air formed in front of my nostrils as the little girl drew closer to the marsh path. Then she started to sing.

I know moonrise, I know star-rise; Lay dis body down.
I walk in de moonlight, I walk in de starlight, To lay dis body down.
I'll walk in de graveyard, I'll walk through de graveyard, To lay dis body down.
I'll lie in de grave and stretch out my arms; Lay dis body down.
I go to de judgment in de evenin' of de day, When I lay dis body down.
And my soul and your soul will meet in de day, When I lay dis body down.

Suddenly I relaxed, lovely pictures floating through my head. I saw myself saving the life of the Master, who was so pleased with me that he set me free. Now a free boy, I went to school, studying long hours into the night to earn a place at university. Then I saw myself as an important lawyer, earning enough money to buy Mama and Pa from the Master and set them free. I ran to the old cabin where I once lived with Mama and Pa to tell them the great news. Mama stood at the far side of the room and I called out to her, but she didn't hear me. She held a hand to her ear and beckoned me closer. I hurried toward her, splashing through water that came to my knees, my waist, my chest. There was only one thought in my head. I must reach Mama and tell her that she was free. I shouted the words as loud as I could, but my mouth filled with water and I choked. "Mama!" I called, stretching strangely heavy arms toward her. She reached toward me, and I was overwhelmed by the stink of stagnant marsh water. My heart froze in fear, for Mama's eyes were glowing silver. The world went dark.

I woke gasping as someone pounded me on the chest. I choked and threw up all over the person who was thumping my ribs. The muddy water coming from my mouth tasted as foul as it smelled. I vomited again, this time vomiting my lunch along with the marsh water. I could hear Jimmy blubbering in the background but felt too ill to open my eyes. Then I heard Pa's voice: "Son? You all right? Son!"

I opened my eyes and saw my pa's face above me in the shimmering moonlight. I was soaked to the skin, and my whole body trembled with cold and shock. "I saw her, Pa," I gasped. "She sang to me. She sang. . . ."

I lost consciousness again. When I woke I was in my bed and Mama was holding my hand and weeping. I stared up at her, vowing then and there that I would never again do anything to make my mama cry. I squeezed her hand and she looked up, startled, when she realized I was awake. She hugged me so tight I could barely breathe and scolded me something fierce for disobeying her. I promised her that I would never walk the marsh path again, and I kept that promise.

But after that night I had to leave the rice fields whenever the workers sang "I Know Moonlight." Hearing the tune made my whole body shake and my mouth taste of rotting marsh water.

16

The Handshake

Polly was the sweetest, prettiest girl in Goldsboro, yes sir. All the local boys were chasing her, and quite a number of the fellows from the surrounding countryside were too. All the girls were jealous of Polly 'cause they didn't have no sweethearts to take them to the local dances, but even they couldn't help liking her. Polly would give someone the shirt off her back if they needed it. That's just the way she was. Of course, the girls all wanted Polly to choose her man so things could go back to normal. But Polly was picky. None of the local boys suited her, and neither did the fellows from the backcountry.

Then one day, George Dean came home from university, and Polly was smitten. He was handsome, tall, and mysterious. He didn't chase her like the other fellows. He seemed to favor the other girls. For weeks Polly fumed as George played beau to first one pretty girl then another. Didn't he see her at all? She was in a real tizzy by the time handsome George Dean wandered up to her front porch one evening and asked if she'd care to take a stroll down the lane. Polly sniffed and acted haughty at first, but finally she allowed that a stroll might not come amiss.

From that moment on, Polly and George were inseparable. You couldn't turn around without bumping into them at one social event or another. Polly completely dropped all her other beaus, much to the relief of the local girls, and soon the town was filled with the laughter of many courting couples. The Saturday night dances were particularly popular, and it was at one of those that George proposed and Polly accepted. There was great rejoicing—particularly among the eligible young females, who'd been afeared of what might happen if Polly broke it off with George.

A day was set, and Polly started making preparations for the wedding and shopping for items to fill her new home. George wasn't too interested in all the fripperies and wedding details. He left the womenfolk to get on with it and started spending time down at the pool hall with some of his buddies. And that's where he met Helene, the owner's saucy daughter. She had bold black eyes and ruby-red lips, and a bad-girl air that fascinated George. He spent more and more time at the pool hall, and less and less time with Polly, who finally noticed in spite of all the hustle and bustle.

She made a few inquiries, and Cindy—a girl who'd lost her favorite beau to Polly a few years back—told her *all about* Helene. In detail.

Of course, Polly was furious. She immediately confronted George with the story, and he couldn't deny it. Suddenly, George had to toe the mark. His pool-hall visits were over, and he spent every free hour he wasn't at work by her side. That didn't sit well with George, but his family backed Polly up, so he went along with it.

The day of the wedding dawned clear and bright. Polly and her bridesmaids went to the church to get dressed in their finery, whispering excitedly together. The guests filled the sanctuary, and the pastor and the best man waited patiently in the antechamber for the groom's arrival. They waited. And waited. And waited some more. But George didn't come.

The best man hurried into the sanctuary to talk to the groom's father, who hustled back to the house right quick to check on his son. Still no George. Had he been in an accident? Was he hurt? No one knew the answer.

George's brothers went searching for him, calling in at the police, at the hospital. His youngest brother even went to the pool hall. And that's when he found out that Helene was missing too. Helene's youngest sister told George's youngest brother that she'd seen them leave the pool hall together about an hour before the wedding. So that was that.

With dread, Polly's mother went to tell her daughter what had happened. Polly, all bright and shining and lovely in her long white dress and soft wedding veil, turned pale when her mother broke the news.

"It couldn't be. George would never do that!" she exclaimed. She stared blankly at her mother, swayed a bit, and then stiffened, grabbing her left arm as a sudden pain ripped through it. She was dead from a massive heart attack before she hit the floor.

And so Polly's wedding became—in essence—Polly's wake. Her family was furious. George's family was furious and embarrassed. And the guests were furious too. George's unthinking actions had killed the sweetest, prettiest girl in Goldsboro. If he was going to jilt her, the gossips all agreed, he should have done it privately. He shouldn't have left her at the altar.

A few days later Polly was buried in the churchyard, still wearing her white wedding dress and veil. The whole town came to the funeral and wept at the passing of such a beautiful young girl. George and Helene, who had spent the week happily honeymooning in the Outer Banks, arrived home at the very moment that the black-clad crowd exited the churchyard. Their arrival caused a commotion. The minister had to pull Polly's father off George before he killed him. And George's family disowned him right there in the street in front of everyone. Even the attorneys at the law office where George worked turned him away, knowing that no one in town would do business with them as long as George remained on their staff.

Helene's family was equally embarrassed. No one was visiting the pool hall anymore, and it looked like they would have to move away from town. They refused to open their door to their daughter and her new husband. Only Helene's youngest sister relented enough to open the upper window of the pool hall and speak to her sister. She dropped a bundle of clothes down to Helene and then slammed the window shut immediately afterward to make her position clear. So George and Helene left town in disgrace to make a new life for themselves elsewhere.

Life moved on. The scandal grew cold, and new ones took its place as new interests arose among the young people and the gossips. Polly and George and Helene were forgotten. Then, a year after Polly's death, George's father passed and was buried in the local churchyard just a few plots away from the girl who had almost become his daughter-in-law. This event triggered gossip about the fatal wedding day. For a few days the story of Polly and George was revived and much discussed.

Everyone in town turned out for the funeral of the elder Mr. Dean. Everyone was waiting to see if George would show his face. But George was too clever for them. He waited at an inn outside of town until it was dark, and then he went to the churchyard to pay his last respects to his father.

George Junior stood by the freshly dug grave and told his father that things weren't going so well. His old law firm had refused to give him a reference, and word of Polly's death had reached those at his former university who might have once helped him. So he was working as a farmhand, barely able to feed and clothe himself and his wife, who flagrantly chased after other men.

As he unburdened himself at his father's graveside, George heard a sweet female voice calling his name. "George. Sweetheart." George looked up in sudden hope. Was that his mother, come to forgive him? But no, the voice was pitched too high to be his mother, who sang contralto in the church choir.

"George," the voice called again. Puzzled, George turned toward the sound. And then he saw, rising up from a grassy mound under a spreading oak tree, a figure in a long white gown and a soft veil. Her eyes and her lips were yellow flames beneath the veil, and the rotted wedding dress glowed with a white-yellow light. It was Polly.

George's body stiffened, shudders of fear coursing up and down his arms and legs. Every hair on his neck prickled, and bile rose up into his throat until he retched and threw up on his father's grave. He put a shaking hand to his mouth and staggered backward, the other hand outstretched to ward off the specter floating toward him.

The spectral bride cackled with angry laughter and swooped forward until her hand closed over George's outstretched one in a terrible parody of a handshake. The grip of the spectral bride was so cold that it burned the skin, and so hard that the bones crunched as she squeezed. "Come along into the church, George," the glowing bride whispered. Through the veil, George could see maggots crawling in and out of Polly's flaming eye sockets.

"Nooo! Polly, no!" George screamed in terror, but he could not wrench his hand free. The ghost dragged him step by halting step toward the front door of the church. His hand was a red-hot agony of pain, though the rest of his body was shaking with cold. The agony was spreading now, up his arm to his shoulder.

"No!" George gave a final cry of despair and wrenched again at his hand. And suddenly, he was free. The spectral bride gave a roar of rage as George ran pell-mell down the church lane and out into the street.

"You're mine, George Dean! If not in this world, then in the next," the spectral bride howled after him. Her glowing form swelled upward until it was taller than the treetops. George looked back once and fell headlong when he saw the massive form with its flaming yellow eyes and lips and the moldering rags of its white wedding dress. He picked himself up, terror lending him speed. Clutching his aching hand, he ran all the way back to the inn.

By the time George reached his room, the fiery pain in his hand and arm was seeping through his entire body. He rang desperately for the housemaid and begged her to send for a doctor. Then he fell into bed and stared at his hand, which was black and withered, as if it had been scorched long ago by a fire. Black and red streaks were climbing up his arm so fast that he could almost see them move.

George was unconscious when the doctor arrived, and the swelling was already extending into his chest and neck. There was nothing the physician could do. The injury was too severe and had spread too far. Within two days George was dead. Polly had gotten her man at last.

17

The Wraith of the Creek

He left his tribe to work with the white lumbermen in Alger, changing his name to William Cloud. He even dressed in white man's attire and attended the local church on Sunday. It was a new life for him, and he was grateful when the lumbermen accepted him with little regard for his color or his birth. The lumberjacks started calling him "Cloudy," and they occasionally asked him to tell them some of the traditional stories from his tribe when they gathered around the fire at night.

The story they liked best was about the wraith that lived in the creek that powered the local log chute. The wraith was an evil creature that desired nothing more than to wrap its long arms around humans or animals and pull them down into the water to drown. At dusk, the wraith would slip out of the creek and hunt along its banks. Anyone passing near the creek from dusk until midnight should walk wary indeed, Cloudy told them, for the claws of the wraith could tear a grown man to bits in a few sharp blows.

The lumbermen liked to tease Cloudy about the wraith. Whenever he worked down on the log chute, some jokester would leap out at him from behind a tree, hands extended like claws, and grab him. Cloudy took the teasing in the good-natured spirit that it was intended, but he made a point of never going near the chute after dark. His uncle had been taken by the wraith when Cloudy was a small boy, and he would never forget the sight of his uncle's mangled body when his father and the other tribesmen pulled it from the creek.

It rained heavy and long that spring, and the creek was flooded almost to capacity. A large raft of logs was floated down to the chute, but the foreman decided to hold them back with a gate until the creek rose high enough to send them through in a mass. The order to lower the gate came through about 9:00 p.m. one stormy night in early April. Thunder was booming constantly, such that the lumbermen waiting in the cabin could hardly hear each other speak. Jagged lightning blazed across the sky, and the rain fell in heavy, chilly sheets. The thought of going outside in the storm did not appeal to anyone. Finally, the men drew straws, and Cloudy came up with the short one.

"Bad luck, ol' chap," said Ethan, a British man who was new to the lumber camp. "Watch out for that wraith of yours. It hunts the banks of the stream at this time of night, and this is just the sort of weather it likes best."

Cloudy glanced briefly at his comrade and nodded wordlessly. He clapped on his cap and slipped out the door before anyone else could speak. He knew that the Englishman meant no harm, but it was dangerous to speak of the wraith before going to the creek. Such careless speech might draw the attention of the very creature he hoped to avoid.

Cloudy was instantly soaked by the heavy rain and cut to the bone by the chilly wind. He hugged his coat tightly around him as he made his way silently through the pitch-black night toward the log chute and the waiting raft. It would take only a moment to lower the gate, and then he would run as fast as he could back to the safety of the cabin. He comforted himself with this thought as he approached the creek bank. He could hear the roar of the flooded stream long before he saw it, and within moments he was at the gate and tugging at the iron pins that held it above the water.

As he released the first pin, he heard a foul hissing sound from beside the floating raft of logs. Cloudy turned his head and saw a grotesque form rising from the swirling stream. It had a cat-like face, glowing yellow eyes, and long teeth. Its face was framed by wild, weed-strewn hair. Sharp spikes protruded from its spine, and dark slimy scales covered its lithesome body.

Cloudy gave a loud shout, hoping to scare the creature away. He tugged at the final pin, but it got stuck halfway out. Suddenly, the creature lunged out of the water. Cloudy leapt back, abandoning the recalcitrant pin to flee back up the path toward the distant cabin and safety. Behind him, the wraith howled once: a long, threatening shriek. Cloudy increased his speed, running blindly in the darkness as tree branches slapped at him and roots tripped his feet.

From behind him, he heard the sound of claws raking the muddy path as the wraith pursued him. The creature howled again, a sound that froze his blood even as it made his heart thump so hard that it hurt his chest. He heard the creature veer off the path suddenly, and then the sounds of pursuit ceased. Cloudy gasped and pushed himself harder, more frightened by the sudden silence than he had been when he saw the creature first rise from the waters.

Then the wraith dropped down from the branches of a tree right in front of him, blocking his way. Its yellow eyes glowed, and moonlight glinted against its slimy skin. Cloudy saw its long, thin arms stretch out toward him through the raging storm, claws

extended. He gave one loud shout of despair, thrashing at the monster with his hands and feet. His cry was cut off suddenly by the lightning-fast movement of a razor-sharp claw, and the woods were suddenly still again, save for the sound of the chilly April rain.

Back in the cabin, the lumbermen waited with increasing unease for Cloudy to return. At first, they joked about the wraith. One man wondered aloud if Cloudy was hiding somewhere until after midnight, when the creature was said to return to its underwater den to sleep. But as the minutes ticked by, the men grew somber. Finally, Ethan volunteered to go down to the log chute and look for his friend. Several other loggers decided to accompany him. Though no one said anything aloud about the wraith, the men all loaded their guns before stepping out into the rainy night.

Within ten minutes, the men were standing next to the lowered gate, watching the water rushing down the chute. There was no sign of Cloudy, but after a moment, Ethan realized that the gate had not settled fully into the water. The men lowered the lantern to the level of the rushing water and peered into the depths at a large object partially obstructing the gate. It moved slightly in the current, and Ethan gave a sudden sharp cry as it flipped over, revealing the mangled face of Cloudy.

The loggers lifted the gate slightly and drew Cloudy up with pike poles. His body had been sliced to ribbons, and his head was almost completely severed. They could see teeth marks on his face, and parts of his arms and legs had been ripped away completely. Ethan picked up his friend's body while the other men stood in a ring around him, guns pointing in every direction. Keeping a sharp lookout for any sign of the creature that had killed Cloudy, the loggers hurried back to the safety of the cabin.

The next day, Cloudy's body was buried in a small clearing in the woods, far away from where the feared wraith lurked. The foreman instructed everyone working at the creek to keep their guns with them at all times, and no one was to go near the log chute after dark unaccompanied. News of the murderous wraith in the creek quickly spread through the lumber camp and the nearby village. Many of the loggers quit their jobs rather than risk their lives.

One night, a week after Cloudy's death, Ethan was awakened by a strange blue light hovering above his bed. He opened his eyes and found himself gazing into the shining face of William Cloud. The spirit warned Ethan to leave the lumber camp at once. The wraith had marked Ethan for its next victim the night he came down to the stream to look for his friend. If the Englishman stayed at the camp, he would share the same fate as Cloudy. Terrified, Ethan promised the apparition that he would depart at sunrise. Cloudy's ghost nodded gravely and disappeared, leaving the Englishman trembling in the darkness.

At daybreak, Ethan packed his belongings and left the camp. On his way out, he confided his story to the men who had helped him retrieve Cloudy's body. Soon word of Cloudy's warning spread throughout the camp, and by sundown, it was completely deserted.

With no one left to maintain it, the log chute fell into disrepair and slowly crumbled away, never to be replaced. In the depths of the stream, the wraith still lurks, watching for another victim. But it waits in vain, for the ghost of Cloudy appears to anyone foolish enough to wander near the stream, warning them away with terrible groans and piercing screams.

18

The Face

He toppled into love the moment he set eyes on the new transfer student in late August when classes started for the semester. She was an art major, and he was a poor medical student who didn't talk much about his family, on account of his father. His father had gone insane in traffic one day and tried to run over several pedestrians who were blocking the street. His father had been locked away in an asylum, and the family never mentioned him.

But his father was not on his mind the day he met Sheila. She was a lovely girl with masses of long, black hair and eyelashes so long they got tangled in her curls when she leaned over her desk. He had a withdrawn nature, though not by inclination. He'd learned the hard way that friends started acting funny when they learned about his insane father. So he'd stopped having friends. If anyone inquired about his family, he told them his father was dead rather than admit the truth. Now, he had to overcome his taciturn nature or risk losing Sheila to one of the other fellows who panted after her.

He studied her habits as closely as she studied her books, and soon he found a way to be close to her. She had a favorite spot in the library where she always studied between classes. He started studying in a cubicle nearby, and a couple of "chance" encounters between them turned into a conversation. Then, he volunteered to tutor her in one of her classes. From there, it was easy. Sheila toppled into love with him, too, almost as madly as he had fallen for her.

The new college sweethearts went everywhere together, hardly bearing to part for classes. He lived in a bubble of joy . . . until the Tuesday he saw her leaving her history class next to a good-looking fellow who lived in the same dorm. They were laughing together over something the professor had said in class, and a shaft of sheer jealousy pierced his gut. How dare she laugh with another man?

The boyfriend confronted his wayward girlfriend with her perceived trespass, and she stared at him incredulously. "You're crazy!" she said.

He winced, reminded of his father. That set him off. He started yelling at her, accusing her of all sorts of things, and she stalked off in a rage. He huddled in his dorm room, feeling miserable and vowing to forget her. But they made up over dinner, and things were fine for a while.

But one day the boyfriend saw her borrowing a pen from a handsome blond fellow at the library. That set him off again. The two young lovers hissed angry words at each other until the librarian kicked them out. Again, Sheila stalked off in a rage, as he shouted nasty things at her retreating back. Again, he huddled on the narrow bed in his dorm room, feeling miserable and vowing to forget her, until the black anger gave way to common sense. He called Sheila and apologized. She accepted his apology, and they agreed to get back together. In a flush of excited relief, he asked her to the dance on Friday, and she accepted.

The boyfriend's hands trembled with excitement as he packed his medical bag after class on Friday. He rushed back to the dorm, threw his bag on the desk, and dressed in his best. He picked Sheila up at her dorm room and escorted her to the dance. It was a wonderful night. Sheila had bought a new yellow dress—a lovely concoction with a swirling skirt and a little bit of a top. She looked stunning. The boyfriend's head whirled at the sight of her, and he could hardly keep his hands away from her. They danced, drank, and ate appetizers until Sheila called a laughing halt to the eating, saying she'd gained ten pounds in the last ten minutes. He'd laughed along with her and told her they would dance it off, which they did. They left early and walked hand-in-hand back to his dorm room for a nightcap.

When they reached the entrance to the dorm, Sheila veered off for a moment to speak with a red-haired fellow who was in one of her art classes, wanting to know about an assignment that was due the next day. The boyfriend stood impatiently just inside the door, frowning as the art student beamed at Sheila in the gorgeous, little yellow dress. When she smiled back at him, the red-haired art student looked stunned.

The inside of the boyfriend's skull throbbed from a sudden headache, brought on by too much alcohol combined with gut-gnawing jealousy. When Sheila rejoined him, he grabbed her hand roughly and hustled her upstairs to his room.

"Stop rushing! You're hurting my hand!" Sheila protested as he swept them both inside.

A quick glance told him that his roommate was out. Good. He rounded on Sheila and shouted, "You are hurting my heart! You flirt with every man you meet, you tramp!"

Sheila's face flushed scarlet with fury, and she shouted back at him, accusing him of flirting with the female medical students and of being so jealous she couldn't ask a seventy-year-old man for directions without setting him off. "You are crazy!" she shouted at him. "Stark raving mad!"

The boyfriend saw red. It rose around the edges of his eyesight, billowing like clouds. He groped through the red mists, and his hands found his medical bag. "Don't call me mad!" he said through gritted teeth, and his hands closed on a scalpel.

When the mists cleared from his eyes, Sheila lay dead at his feet, her throat cut from ear to ear. The whole room was covered with red gore, and her masses of black hair lay in a pool of streaming blood.

It had been a silent murder. Sheila hadn't believed her eyes until it was too late to scream . . . too late to do anything but die. The boyfriend had cut her windpipe with medical precision, though he didn't remember anything that happened after the red mist had obscured his eyesight.

His brain went into overdrive. Hide the body. Clean up the blood. Invent an alibi. But first . . . he stared at the face he loved so much. Dead now. Gone, out of his reach. The red mist rose a little in his mind as he knelt beside the body and slowly cut off her face. He wrapped the face carefully in plastic before putting it in his desk drawer. Then, he cleaned up the blood, tucked the body into a blanket, and stuck it under his bed until the middle of the night, when he carried it downstairs and hid it in the tunnel near the laundry room.

The next day, the boyfriend told his roommate that he and Sheila had broken up and she'd gone home in a snit without finishing her classes. He patted his desk drawer absently as he spoke. Once his roommate turned back to his books, he peered at the face inside. Yes, Sheila was still there.

The face seemed to draw him, just as Sheila's presence had once done. The boyfriend kept wandering over to the desk to peer inside several times an hour. His roommate sat studying on the other bed and didn't seem to notice his restlessness, which was just as well. He had to get a grip on himself, start studying for final exams.

Finally, the boyfriend went to the vending machine to buy a soda. When he got back, his roommate was leaning out the open window, looking ill.

"I think I have the flu," the roommate said when he came in.

"Want me to take a look?" the boyfriend offered, reaching for his medical bag.

His roommate turned white and barked, "No! Thank you! Don't bother. I'll just pick up something at the pharmacy." At that, he hurried out of the room, practically running.

The boyfriend settled down at the desk, peered in the drawer at the face, and then began work on a paper he had due next week. He could feel Sheila's presence beside him. She was helping him with his homework, he thought happily. Downstairs, his roommate was on the phone with the police.

The boyfriend went ballistic when the police came with a warrant to arrest him. They manhandled him out of his chair and over to the door. A grim-faced officer took a look in the desk drawer and then turned around and vomited on the floor. The boyfriend roared at the sacrilege. No other man was allowed to look at his girlfriend's face! It belonged to him! How dare they? He screamed all the way down the stairs and out of the dorm. Students peered out their doors as he fought the hold of the policemen, lunging this way and that in his fury.

When the boyfriend realized they were leaving Sheila's face behind in the dorm where any man might see it, he panicked. "Don't take her away from me," he pleaded with the officer as the man bundled him into the car. "I want her with me always! Don't take her away!" He reached his handcuffed arms toward the man, who backed away and slammed the door on him. The boyfriend lay back against the seat and sobbed in misery: "Sheila . . . Sheila . . . Sheila . . ."

His family had him transferred to the asylum where his father was kept locked up in a padded room. Every day, his enraged father tried to kill his attendants, while the bereft boyfriend wept and stared out the window. The boyfriend kept seeing Sheila's lovely face in the branches of a nearby tree. The face seemed to sway in rhythm to his father's fists pounding on the walls in the room next door to his son.

And in the dorm, the amorphous ghost of a young girl in a bloodstained yellow dress floats along the hallways, looking for her face.

19

Mary Whales

Old Man Whales was a nineteenth-century farmer who loved money more than anything, except his wife. In his lust for wealth, he supplemented his farm income by catching runaway slaves who were escaping to freedom through Indiana. Whales would chain the ex-slaves up in his barn cellar until he could collect the reward on them, and when he couldn't find slaves, he'd capture free men and sell them into slavery. Whales hated just about every human being on Earth except for his Virginia. She was a gentle soul who lived in fear of her stern husband, though she loved him devotedly and had no idea how much he cherished her in return, for he was not a demonstrative man.

Then, things changed. The Civil War ended slavery—a disaster for the evil Whales, who no longer had a profitable source of income to supplement his farm work—and Virginia died in childbirth. Overnight, Whales fell to pieces. He hated the child—a little girl his wife had named Mary—but he raised her for Virginia's sake. As for himself, he withdrew from the world, neglecting his farm and half-starving his child.

Mary was a beautiful girl with lovely blond curls falling in a tangle down her back. She dressed in filthy rags, and when she was in town, she never spoke to anyone except her sullen, angry father. Old Man Whales somehow scratched out a living from his farm—enough to keep himself and his daughter alive. But he took to drinking heavily as the years went by, and Mary did most of the farm work as well as all the cooking and housekeeping.

Whenever she had a moment, Mary escaped into books, where she found a fantasy world much more to her liking than the world she lived in. Sometimes, she wondered if she could do anything to win her father's affection. She tried so hard, but he remained cruel and distant, and his loathing became increasingly more apparent as she grew older. Unbeknownst to the girl, she grew ever lovelier as she neared adulthood, and the resemblance to her dead mother was striking. Whales saw his dead wife every time he looked at the child who had caused her death.

One night, after a hefty bout of drinking, Whales stumbled home with an aching head and a black rage in his heart over the cruelty of a world that would deprive him of Virginia. The person at fault for this dastardly crime lay sleeping peacefully in her bed, and Whales could not stand the thought. Grabbing the knife he used to slaughter his pigs, Whales lumbered into Mary's bedroom and stabbed her to death, flailing at her repeatedly as if she were an attacking bear rather than a sleeping girl. Mary woke screaming and thrashed around in agony, trying to fight off her demonic father as blood spurted everywhere and bits of torn flesh littered the bedclothes and fell to the floor. When she stopped moving, Whales reeled out of the room in satisfaction, leaving a bloody corpse in his wake. Mary's head was nearly severed, and her body lay half-on and half-off the bed, her ragged dress covered in gore, while hanks of her blonde hair trailed in the pool of blood accumulating on the floor beneath her bed.

When Old Man Whales woke the next morning, his head finally clear of the whisky-induced haze, he staggered into the

bedroom to inspect his work. The bloody sight of his dead daughter brought a demonic smile to his lips. He should have killed her years ago, he decided. But she'd made quite a mess, and he didn't want the tramp littering up his house, not even in death. So he slung Mary over his shoulder and carried her down to the basement, where he'd once kept captured slaves. He dug an indifferent grave and tossed her body into it. And that was the end of Mary . . . or so he thought.

Two nights later, when Old Man Whales came back from doing his nightly chores at the barn, he found his daughter Mary Whales standing in the kitchen, her nearly severed head lolling against one shoulder as she stirred an empty kettle. A pool of steaming blood lay beneath her feet, and bits of skin from her knife-slashed face were breaking off and falling into the kettle. Old Man Whales screamed and reeled backward in shock.

At the sound, Mary Whales looked up from her stirring, and a smile crossed her knife-split mouth, widening until it showed shattered teeth. "Faaaaaather . . ." she hissed, and launched herself across the room at her father, the wooden spoon in her hand held like a knife.

Old Man Whales leapt backward out of the kitchen door and fled to the barn. When he chanced a look over his shoulder, the apparition was gone. He spent a sleepless the night in the barn, fortifying himself with a keg of whisky he kept there for emergencies.

In the morning, he staggered into the house carrying his axe for protection. The house was in its customary squalor, and there was no bloody pool on the kitchen floor. The kettle hung demurely from its iron hook at the side of the hearth. Old Man Whales sucked in a terrified breath, and then relaxed. He'd probably been drunk last night and imagined the whole thing, he decided, forgetting he hadn't started drinking until after he'd seen the bloody corpse of his dead daughter.

A week passed. Old Man Whales went about his chores whistling cheerfully, feeling better than he had in years. He brought a newspaper home from the mercantile and sat down by the hearth in the chair he'd favored when Virginia was alive to read it.

As he turned to page two, he glanced up and saw Mary Whales sitting in the chair opposite him, her knife-slashed dress covered in blood. Her pale skin was shattered by knife blows, the cuts raw and bleeding, and her sliced-up hands were busy knitting him a shirt. She had to jerk her half-severed head sideways to look at him with eyes that glowed red with hatred. "Faaaaaather . . ." she hissed through knife-scored lips. Then, she smiled, showing all of her broken teeth, now razor-sharp points that bit down on a tattered tongue. Blood pooled under her chair and fell from her body like rain as she flew across the room toward him, knitting needles held like knives.

Old Man Whales screamed and reeled away, his chair smashing to the floor as he fled from the house. He felt a slashing pain across his back as he leapt through the back door. It was only when he'd safely reached the barn that he stopped to assess the damage. His shirt was in tatters, and two long gashes scored deeply into his back, like the cuts of a butcher's knife . . . or two sharpened knitting needles.

The murderous widower did not go back into the house for days. He slept in the barn and cooked meals around a bonfire he built in the pasture where he kept his cows. Then, he grew tired of this nonsense. It was all his imagination. Too much whisky before bed, he told himself. He allowed himself only one drink before bedding down in the barn that night, and in the morning he marched straight up the weedy walkway and into his house. He'd get cleaned up, shave, and go to town this morning, he decided. It was time he took his place in the community once more.

So he pumped himself a bucket of water at the kitchen sink, washed up, and then took an ewer of water over to the little mirror kept on the far wall for shaving. He set it down on the table and looked into the mirror . . . right into the glowing red eyes of Mary Whales. Her shattered face was knife scored, her once-fair lips were split down the center, and blood dripped from them as she smiled at him. "Faaaaaather . . ." she hissed through razor-sharp, blood-stained teeth. A piece of her lip broke off and fell out of sight below the bottom of the mirror as she spoke. She raised blood-stained fingers, her nails long and sharpened like the claws of a beast, and reached right out of the mirror toward her father; slapping him twice across the face.

Old Man Whales screamed in searing pain as her nails clawed into him, and blood streamed from four slashes, two on either cheek, as he ran from the house toward the safety of the barn. He leapt through the door of the barn, his heart pounding so hard his chest ached with it. He swiped at his bloody cheeks as if wiping away tears, panting desperately. The dust from the hay bales in the loft above tickled his nose, and he sneezed, eyes streaming. He swiped at his eyes with his bloody hand, and they stung as gore leaked into them. "Tramp. Bloody witch," he shouted, half-blinded by blood, tears, and fear.

"Faaaaaather . . ." a voice hissed softly behind him.

Old Man Whales whirled around with a shriek. Mary Whales stood smiling at him through her bloody, razor-sharp teeth, her tattered tongue bleeding from several places, as if it had been scored by a butcher's knife. Her head listed to one side as blood streamed from the wound that had nearly decapitated her. The viscous pool of steaming blood at her feet flowed slowly toward him. She pointed above her head.

Her murderous father lifted his stunned eyes and saw a noose hanging from the rafters beside the ladder to the loft. The rope looked inviting, hanging there in a dust-speckled sunbeam. Hanging there so peaceful and still. Old Man Whales stepped forward and placed his bloody hands on the rung of the ladder. He started to climb. . . .

PART TWO

Dark Tales

Retold By S. E. Schlosser

20

Dance with the Devil

Lacey hurried through her schoolwork as fast as she could. It was the night of the Kingsville high school dance, and she couldn't wait until seven o'clock, the time the dance was to begin. She had purchased a brand-new, sparkly red dress for the occasion. She knew she looked smashing in it. It was going to be the best evening of her life.

Then her mother came in the house, looking pale and determined.

"Lacey, I need to speak with you," her mother said.

Lacey looked up from her books. "What is it, Mama?"

"You are not going to that dance," her mother said.

Lacey was shocked. Not go to the dance? That was ridiculous! All her friends were going. She had bought an expensive new dress just for this occasion.

"But why?" Lacey asked her mother.

"I've just been talking to the preacher. He says the dance is going to be for the devil. You are absolutely forbidden to go," her mother said.

Lacey argued and protested, but her mother remained firm. She would not let Lacey attend the dance. Finally, Lacey nodded as if she accepted her mother's words. But she was determined to go to the dance. As soon as her mother was busy cleaning the kitchen, she put on her brand-new red dress and ran down to the hall where the dance was being held.

As soon as Lacey walked into the room, all the boys turned to look at her. She was startled by all the attention. Normally, no one noticed her. Her mother sometimes accused her of being too awkward to get a boyfriend. But she was not awkward that night. The boys in her class were fighting with each other to dance with her. The other girls watched her with envy. Even her best friend snubbed her. But Lacey didn't care—she was popular at last, and she was going to make the most of it.

Later, Lacey broke away from the crowd and went to the table to get some punch to drink. She heard a sudden hush. The music stopped. When she turned, she saw a handsome man with jet-black hair and clothes standing next to her.

"Dance with me," he said.

Lacey managed to stammer a "yes," completely stunned by this gorgeous man. The man led her out on the dance floor. The music sprang up at once. She found herself dancing better than she had ever danced before. Slowly everyone else stopped dancing to watch them. Lacey was elated. They were the center of attention.

Then the man spun Lacey around and around. She gasped for breath, trying to step out of the spin. But her partner spun her faster and faster, until her feet felt hot and the floor seemed to melt under her. Lacey's eyes fixed in horror on the man's face as he twirled her even faster. She saw his eyes burning with red fire, as he gave her a smile of pure evil. For the first time, she noticed two horns protruding from his forehead. Lacey gasped desperately for breath, terrified because she now knew with whom she was dancing.

THE DANCE

The man in black spun Lacey so fast that a cloud of dust flew up around them both, hiding them from the crowd. When the dust settled, Lacey was gone. The man in black bowed once to the assembled students and teachers, then vanished. The devil had come to the party, and he had spun Lacey all the way to hell.

21

Morning Star

Gray Wolf was the handsomest of the warriors; tall, broad, and strong, fleet of foot, and a good hunter. Many of the nubile maidens of his tribe had cast their eyes upon him with favor, but as yet he had chosen none of them to be his wife. His mother scolded Gray Wolf about his reluctance to marry, but he only chuckled and told her that he would marry when he found a maiden who suited him. His nonchalance irritated his mother, but Gray Wolf was her only son and she loved him dearly, so she held her peace.

There came a time when the white men, following a great chief named Penn, began settling on the tribal lands. The tribe grew afraid that they would be driven away from the bones of their fathers. The chief of the tribe summoned Gray Wolf, whose fleetness of foot made him a good messenger, and sent him to the neighboring tribes to request their attendance at a council to discuss the matter.

Gray Wolf was gone for four sunsets. On the morning of the fifth day, the warrior staggered into the village, covered with grievous wounds and the bite marks of a large beast of prey. Gray Wolf was feverish and too ill to speak with any sense. His mother and sisters tended his wounds with the herbs given to them by the medicine man.

When the prayers of his family and the herbs had succeeded in restoring some measure of health to the handsome warrior, Gray Wolf told the council that he had been attacked by a large black cat with glowing eyes the color of the moon. The beast had invaded his campsite one evening shortly after he had gone to sleep and had mauled him, clawing his chest and face and biting his shoulders and arms.

Gray Wolf had struggled desperately with the creature, fighting to keep its teeth away from his neck. Finally, his hand had closed over his quiver, and he drew forth an arrow and thrust it into the beast's chest. The cat had howled in pain and had retreated back into the forest, leaving the warrior to bind up his wounds as best he could and stagger back to the village to find help.

Thus went the tale that Gray Wolf told the elders of his tribe. To Running Water, who was his best friend, the warrior confided a slightly different story. When he plunged the arrow into the chest of the beast, it had wailed in the voice of a human woman. Gray Wolf had heard distinct words in her cry as the black cat flung herself away from him and ran back into the forest. It had been Gray Wolf's intention to pursue the beast wherever it fled and to kill it, but he was shaken by her strange voice, and instead he had built up the fire, tended his wounds, and slept. In the morning, Gray Wolf had found a broken necklace on the ground where he had been attacked. The amulet took the form of a sunburst and was made out of beads and human finger bones. It was a horrible thing to look upon. When Gray Wolf showed the amulet to his friend, Running Water shuddered and turned away, refusing to touch such a defiled object.

In the days that followed, Gray Wolf grew restless and dreamy eyed. Though his wounds were closed, the vigor and health he

once had did not return. He grew careless of his appearance and spent much of his time alone in the woods and thickets rather than hunting with his friends. Finally, Running Water confronted Gray Wolf and asked him what was happening. Gray Wolf's face lit up with a dreamy, strange delight, and he told his friend that he had fallen in love at last. Something about Gray Wolf's statement worried Running Water. He had not seen his friend with any of the village maidens, and there were no other villages nearby.

Running Water carefully inquired about the maiden he had chosen, and Gray Wolf launched into a paean of delight regarding her beautiful skin, her glowing eyes, her long dark hair, her luscious mouth. Her name was Morning Star, and she lived alone in the woods because her family had all been killed by the white men. While hunting one early morning, Gray Wolf had seen her on her way to the stream to bathe. Although he should have turned his eyes away from her unclothed form, Gray Wolf had been transfixed by her beauty. He had followed her and spoken to her while she bathed. She had been annoyed by his presence at first, but Gray Wolf had appeased her with the offering of several rabbits, and at last she had allowed him to know her. He had visited her every day since then, and his heart was sick with love for his Morning Star.

Running Water studied his friend intently. Gray Wolf did indeed look heart-sick. He was pale and wan, and the muscles of his body were losing their tone. His hair had come loose from its bindings and was in disarray. Running Water was afraid of this Morning Star. If she were a normal maiden, surely she would have sought out another village after her family had perished.

Lightly, so as not to offend his friend, Running Water suggested that he might try sleeping a little more and seeing a little less of his beloved Morning Star, else he was likely to die of love sickness. Gray Wolf's face clouded, and he shook his head. "I cannot sleep," he told Running Water. "Every night, I dream of the black cat. It comes to me, licks open my wounds, and drinks my blood." He rubbed his throat unconsciously, and his hair swung back, revealing two swollen marks where the black cat's teeth had bitten him.

Running Water felt his heart begin to pound within him. He was filled with apprehension and fear for his friend. Remembering Gray Wolf's story of the black cat with a woman's voice, and the evil necklace of human finger bones Gray Wolf had found at the place where he was attacked, Running Water was sure that Morning Star and the black cat were one and the same entity. Running Water urged his friend to bring the maiden to live in the village with him, or else to forsake her and look to his own health instead. His words angered Gray Wolf, and they parted bitterly.

Still, Running Water was concerned for his friend. He spent the next night in the woods outside Gray Wolf's home, waiting and watching. At length, he heard the soft padding of large feet, and a huge black cat slunk into the village and crept into the home of the warrior. It cried out in a voice that was neither that of beast nor woman, and Running Water expected the village to rouse at the terrible sound, but an uncanny stillness lay over everything, and no one stirred.

Then Gray Wolf emerged from his shelter, with the black cat twining and purring around him. His eyes were glazed and unfocused as he followed the creature into the woods. Running Water aimed an arrow at the creature, but it kept Gray Wolf's body between itself and Running Water at all times, as if sensing he were near. So Running Water followed them into the woods, keeping knife and bow at hand, seeking a chance to kill the evil thing that had ensorcelled his friend.

The creature led Gray Wolf to a small clearing outside a cave. Then it rose on its hind legs and pawed at the warrior's shirt until the laces came open, revealing the wounds at his throat. Running Water tried to draw an arrow but found to his horror that his body was fixed in one place. Unable to do more than watch, he saw the creature open the wounds with its rough tongue. Then, before his eyes, it transformed into a beautiful, sensuous, unclothed woman who drank the blood of the warrior as Gray Wolf stood transfixed in the clearing before her cave. Such was the look of extreme pain and delight that appeared on Gray Wolf's face that Running Water wanted to cry out, but he could not.

Running Water's eyes remain riveted on the beautiful woman, and he felt desire running through him, terrible and fierce. For a moment, he sensed a little of what his friend must be feeling, and it terrified and entranced him. Then the woman looked straight at him, her mouth covered with blood, and smiled. Her eyes glowed with the color of the moon. They were the eyes of a beast. She had known he was there all along. Turning to Gray Wolf, she struck him in the chest, her arm entering through his flesh as if it were not there. Gray Wolf came out of his trance and stared in horror down at the beautiful, naked woman before him as she ripped out his heart.

"No, Morning Star," Running Water shouted, horror releasing his voice from the creature's spell. "No!"

"It tastes better with the fear," she said, as she held Gray Wolf's still-beating heart in her bloody hand. Before her, Gray Wolf staggered backward and fell dead to the ground. Morning Star turned gloatingly toward Running Water and raised his friend's heart to her lips. Running Water strained desperately against the spell that still bound his body, but it held him transfixed. Then he felt the spell cover him thickly, suffocatingly, as if a blanket were thrust over his mouth and nose. He gasped desperately for breath and fell senseless to the ground.

Running Water awoke to the sound of horrified voices and looked up into the faces of his people. He lay at the very edge of the village, unharmed save for the bloody handprints upon his shirt, and he knew that Morning Star had carried his unconscious body home after her terrible feast.

Running Water stood before the council and told them the whole terrible story. A search was mounted at once, but Morning Star had disappeared, and Gray Wolf's body with her. It was found a moon later, wrapped in elk bark just outside the cave where Morning Star once lived. In his chest was a gaping hole where the heart had been ripped out, but the body was entirely drained of blood. Around his neck was a sunburst necklace made of beads and human finger bones.

Thereafter, the warriors were all instructed to hunt in pairs, and to beware of a black cat with eyes that shone the color of the moon. But Morning Star was not seen again in those parts.

Many years passed, and gradually the story of Morning Star was forgotten as new tales of life and love and death were created within the village. Then one morning, Running Water, who was a venerable old man and very full of years, woke from a deep sleep to find a newly made sunburst necklace made of beads and human finger bones lying mockingly beside him on his sleeping mat.

Morning Star had returned.

22

Laughing Devil

'Round about 1850 or so, a grandpa and his boy living in the Willamette Valley heard from a passing tradesman that gold had been found in the hills along the Rogue River. Gold fever hit them two bachelors within minutes of hearing the report, and they decided they'd best get in a claim lickety-split before any of them forty-niners down in Cally-fornia heard about it. They hightailed it to the coast and went straight to the closest general store to stock up on food and placer mining supplies. Cost them a mint, but they didn't care. Soon they'd be rich!

While they were at the store, the owner came out of the back to chat with the new prospectors. During the visit, he warned them to avoid Laughing Devil Canyon. It was said to be haunted by an evil spirit that twisted the heads off anyone roaming through the canyon after dark, dragging their bodies up to its lair and gnawing on their bones.

The prospectors burst out laughing when they heard this load of hokum. A laughing devil! What was a devil or two when gold was on the line? The storekeeper shook his head and handed them their parcels. He'd warned them. That was all he could do.

"What say we jog on up to Laughing Devil Canyon tonight, partner?" said the grizzle-haired, red-faced prospector to his grandson, who he'd raised as his own son after his daughter and her husband died in a fire.

"Sure thing, Pa!" said the curly-haired imp. "Betcha that story was put out by a gold miner who didn't want anyone stealing his claim!"

"Bet yer right," said his grandpa.

Chuckling happily, the old man and the young boy stomped out into the hills, keeping their eyes open for any promising sparkles in the streams or interesting-looking seams in the jutting rocks. They'd obtained directions to Laughing Devil Canyon from the lady who ran the post office, and they headed straight there.

It was about noon when they entered the narrow canyon and started making their way through the dim light that filtered down from the high walls above.

"Gloomy," said the boy cheerfully. "Makes a body think there might be somethin' in that Devil story after all!"

"'Bout a million dollars in gold, I'm thinkin'," said his grandpa. "Jest you keep prospecting!"

Slowly, the boy and his grandpa made their way through the deep gulch, searching the walls and streambed for tell-tale signs of gold.

Round about dusk, the boy let out a yelp of excitement and started shouting for his grandpa. "I've found it! I've found me some gold!"

The old man came a-running, his red face glowing almost as bright as the setting sun. Man and boy started panning in the stream, and gee-whilikers if they didn't find a mess of gold right then and there!

"We got ourselves a claim!" shouted Grandpa, tearing off his hat and throwing it in the air.

"Gold!" shouted the boy. "Gold!"

They danced around in the streambed, throwing water into the air for sheer joy.

And that's when the laughter began. It started low; just an evil-sounding chuckle that raised the hair on the back of the neck and froze the limbs in place. The miners stared at one another, droplets of water falling all around them, as the laughter got louder and louder, bouncing off the walls of the narrow gulch. It didn't sound human. It had strange undertones that made the whole body shiver and shake and set the feet to running before the mind could register the movement.

Abandoning packs, gold, and reason, the boy and his grandpa raced out of the stream and down the length of the gulch as the laughter grew louder and louder, hurting their ears and making tears of pain sting their eyes. Darkness was falling swiftly around them as they stumbled over rocks and jumped fallen trees in sheer panic.

Then the boy let out a scream of terror and started backpedaling as a huge, winged shape shot over his head and landed right in front of him, blocking the path through the narrow canyon. It was a foul creature, more skeleton than living flesh. It towered ten feet above them, and it had giant leathery wings like a bat and a narrow, evil face like a crocodile, with the same sharp teeth.

Grandpa ground to a halt behind the boy and grabbed hold of his shoulders, trying to stay upright. The two ended up in a heap at the feet of the Laughing Devil, and the beast started chuckling again in the same horrible, rumbling tone that made their bones vibrate with terror. Reaching down casually with one claw, it ripped the head right off the struggling boy and ate it in

one bite. His Grandpa gave a scream of rage as his grandson's blood spilled out all over his head and body. He launched himself at the creature, batting at it fiercely with his fists. The Laughing Devil grabbed him with both claws and ripped him cleanly in two. Blood and guts spilled all over the ground, soiling the headless body of the boy. The Laughing Devil chuckled again, its laughter getting louder and louder as darkness encompassed the canyon. It wrapped its tail around the boy's body and leapt into the air, carrying the corpses up and up to its den, hot blood dripping onto the earth far below.

The next morning, the storekeeper and two of his employees came to the Laughing Devil Canyon and walked upstream until they found the prospectors' packs and mining gear. Quietly, they packed everything up and carted it down the canyon and back to town to sell to the next greedy fool who passed that way. The last man in line carefully kicked sand over the blood on the ground and made sure the fake gold deposits were back in place. Then he hurried after the storekeeper, grinning to himself as he ran. The boss was right, as usual. Greenhorns always came to the canyon to pan for gold, in spite of their warnings. They were making a fortune off this place!

Up in its aerie on top of the canyon wall, the Laughing Devil burped contentedly. Pulling another bone off its pile, it started to gnaw.

23

The New Neighbor

I told Millie right from the start that our new neighbor was a
bad one. Mr. Elgin lived in an apartment over his new dry goods
store, and he seemed to prefer the nighttime. We never saw him
out in the street before dusk. He was a tall, darkly handsome man
with a face as white as new milk and a bit of an accent I couldn't
place. He was very thin but very strong, almost supernaturally so.

I watched him on the evening he moved into the apartment
next door to our boardinghouse. He got very angry with the
movers when they jostled the six-foot-long box he had most
carefully placed in the center of the wagon. I hated that box on
sight. It looked just like a coffin to me, and my eyes burned red
for several minutes after seeing it for the first time.

Mr. Elgin hired a local boy to take care of his store during
the day. Billy was a good lad who'd grown up on a ranch outside
town, but he wasn't bright enough to question his employer's
odd habits. Billy took a room in our boardinghouse, and Millie
took a motherly interest in him and made sure he was well fed.

I soon noticed that Mr. Elgin had a rather hypnotic effect
on people. Whenever he appeared in the store after dusk, folks
bought twice as many items as they intended. And many of the
women ended up inviting him to dinner at the local restaurant,

which was very strange, considering many of them were happily married.

Millie tutted over the situation, but what could you do? It was a free country, and if the local ladies wanted to make fools of themselves over a tall, dark stranger, that was their business—and their husbands'.

Mr. Elgin tried his hypnotism on me one late afternoon when I went next door to buy some nails to fix up the new-fangled water closet my wife insisted on having in the house for our boarders, but I was immune to those dark eyes with the red glint in their center. He looked rather chagrined that he couldn't persuade me to buy a very expensive and completely unnecessary plow for the farm-garden Millie kept in back of the boardinghouse. "What do we need a plow for? A spade and shovel work just fine," I told Mr. Elgin crisply as I paid a few pennies for the nails. That was the last time I patronized his store, and I forbade Millie to step foot inside it. Better to jog across town to the other dry goods store than to put oneself voluntarily in the presence of Mr. Elgin.

Millie laughed at me, but she could tell I was truly worried about the man, so she promised to keep away. She had enough to do cooking and cleaning up after the boarders. So that was all right.

It wasn't long after Mr. Elgin appeared that an illness spread through town. It mostly affected the womenfolk. They'd go all white and glassy-eyed, and red marks would appear on their throats or sometimes their wrists. The local doctors were baffled and tried every remedy they knew, to no avail. The disease continued to spread.

You could tell folks had the disease by the languid way they walked about town, and their too-pale faces. A couple of the ladies died after the local doctor tried bleeding the disease out of their bodies. So they stopped that technique and tried using elixirs to strengthen the blood. This seemed to offer the stricken some relief, but the epidemic continued to grow, in spite of the new treatment, and two more people died, their bodies white and stiff as if drained of all blood.

I quickly noticed that Mr. Elgin grew almost ruddy in appearance whenever someone in town fell ill. I also noticed that it was most often the women who invited him to dinner that suffered from the mysterious disease. I grew suspicious then and decided to check up on things myself.

Kissing Millie goodbye, I harnessed our two big workhorses and drove all the way out to the family ranch to visit my little Scottish grandmother. When I was a wee fellow, she'd told me stories about evil creatures that only came out at night and drank the blood of humans, and I was beginning to wonder if Mr. Elgin might be one of them.

Granny was thrilled to see me, but not so thrilled when she heard about Mr. Elgin. Her face grew positively grim when I told her about the illness sweeping through the town and the symptoms exhibited by the afflicted. Together, we consulted an old tome she'd brought west with her when she and granddad traveled the Oregon Trail. Granny turned to the section entitled "On Dark and Foul Creatures" and read me the passage aloud. In summary, it said that there were evil creatures called *vampyren* or *revenants* that returned from the grave to prey upon the living. They slept during the day in coffins filled with the dirt from their grave and walked abroad at night. To stave off a return to death, they drank the blood of living humans. You could protect yourself against the beings using garlic and holy objects, according to the book, but you could kill them only by plunging a wooden stake through their heart and removing their head.

"Sounds like your Mr. Elgin," Granny said, closing the book. I nodded grimly. So it did. I felt a sudden sense of urgency to return home. Millie was surrounded by all the boarders living in our house, but I still didn't like the thought of her living and working next door to Mr. Elgin. Our source said that vampires often killed their victims. The thought terrified me.

It was late, and I was forced to spend the night with my grandparents. But I woke at dawn, harnessed the horses, and headed for Baker City as fast as I could. It was dusk when I turned down the little alley behind the boardinghouse and pulled to a stop outside the barn. As I jumped off the seat of the wagon, Billy came running up to me.

"Oh, Mr. Porter, your wife is sick," he exclaimed. "She took sick last night after you left, and the doctor thinks she's got the plague, same as the other folks in town."

Alarmed, I threw the reins to Billy and asked him to put away the horses and the wagon. Then I ran into the boardinghouse, heading for the rooms reserved for Millie and me. Millie lay sleeping in bed, and from the doorway I could see the red marks on her throat where Mr. Elgin had sucked her blood. I was filled with a blinding fury, and it took several moments to calm down enough to wake my wife and find out what had happened. I could tell at once that Millie had been hypnotized by the creature calling itself Mr. Elgin. She spoke in fits and starts, saying she was out picking tomatoes for dinner the previous evening and could remember nothing after greeting Mr. Elgin, who was taking the

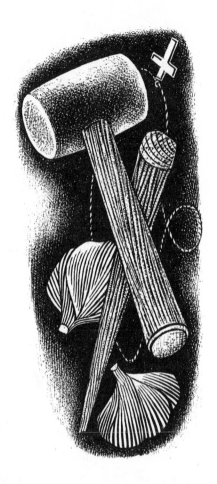

night air in the backyard of the dry goods store. Frankly, I was surprised she remembered that much.

Tenderly, I laid Millie back down to sleep. I tucked a great many cloves of garlic in the bed with her and placed Granny's cross around her neck. Then I went out back to the woodpile and started splitting logs and filing the pieces down into very, very sharp stakes. I was going vampire hunting. If Granny's book was correct, the vampire might very well visit Millie again tonight. And I would be ready for him.

It was almost midnight when I heard the first hypnotic sounds coming from the backyard. It sounded like someone humming a high-pitched tune, and it had a startling effect on Millie. Her eyes popped open, and she sat bolt upright. Her gaze was misty and unseeing, yet she hopped out of bed with ease and floated gracefully across the floor. I followed her, wooden stake in one hand and mallet in the other. Millie swept quickly through the large kitchen and out the back door. The strange, almost-singing sound increased in intensity as I hurried after her, and then stopped as Millie stepped into the vegetable garden. A dark figure in a sweeping black cloak was waiting for her. Its back was to me as it swept Millie into its arms. It bent its head, sharp canines gleaming in the moonlight, and then recoiled when it saw Granny's silver cross around my wife's neck.

I took two silent steps forward and thrust the stake into the creature's heart with all my strength. It started bolt upright in pain, dropping Millie to the ground. I smashed the mallet against the stake, forcing it deeper into the vampire. Mr. Elgin gave a single, high-pitched whine like that of a wolf in pain and then collapsed onto the ground. I grabbed my axe and lopped off his head right then and there. There was no blood on the axe when I returned it to the woodpile. Mr. Elgin had no blood of his own, I reasoned. Only that of his victims. I carried Millie into the house and tucked her back into bed. Then I wrapped Mr. Elgin's head and body in a couple of thick blankets, put them in the wagon, and drove the dead vampire out of town to a distant canyon. There, I set the body afire and watched it burn through much of the night. And that was the end of Mr. Elgin.

The local doctors were amazed at the way the plague suddenly vanished from Baker City. All the victims soon were better, and no one ever associated disease with the appearance or disappearance of the mysterious Mr. Elgin. Folks just assumed he'd gotten tired of life in the Wild West and headed back East. The only ones who ever knew the truth of the matter were Millie and my old Granny. And they never told a soul.

24

White Wolf

She snapped awake suddenly out of a deep sleep, every muscle tense, ears straining. What had she heard? Something was out of place, and the thought terrified her. She kept very still, barely breathing as she listened for the sound that had alarmed her. The house was silent. There was not even the soft sigh of the wind against the weathered boards of the farmhouse.

Then it came again. Sniff, sniff, sniff. A quick snuffling sound down the hall, near the front staircase. Pad, pad—click, click. It sounded like the paws of a giant creature. Pant, pant, pant. Soft sounds. Menacing sounds. Some animal—a large animal—was in the house with her.

Hide, hide. The instinct screamed at her to burrow under the covers, slide under the bed, tuck herself into her closet. Find somewhere safe to hide. Electricity screamed through every nerve, making her body sing with awareness and tense fear. But her mind ran quicker even then the lightning shafts tensing her body for action. If she stayed in this room she would be trapped with the creature. There was nothing to fight it with. Tennis rackets, baseball bats, old lengths of pipe—these were all out in the shed, not in her far-too-pristine bedroom with its pink ruffled femininity and display of stuffed animals still proudly sitting on a shelf over the desk.

Pant, pant, pant. Click, click. The creature was getting closer now, stalking her. Its breath came faster as it approached, and instinct told her that when it found her, it would kill. It had smelled her. It knew she was here, alone in the large house while her parents lingered long over their anniversary dinner.

Before her conscious mind connected with a thought, her body already had her slipping out of bed, nightdress fluttering around her as she sped through the connecting bathroom, out the door at the far end of the hall, and down the back staircase. She heard a soft growl and then the sound of animal feet pursuing her as she raced down the steps so fast she almost fell, leaping over the last four. She sank nearly to her knees at the impact with the kitchen floor, then terror led her past the cupboards with their too-dull butter knives to the back door. She fumbled with the handle, her straining eyes glancing in the glass of the windows for a horrible, curious moment to see what it was that was stalking her. She caught a glimpse of maddened red eyes over a narrow white snout. Pricked ears. And white speed. A wolf. A giant wolf. The door swung open and she was through, but it was caught before it latched by the body of the beast.

Then she was running, running through the cool, dark autumn night. Get to the tool shed, her brain screamed. Get a baseball bat. A tennis racket. Something to hit it with. But her feet were already skidding to a halt, changing direction as soon as the shed came into view. It was padlocked. Her father had decided to lock it this night of all nights, since a rash of petty thievery had overtaken their neighborhood. Her legs were even faster than her conscious mind, which was so numb with terror that she couldn't keep up. They had turned her body and she was racing away around the house, the terrifying almost-silent

sound of the creature's pounding feet and panting breath loud in her ears. The shivering of her spine told her that it was close behind. Almost, she could feel the hot, humid touch of its breath on her body as she ran.

Faster, faster, she commanded her legs, gasping desperately against the fear choking her, against the stitch forming in her side. Run around the house and down the driveway. Over to the neighbor's house. She turned the third corner of her house, and realized she'd never make it across the street in time. The wolf was too close. Perhaps she could run back inside and lock the creature out. But how could she keep it out when she had no idea how the white wolf had gotten inside? And the creature was gaining on her. She felt it snap at her back leg, felt the sting of teeth scraping calf muscle, and put on speed. Around one more corner to the front of the house. Then it veered away from her suddenly, and her heart pounded with hope. Maybe it had heard her parents' car! She kept running, around the last corner to the front of the house, past the rickety old well house that her father always promised to tear down and never did.

The wolf was there, springing on her from the top of the well house, teeth ripping, tearing out her throat in a single brutal moment. Her mind screamed in shock, but she had no voice left to echo the horror drumming through every cell in her body as her brain functions dulled. She felt her body thud to the ground, borne down by the weight of the white wolf, but the impact did not register. Nor did the continuous tearing of its teeth against skin and muscle and bone. It was eating her, she thought dispassionately as the blackness fell across her vision. But she had no voice left to scream.

She woke suddenly as her shoulder was shaken by trembling hands. She looked up into the frightened face of her mother, her father hovering just behind. "Celia, what's wrong, honey? Did you have a bad dream?"

Celia leapt into her mother's arms, sobbing incoherently about a wolf and no throat and the old well house. Her mother couldn't catch the whole story; nor did she try. She just soothed Celia, and her father got her a hot drink. Finally she went back to sleep, reassured because it had only been a dream after all, and her parents were sleeping in their bedroom down the hall.

Everything was completely normal the next day, her parents' anniversary. Breakfast was normal, school was normal—though her friends remarked on her paleness and tendency to gasp and jump at the least little noise—and the ride home from school on her bike was normal. All was well, until the moment her mother reminded Celia over milk and cookies that she and Celia's father would be going out that night again to celebrate their anniversary. Celia turned milk-white. In her dream, the white wolf had come to kill her while her parents were out celebrating their anniversary! She started shaking, and, to her own shame, heard herself begging almost hysterically for her mother not to go.

Celia's mother was impatient with this childish behavior. After all, Celia was sixteen, not a baby. She had her parents' cell phone number, and the neighbors were nearby. She had been left alone many times before; had even babysat for the neighbor's children. Celia allowed herself to be shamed into staying home that night, alone in the big house that had never frightened her before. But she had never had such a dream before, either. The thought of the coming of the white wolf terrified her.

She locked herself into the house as soon as her parents left, checking every door, every window, carrying her father's old baseball bat with her for protection. She knew it was silly, but she kept looking out the windows, trying to see if anything . . . if it was coming. Once she caught a glimpse of white, and her heart almost stopped in terror until she realized it was the reflection of her own face in the window. She laughed shakily then and went up to bed. Just before she turned off the light, she set the baseball bat carefully against the foot of her bed where she could easily reach it. Then she rolled over to sleep. As dark fog descended over her mind, she ignored the small thumping and bumping sounds the baseball bat made as it fell to the floor and rolled under her bed.

She snapped awake suddenly out of a deep sleep, every muscle tense, ears straining. Then she heard the tinkling of falling glass from a broken window, and the snuffling sound of a snout pressed to the floor. Pad-pad-pad went large feet as they negotiated the stairs. It was the sound of a hunting wolf. Werewolf, her treacherous mind corrected her in a calm, clinical way. It was a werewolf. Real wolves did not break into houses when there was plenty of game outside for them to eat. She could hear the click-clicking of the creature's claws on the wooden floor. The musky, foul smell of wet animal fur combined with the meaty breath of a carnivore drifted faintly into the room, making her gag.

But she was ready this time. The dream of the previous night had warned her. Trying to stay calm, she reached for the baseball bat at the foot of her bed. Her fingers grasped empty air, and she felt the first seeds of panic grip her. For a moment, she felt the blood thundering in her veins, felt her skin go clammy with fear. Where was the baseball bat? She could hear the werewolf's panting breath right outside her bedroom, dimly see the door handle turning as the clever creature pawed at it. The stench of meat-breath and animal sweat filled the room. She felt panic grip her, remembering suddenly the thud of the falling bat as she fell asleep. There was no time to search for it now. No time!

Her body was already out of bed, nightdress fluttering around her as she sped once again through the bathroom and down the back stairs. She heard a soft growl and then the sound of animal feet pursuing her as she raced down the steps, nearly collapsing onto the kitchen floor as she tore open the back door. A glance at the window beside her showed a reflection of the werewolf leaping down the last few steps behind her.

Then cool autumn air smacked against her face, her bare legs, her skin. Her feet screamed in protest as she ran painfully across the sharp gravel driveway toward the tool shed. And skidded to a halt a second time at the sight of the padlock. The huge, red-eyed wolf was between her and the driveway now, stalking toward her with every hair on its white coat standing erect, forming a great white ridge running the length of its back. The cold wind pierced her skin as she turned and fled around the side of the house. She gasped as the white wolf howled and took off after her. She could hear the terrifying sound of the creature's pounding feet and feel its hot, panting breath against her thin legs, exposed by her short nightgown.

Faster, faster, she commanded her legs, gasping desperately against the fear choking her, against the stitch forming in her side. Run around the house and back down the driveway. She felt the wolf snap at her back leg, felt the sting of teeth, felt hot blood pouring down. She put on speed. Around one more corner to the front of the house.

The wolf veered away from her suddenly, and she felt a rush of hope. But then she remembered the trap at the well house from her dream and whirled around to run back the other way, away from the trap. She couldn't hear the wolf now, couldn't see it in the cloud-darkened night. She kept running, this time back toward the locked tool shed. To her intense relief, she saw headlights pulling in to the bottom of the long driveway.

Then her heart stopped in panic as the headlights illuminated the shape of the white wolf balanced on the porch railing right in front of her. It sprang upon her, huge teeth tearing, ripping into her throat as she fell to the ground under the weight of its body in the pool of light created by her parent's approaching car.

25

Old Granny Tucker

There were just the three of us when I was growing up—Mama, Nicholas, and me. My name is Carrie. Papa died when Nicholas was two and I was five. I barely remembered him. There were no other relatives on Papa's side of the family, and the only relative we had on Mama's side was old Granny Tucker, whom we never saw. So we were all alone in the world, and Mama had to work hard as a seamstress to keep food on the table and a roof over our heads.

When I was a little girl, I never thought about Granny Tucker. I was too busy playing with Nicholas and helping Mama around the house. But as I grew older, I began wondering why we never saw her. She lived just outside the village, only a few miles from our little house. Other families visited back and forth with their relatives, even when they lived far apart. But Mama never talked about Granny Tucker, and she never took us to visit her.

I wanted to ask Mama about her, but somehow I could never get the words out. Whenever Mama heard one of our neighbors mention Granny Tucker, her lips thinned, and she frowned fiercely. I was very curious, and so I started eavesdropping on conversations anytime I heard the name Tucker mentioned.

It did not take me long to realize why Mama frowned whenever she heard her mother's name. Granny Tucker was a witch. From what I overheard, the townsfolk often visited Granny

Tucker's cottage to buy love potions or to ask her to hex someone who offended them. They also blamed her for everything that went wrong, from spoiled stews to missing animals. They said that Granny Tucker could find anyone she wanted to hex, even if they hid from her. She had a magic ball that she used to find people, and it was never wrong.

One day, I listened to a few neighborhood women talking in the dry goods store about Granny. One woman described the way Granny would shed her skin at night and her spirit would fly on the evening wind. When she returned to her home before dawn, she would say, "Skin, skin, let me in." Then she would slide back into her skin and be a woman again. Another spoke of Granny turning herself into a cat and roaming over the land doing evil things. The third woman spoke of the children living with Granny Tucker. No one knew where they came from or who they were or if they really belonged to Granny, since she was not married. I saw the woman glance toward me as she spoke, and I knew she was thinking about Mama.

As I walked home with my packages, I wondered how Mama had managed to escape Granny Tucker without being cursed. Then I thought of how Papa had died so young, and I wondered if she really had escaped. I talked the matter over with Nicholas, who is very wise. He thought that Papa must have bribed Granny Tucker somehow, and that is why she allowed him to marry Mama. Neither of us had enough nerve to ask Mama about it.

Nicholas and I were very curious to see Granny Tucker. I wanted to judge for myself whether or not she was a witch. She might, I told Nicholas, just be some poor misunderstood old woman. Nicholas laughed when I said that. He was sure she was a witch, and he wanted to see her do magic.

Finally, I worked up enough courage to ask Mama if Nicholas and I could visit our grandmother. As soon as she heard my question, Mama turned pale and clutched at the doorframe. For a long moment, she didn't speak. I stood waiting nervously for her response.

"You want to visit your grandmother?" she asked, sitting down abruptly on a kitchen chair.

"Yes, Mama," I replied. "Nicholas and I can walk to her house after school and spend the night."

"Carrie, I cannot allow you to go," Mama said. "No child has ever returned from that house except me. And your father had to pay Mother a hundred dollars for me before she let me go."

So Nicholas was right, I thought.

I didn't say anything more that day. But every day after that, either Nicholas or I would ask Mama if we could visit Granny Tucker. Mama was afraid for us, I knew. But I would not be satisfied with rumors. I had to see for myself what kind of grandmother I had. Nicholas felt the same way.

Finally, Mama said we could visit Granny Tucker on the following Saturday. Mama spent every night that week teaching us all the spells that she had learned when she lived with Granny, so we could protect ourselves should the need arise. It was the first time Mama had ever admitted that she knew magic.

Nicholas also devised an escape plan, just in case anything went wrong. He said to Mama, "I am going to put the dogs into a pen next to the house. If anything happens to Carrie or me, I will whistle the magic spell you taught us. When the dogs hear it, they will bark. Let them out when they bark, and they will come and rescue us."

A little of the tension left Mama's face when she heard Nicholas's plan. I hated making Mama worry, but I was determined to visit Granny Tucker.

We left our house around noon, and after walking for an hour, we came up to Granny's gate. I saw Granny Tucker at once. She was a little bent old woman with white hair and wicked black eyes. She was digging in a twisted little garden at the side of her house. She straightened up and looked right at us. She knew who we were and welcomed us by name.

"So, Carrie and Nicholas have come at last to visit with their old granny," she said.

There was nothing terrible about her words, but something in her tone gave me goose bumps. I glanced at Nicholas. He was regarding Granny Tucker calmly. Nothing ever upset Nicholas.

"Good day, Granny Tucker," I said, curtsying politely.

Granny beckoned for us to come into her garden. We walked through the gate and met Granny on the walk in front of her house. She studied us with a little smile that made me want to run away. Then she called her children to come and meet us and sent us into the back pasture to play.

I didn't like Granny's children. There was a boy my age and a girl who was a little younger than Nicholas. They both had a sly look in their eyes, and their skin had a little too much hair. They had strange ears that ended in a point, and when they smiled, their teeth were pointed and looked very sharp.

The children didn't know any of the games we played at school. They were very rough and didn't seem to mind hurting us. I think they liked hearing us cry out in pain when they knocked us down or stepped on our feet. Nicholas hated them from the moment he saw them. Nicholas is always very formal and polite

with people he hates. By the time we went in to supper, Nicholas was speaking in such a formal manner that he sounded like a politician.

After supper, Granny Tucker sat in a corner, sharpening her knife. She asked Nicholas to turn the grindstone for her. When Nicholas asked her what she was going to do with the knife, Granny replied, "I am going to kill a wild hog I have penned outside."

I had seen nothing in the pen except a few chicken feathers. My heart gave a frightened little leap. Nicholas's face became inscrutable. Whenever Nicholas looked like that, it meant he was worried.

Once the knife was sharpened, Granny Tucker had me fill the large pot with water and hang it over the fire to boil. Then she sent us all to bed in the loft. She put her two children in one pallet, covered with a dark sheet. Then she put Nicholas and me into the other pallet and covered us with a white sheet.

Granny's children fell asleep right away. They grunted and snorted in their sleep like a pair of animals. I knew I would not sleep that night, but I pretended to doze. Nicholas just lay with his eyes wide open, staring at the ceiling. Finally, Granny asked him why he didn't go to sleep. Nicholas said, "Mama always lets me play the fiddle before bed. Playing the fiddle helps me relax."

Granny Tucker took the fiddle down from its place over the mantelpiece and gave it to Nicholas. He started playing softly, sweet lullabies and gentle songs about love. As he played, I watched Granny Tucker. She sat near the steps, waiting patiently for Nicholas to fall asleep. I saw her fingering something hidden under her apron. I knew it was the sharpened knife. I was so frightened I could hardly breathe. Beside me, Nicholas played the fiddle better than he had ever played it before. I knew he was frightened too. Downstairs, Granny Tucker's head began to nod. At last, she fell asleep in her chair.

Nicholas put down the fiddle and motioned for me to get out of bed. While Nicholas removed the dark sheet from the sleeping children, I placed several bundles in our pallet to make it look like two people were sleeping there. We covered our pallet with the dark sheet and put the white sheet over Granny's children. Then we snuck down the stairs and out the door into the moonlight.

As soon as we were out of sight of the house, we ran as fast as we could go. It was not long before we heard a shriek of rage and horror coming from the house. Granny Tucker must have used the sharp knife on the children under the white sheet, not knowing until now that they were her own.

Nicholas grabbed my hand, and we ran even faster, taking side roads and twisting back and forth so as not to be found. I was winded and had a cramp in my side, but I did not dare stop. I kept remembering Granny's magic ball that could track anyone. If we did not reach our house soon, then Granny would track us down and kill us.

Suddenly, I heard a rumbling behind us. I looked back and saw a glowing ball following us in the moonlight.

"She's found us," I called to Nicholas. He nodded, too breathless to speak. Then he pulled me over to a large tree and thrust me up into the branches. I climbed up as fast as I could go, right to the top. Nicholas gave the emergency whistle for his dogs and then climbed up after me.

I could hear Granny Tucker muttering angrily to herself as she came down the road. She had a clear view of us silhouetted against the moonlit sky and came right to the bottom of our tree.

She was carrying an axe. I hoped with all my heart that Mama had heard the dogs barking and turned them loose. It was our only chance.

Below us, Granny Tucker started chopping down the tree. With each blow, she chanted: "Wham, bam, jenny-mo-jam. Wham, bam, jenny-mo-jam."

I closed my eyes, remembering one of the spells Mama taught us. "Tree, tree, when the ax goes 'chop,' grow big at the bottom, grow little at the top," I sang.

"It's working," Nicholas said, gazing down at Granny Tucker. "The chopped bits are growing back. Keep singing!"

So I kept singing, "Tree, tree, when the ax goes 'chop,' grow big at the bottom, grow little at the top." Below us, Granny kept chanting, "Wham, bam, jenny-mo-jam. Wham, bam, jenny-mo-jam." She was chopping as fast as she could.

Then I heard the baying of Nicholas's hounds. They came running up the road in a bunch and attacked Granny Tucker. A terrible fight ensued. Granny slashed at the dogs with the ax, and when she dropped that, she took out the sharp knife. One, two, three dogs fell to the ground, dead from stab wounds. She cut the throat of the fourth. Nicholas was shouting and cursing Granny, tears running down his cheeks as he watched his dogs die. Goldie, the oldest hound and Nicholas's first pet, had been at the back of the pack when they attacked. She was too old to keep up with the younger dogs. But she saw her chance when Granny slashed the throats of two of the younger dogs. Goldie leaped upon her and tore out her throat. Granny Tucker flailed about for a moment longer with her knife, then died.

Nicholas was so distraught by the slaughter that I had to drag him down out of the tree. As he sat weeping between the bodies of two of his hounds, I knelt beside Granny and took her knife. Mama had taught us one spell that good people should not use. But in this case, I thought I could make an exception.

The thought of what I had to do made my stomach heave, but I gritted my teeth and cut out Granny Tucker's heart. Goldie lay nearby, nuzzling the corpse of one of her pups. She whined a little as I took Granny's heart and walked over to her. I rubbed the heart on the dead pup's nose and watched as the hound came back to life. Quickly, I did the same for all the dogs. Nicholas observed me in silence. When they were all alive again, I dropped the heart to the ground, ran into the bushes, and was sick. When I was done being sick, Nicholas led me over to a nearby stream so I could wash off that wicked woman's blood. Then he and the dogs took me home.

Mama and Nicholas went back the next day and buried Granny and the children. They told the neighbors that the whole household had died of scarlet fever. No one questioned the truth of this statement. I think the whole neighborhood was relieved that they were gone.

I was ill for a week following that night. Once I was out of danger, I had a long talk with Mama, and then with the priest. I never did magic again.

26

No Trespassing

They were driving down a lonely stretch of highway at dusk when the thunderstorm came crashing down on them. The wind whipped the car crazily, making it hard to steer, and the gusts of rain made it hard to see. Peggy's boyfriend, Tommy, slowed the car until they were barely moving forward. They crept their way past the only house they'd seen for miles, a formidable, dilapidated structure with a sagging tower in one corner and a warped wrap-around porch. The front yard was surrounded by barbed wire fences. Plastered all over the fences and on every available tree in the overgrown yard were NO TRESPASSING signs. A single light shown in a dirty, cracked downstairs window, but it did not look welcoming, not even in the early dusk brought on by the howling storm.

The house was so creepy that Tommy automatically sped up a little to get away from it, and Peggy didn't blame him a bit. The rain was still heavy, but the wind was letting up a little, although the lightning flashes and thunder out in the long fields surrounding the road were still quite spectacular.

They were about a mile past the house when the car hydroplaned. Peggy screamed as the car turned a complete circle and then slid off the road, plunging down into a gully on the

opposite side of the road. The car slammed into a large boulder, throwing Peggy violently into the door.

Her head banged against the window, and a stabbing pain shot through her shoulder and arm as the car bounced off the boulder and kept sliding down the incline. It bounced off another small boulder, spun around, and then slid sideways until it came to a shuddering halt under a large pecan tree. Peggy's head was spinning, and she felt hot, sticky liquid pouring down into her eyes. Blood. The sharp flashes of pain coming from her arm and shoulder made her feel sick to her stomach, but the pain soon faded as dots of bright light flickered across her vision and she lost consciousness.

She was jolted awake by a sudden sharp pain as her boyfriend shook her by the shoulder, calling her name desperately above the heavy thunder of rain against the roof. Tommy probably thought she was dead, she thought hazily, considering all the blood covering her face. She managed to open her eyes and say his name, and she saw relief spread across his freckled face. He rubbed a hand frantically through his short red hair and said: "Are you all right? You're bleeding!"

"Bumped my head," Peggy managed to gasp. "Arm, shoulder feel bad."

Tommy glanced cautiously at her right arm and then went completely white in the semidarkness inside the car. "Your arm is all twisted," he said. "I think it's broken."

"Yes," Peggy whispered, unable to nod her head for fear it would fall off completely.

Tommy tore a strip off his shirt and pressed it to the cut on her head. "I'm going to call for help," he said when it became obvious that the bleeding was not going to stop right away.

He grabbed his cell phone off his belt with shaking hands. Then he swore and frantically pushed at the on button several times. Peggy closed her eyes, in too much pain to care. But she opened them again when Tommy cried: "The battery's dead. Peggy, where's your cell phone?"

"Forgot . . . it . . . at . . . home," she managed to say against the throbbing in her head.

"Oh, Lord!" Tommy exclaimed. "I'll have to go for help. There was a light in that house we just passed. They'll have a phone I can use."

Peggy's eyes popped wide open at this statement. Even through the haze of pain, she remembered how strange and creepy the house had looked. "No, Tommy. Stay here. A . . . car . . . will come," Peggy had to strain through the darkness that was slowly eclipsing her mind in order to say the last few words.

"I can't stay, Peggy," Tommy said, running his hands worriedly through his red hair, making it stand on end. "It could take hours for another car to come, and you might bleed to death."

Peggy couldn't speak against a sudden sharp pain stabbing through her arm and shoulder. She just gasped and curled in onto herself, wishing she could pass out so the pain would go away.

"I'm going to lay you down," Tommy said. "I'll try not to move your arm."

Very carefully, he adjusted the passenger seat back until it was as flat as he could make it. In spite of his care, she cried out once as the movement jostled her broken arm.

"Your shoulder looks funny too," Tommy whispered, as if to himself. "I think it's dislocated."

He managed to wrench open the badly dented driver's door and ran through the heavy rain to get a couple of blankets out of the trunk. He tucked the blankets around her until she was cocooned in them. Then he wiped more blood from her face and gingerly put a new, clean piece of his shirt against the cut on her head, which was swelling up.

"I'll be back as soon as I can," Tommy said. "Don't try to move until I come back with help."

"I won't," Peggy mumbled through the pain. Then Tommy was racing out into the storm, shutting the dented car door behind him as gently as possible so as not to jar her further.

For a few moments Peggy drifted in a kind of daze, but something at the back of her mind was urging her to wake up. She was uneasy about that strange house where Tommy was going to seek aid. It looked very threatening, and here she was alone and helpless beside the road. Some instinct made her pull the blanket up over her head and scrunch down into the seat as if she were just a spare pile of clothing rather than a person. The movement made her arm throb so horribly that she almost threw up, but she did it anyway. No need for anyone to know she was here in the car if they came poking around. It was a silly thought, of course, brought on by the pain she was in. But she kept on sliding down the seat until most of her body was on the floor under the dashboard, and her head under the blanket lay cushioned on the seat. The steady thudding of the rain on the roof of the car lulled her, then, and she allowed the tearing weariness caused by her wounds to pull her deep into sleep.

Peggy wasn't sure what woke her. Had a beam of light shown briefly through the blanket? Did she hear someone curse outside? She strained eyes and ears but heard nothing save the soft thudding of the rain, and no light shown through the blanket now. If Tommy had arrived with the rescue squad, surely there would be noise and light and voices. But she heard nothing save the swish of the rain and an occasional thumping noise which she put down to the rubbing of the branches of the pecan tree in the wind. The sound should have been comforting, but it was not. Goose bumps crawled across her arms—even the broken one—and she almost ceased breathing for some time as some deep part of her inner mind instructed her to freeze and not make a sound.

She didn't know how long fear kept her immobile. But suddenly the raw terror ceased, replaced by cold shivers of apprehension and a sick coil in her stomach that had nothing to do with her injuries. Something terrible had happened, she thought wearily, fear adding yet more fatigue to her already-wounded body. Then she scolded herself for being a ninny. It was just her sore head making her imagine things. Somewhat comforted by this thought, she dozed again, only vaguely aware of a new sound that had not been there before; a soft thud-thud, as of something gently tapping the roof. Thud-thud. Pattering of the rain. Thud-thud. Silence. Sometimes she would almost waken and listen to it in a puzzled manner. Thud-thud. Patter of rain. Thud-thud. Had a branch dislodged from the tree?

Peggy wasn't sure how long she'd been unconscious when she was awoken by a bright light blazing through the window of the car, and the sound of male voices exclaiming in horror. A door was wrenched open, and someone crawled inside just as she lifted her head and clawed the blanket off. She looked up into the blue eyes of a young state policeman. He reeled back a little in surprise, nearly knocking off his hat, and then cried out when he saw her blood-stained face.

"Miss, are you all right?" he asked, then turned over his shoulder to call for help without waiting for her response.

Within moments, she was being carefully lifted onto the seat and examined. An ambulance was called, and the officers did what they could to make her comfortable until it arrived, though for some strange reason one or the other would pop outside the car to look at something before returning to her side. Peggy managed to tell the officers her story while they waited, and then begged them to tell her where Tommy was. Surely he had come back with them to find her? Or had he been injured in the storm? Both officers deftly avoided answering her questions about Tommy, and just kept reassuring her that help was on its way.

The paramedics arrived promptly. Within a few rather painful minutes, Peggy was strapped to a stretcher and eased out of the ruined car and into the light mist that was all that remained of the rain. It was only as they carried her carefully up the slope of the incline that she thought to look back at the car—and saw the grotesque figure hanging from a branch of the pecan tree. For a moment, her brain couldn't decipher what she was seeing in the bright lights of the police car parked at the side of the road. Then she heard a thud-thud sound as the foot of the figure scraped the top of the totaled car, and she started screaming over and over in horror. One of the police officers hastened to block her view, and a paramedic fumbled for some valium to give her as her mind finally registered what she had seen. Tommy's mangled, dead body was hanging from the pecan tree just above the car. Nailed to the center of his chest was a NO TRESPASSING sign.

27

Black Magic

He was a strange man; wild-eyed and hook-nosed, with a shock
of black curls streaked with gray and the loping walk and crazy
laugh of the insane. Folks in town avoided Mad Henry, who
engaged in no visible profession yet somehow always had money.
He lived in a large, decrepit mansion, from which strange lights
shone at night. Folks said he was a black magician who called
upon the powers of darkness to wreak havoc upon his neighbors.
Others claimed he was a mad doctor trying to restore life to foul
corpses he dug up from the local cemetery. Rumors spread across
the whole region regarding Mad Henry, but no one ever dared
ask him what it was he did in his lonely mansion at night.

Young boys looking for a thrill looked no further than the
windows of that benighted dwelling. Strange and grotesque
shapes could be seen through the curtains when the moon was
full, and many a tough lad went running from the place, weeping
with fright. Most of them spent the next month plagued by the
nightmarish memories of what they had seen.

Now it happened one year that a new attorney opened an
office in town, bringing with him his young family. The eldest
daughter, Rachel, was a beauty and soon became the belle of
local society. Mad Henry saw her through his bedroom window
one night as she strolled arm-in-arm with two of her girlfriends,

and he fell in love with the red-haired minx at once with all the passion in his twisted soul. The very next evening, he showed up on her doorstep carrying a bunch of red roses that gleamed with their own inner light and left dewdrops of pure gold on the maiden's mantelpiece long after their giver made his way home.

Rachel was both intrigued and frightened by her strange suitor, who was so very much older than she. Her father was pleased by her new beau. Yes, Mad Henry was a strange fellow, but he was obviously well-off and could keep his daughter in the style she deserved. And he showered the lovely red-haired maiden with gifts—goblets of pure gold, necklaces of pearl and diamond, and stranger things too. Like the statue of a small dog that could actually bark and wag its tail; a mirror that reflected far-off vistas when it was not being used by its owner; and a pot of daisies—Rachel's favorite flower—that never grew old nor dropped a single petal, even if it was not watered for a week.

The gifts made Rachel uneasy. She couldn't help wondering what price their owner had paid to create them. Folks in town whispered that Mad Henry had sold his soul to the Devil in exchange for the ability to turn lead into gold. Alchemist, they called him, and other, darker names. He never invited Rachel or her parents into his home. He never brought anyone there, and Rachel was afraid to ask why.

About this time, young Geoffrey Simmons, the son of a prominent businessman in town, came home from university, where he was studying to be a doctor. He met Rachel at a party given in his honor and fell head-over-heels for the attorney's daughter. Rachel found his simple love much easier to accept than the complex adoration offered to her by the alchemist. A week after they met, Geoffrey and Rachel eloped, leaving behind a bewildered and angry father and a stunned alchemist.

The elopement was a nine-day wonder in town. By the time Geoffrey and Rachel returned from their honeymoon, their marriage was an accepted fact, and though they were teased about its suddenness, everyone was happy for them. Rachel's parents threw a big ball for the newlyweds and invited everyone in town. It was a festive, happy occasion with music and dancing and special performers brought to town for the festivities.

Rachel had been acting jittery all evening, looking over her shoulder again and again, sitting out the dances, and laughing with a too-high pitch that suggested the red-haired bride was not really happy at all. Geoffrey noticed and pulled her into a small alcove to kiss and comfort her.

"Are you worried about Henry?" Geoffrey asked.

Rachel turned her head and nodded in agreement.

"Henry won't come," Geoffrey said. "He's a gentleman and will leave you alone."

"You don't know him," Rachel told her new husband. "He is not quite sane, Geoffrey. He will come for me."

"Nonsense!" Geoffrey scoffed gently. He gave her another kiss and then the couple returned to the dance.

Rachel was waltzing with her father when she heard the first clap of thunder. It boomed in the distance and gradually got louder until it became a continuous roar in the sky above the dance hall. Lightning flashed again and again, sizzling the air, but no rain fell. It was not that kind of storm.

The guests murmured in fear as the sound of the storm grew louder than the orchestra, and the music twanged and limped to a halt when lightning struck a tree directly outside the hall.

Suddenly, the double doors blew open and a sharp, nasty breeze whirled in, bringing with it the smell of dead, decaying things and just a whiff of acrid chemicals. And then Mad Henry loomed in the doorway, black cape flapping in the foul breeze, pupils gleaming red with anger, wild black curls streaked with gray standing on end. He raised his arms above his head and shouted aloud in a language that made the eyes burn and the skin shiver.

There came a sharp clanking sound, and the grotesque figures of the dead came marching two by two into the room, decaying skeletons with bits of skin and dirt still clinging to them. Their eye sockets glowed with blue fire as they surrounded the room. Guests screamed aloud in terror and raced to escape out of every door and window. The boldest tried to attack the invaders, but those who tried found themselves pinned against the walls by hands of stretched gray skin and white bone.

Two of the creatures captured Geoffrey and threw him down at the feet of their lord amidst a shower of dirt and bits of gray skin that flaked from their foul forms. Geoffrey's head banged against the stone floor with a crack that left him stunned and helpless before the alchemist. Mad Henry stared at his rival with a gentle smile that boded ill for the university student. "Kill him," he ordered. "And bring me his widow."

Rachel screamed then, a terrible sound that made even the wild skeletons flinch. She ran forward, pushing through the confining ring of the dead, and flung herself upon her trembling young husband.

"Kill us both," she cried desperately, holding her husband close. "I will not go with you."

Mad Henry smiled grimly and nodded to his dead servants. They plucked the red-haired lass from her husband as if she weighed no more than a small child and marched her out the door. Her father leapt at the cadavers, beating at them with his walking stick; and one struck out with a decaying fist, catching the attorney with a blow that broke his nose and sent shards of bone directly into his brain, killing him instantly. They carried the screaming, beating, writhing Rachel out into the thundering night, and none could stay their progress or pull the girl from their grisly hands.

Red eyes gleaming with evil satisfaction, Mad Henry drew a silver-bladed knife and casually cut the bridegroom's throat from ear to ear. Then he whirled around, cape swirling about him like a black cloud, and strode from the room. Behind him, the army of the dead tossed their battered victims to the floor and followed their master, striding right through the large pool of blood that poured from the dying Geoffrey as he gasped out the final moments of his life. Behind them, the monsters left a trail of blood-stained footprints, half human and half skeleton, that burned themselves permanently into the stone floor of the dance hall.

Geoffrey's parents rushed to his side, and his mother pressed a handkerchief to the gaping wound on his throat in an ineffectual attempt to stop the bleeding. He gazed up at them with glazing eyes and gasped: "Find Rachel." And then he was gone.

The sounds of thunder and lightning were fading away as the alchemist and his dead companions disappeared into the dark night. Geoffrey's father patted his wife clumsily on the shoulder, went home for his gun, and then stalked through the streets of the town, heading toward the house of the local minister, who had stayed home from the party that night with a headache. Geoffrey's father didn't care if the man were dropping dead from consumption. He was determined to rouse the holy man at once and rescue his daughter-in-law.

As Geoffrey's father marched across town, he was joined by Rachel's two brothers, a cousin, and the fathers of her friends. The small mob pounded on the door of the minister's house, waking him and his wife and demanding he come with them at once to the home of the alchemist. They did not even give the poor preacher time to dress, dragging him along with them in nightshirt and cap, his glasses on upside-down and a Bible clutched in his hands.

When they arrived at the alchemist's house, they found it lit from top to bottom, and the stench of chemicals set all the men to gasping for breath and sneezing. Geoffrey's father seemed oblivious to the smell. He leapt into the house with his rifle, shouting aloud for Mad Henry to come down. Inspired by his courage, the mob spread out through the well-lit house, searching for the alchemist and his prisoner. They found nothing. Nothing at all. No furniture, no laboratory, not even dust and cobwebs. The house was completely empty save for the light, which shone from a series of mysterious globes that bobbed near the ceiling of each room. The alchemist had vanished.

The maddened mob torched the empty house and dragged the minister for miles through the surrounding woods and farms and fields, searching for Mad Henry and his prisoner, but they were gone. Search parties scoured the countryside for days, but turned up nothing. Geoffrey and Rachel's father were buried in the local cemetery, and the dance hall, whose stone floor was scored with the footprints of the dead, was torn down. No one in town spoke about what had happened, and no one dared imagine what had become of poor Rachel.

A year to the day after the ball, a timid knock sounded upon the door of Geoffrey's parents' home. When the father opened it, he saw a gaunt, gray figure on the stoop. Her eyes were dull with exhaustion and pain; her once-red hair was pure white and writhed wildly about her head. It took him a moment to realize that it was Rachel, but his wife knew at once and pulled the wretched figure into the house with exclamations of horror and pity. Rachel couldn't speak. Her tongue had been cut out. But she produced a knife from her tattered garments—the knife with a silver blade that they had last seen in the hands of the alchemist—and the gleam of satisfaction in Rachel's eyes told them that the streaks of blood that coated the knife were those of Mad Henry. Then Rachel fell into a dead faint. Geoffrey's parents carried her to Geoffrey's old room and summoned a doctor and her mother. But it was too late. Rachel died in her sleep that night, and upon her ravaged face was a smile of peace.

Inside her tattered dress, they found a note to her mother. It read:

Dearest Mother:

After many months of imprisonment and terrible suffering at the hands of the alchemist, I dug myself out of the stone tower where he kept me, clawing my way through loose mortar and stone until I was free. After his last gruesome visit to my cell, I followed the alchemist to his home deep in the dark woods near the tower. Mad Henry had taken my husband and my youth, and I was determined to take his life. And so I have, using the knife he used to kill my Geoffrey. If this condemns me in the eyes of God, so be it. I will die a murderess, and proud to be. Geoffrey and my father have been avenged, and I leave it to God to judge if I have done right or wrong.

Yours,
Rachel

28

The Brick Wall

There is something very satisfying in the moment when I thrust the tip of my sword into the lying, cheating soldier's heart and watch him fall to the sandy ground outside the walls of Fort Independence, where I currently hold the post of captain. It is a clean blow that will take his life in a few hours. (I am nothing if not an expert swordsman.) Lieutenant Massey writhes a bit at my feet in the chill air of Christmas morning, just before losing consciousness. A job well done, I decide with a little nod, as I turn away from the dying man. The world will be a cleaner place without Robert Massey in it.

As the seconds cluster around the lieutenant, I clean my sword and sheath it. Then I walk away without looking back. Why should I soil my eyes further with the likes of Massey, a man who squeaked by on his charm and then cheated honest soldiers at cards? Good riddance to bad rubbish.

I enjoy the rest of the Christmas season on the base, in spite of the enmity displayed to me by the more common soldiers after Robert Massey dies. They had obviously been fooled by his charm. But not I. I can see through charm to the heart of a man. I pride myself on my ability and feel it is my duty to rid the world of the cheats and liars who worm their way into the military. I have dueled to the death with six other specimens as nasty as this one in the past and anticipate that I will do so again in the future, the world being as corrupt as it is.

The men under my command seem depressed in the weeks following the holiday, and I work them hard. They mention Massey frequently, and to my disgust a monument to the lying lieutenant is commissioned, to be erected upon the spot where he died. I complain but am overruled by my pig-headed superiors.

I retreat to my chambers to sulk and soon am joined by a delegation of my men. Friends of Massey, all, I think they have come to complain about the duel we fought. I am surprised and delighted to learn, instead, that they have come to their senses and now see the lieutenant for the liar and cheat he really was. We share a round of drinks and laugh together over their mistake. One drink leads to another until even I, who am famed for my tolerance of strong alcohol, am feeling rather tipsy.

The other soldiers are worse off than I, of course, and someone suggests as a lark that we explore the lower dungeons. An odd fancy, that, but one that I find alluring after consuming a few more drinks. Everyone sets off in merry spirits, drinking and singing and laughing, our voices echoing through the narrow passages. Deeper and deeper we go, and I suggest we search for phantoms along the way. The men cheer and begin making spooky noises that seem appropriate to the dark and dusty paths we are traveling.

In spite of my good head for spirits, my head is spinning and my legs feel like rubber. I sag a little, and one of the good ol' chaps supports me. I am surprised to see that it is Massey's best friend, but am in too happy a mood to wonder for long. He smiles as we stagger along and sings the words of a bawdy song with me. Another of Massey's cronies grabs my other arm when

I trip, and the three of us chant together to the amusement of the other men.

Things go a bit dim for me at this point. I am afraid I might even have passed out from too much drink—how embarrassing. When I come to, I am lying on my back in one of the dim old dungeons. After a moment, I realize that my wrists and ankles are shackled to the floor. Obviously another lark of some kind, I think, yanking against my restraints.

"Very funny, lads," I call out, turning my head toward the sound of voices and activity at the entrance to the cell. "Now set me free."

The soldiers don't answer me. A moment passes, then two. Then Massey's best friend appears holding mortar and a mason's trowel, and the other men begin handing him bricks. I realize that the soldiers are bricking up the entrance to the cell in which I lay shackled. "Very funny," I say again, louder this time. "Are you trying to teach me a lesson, lads? Is that what this trick is about? Make me sorry that I fought the duel with Massey? Because I'm not."

No one answers me. They work in silence, laying brick after brick until one row is done, then two. They are playing a game

with me, of course. It is only a joke, I think. But something in the men's silence, in the way they build the wall more and more quickly, in the way they watch me with eyes that gleam in the dim light of the lantern makes the hair stand up on my head and brings shivers to my body. If this is a joke, it is a nasty one.

Massey's best friend pauses in his work and looks directly into my eyes. At that moment I realize that this joke is no joke. The soldiers mean to bury me alive in this dungeon. I scream then, tugging hard at the shackles that bind me. Scream after scream rips from my throat as I struggle against my bonds. I hope that my screams will be heard by others who will come and rescue me. But this dungeon is too deep within the fort, I fear. No one will hear. No one will come. I will be entombed alive and written off the books as a deserter.

They are on the final row of bricks. I am reduced to bribery now, but no one speaks. No one heeds me. As the last few bricks are mortared into place, I begin to cry like a pitiful baby and beg the men to spare me this terrible fate. No one answers.

I watch in heart-thudding horror as the last brick is put in place, as the last chink of light fades from my sight. Then I am in utter darkness. I howl in panic, writhing against the iron manacles binding hands and feet and twisting my body this way and that in a frenzy, trying to get free before it is too late—although somewhere in my mind, I know that it is already too late. Eventually I fall back against the floor, spent by my thrashings. My wrists and ankles are wet with my own blood, and the pain of the split skin is an agony almost as deep as that within my mind.

My fingers are torn and throbbing from their intense scrabbling against the hard floor. My mind rails against the darkness, against the utter heartlessness that has trapped me here alive. I find myself weeping angrily, though I have never shed a tear in my lifetime. My lifetime, which can now be counted in hours. Hours! "Oh, God, save me," I whimper. But if my fellow soldiers have not offered me mercy, then how can God?

The agony of the thought sends me writhing again in spite of the horrible pain racking my wrists, ankles, and hands. Daylight. I must see daylight again. One more time. Just once more.

"Don't leave me here to die alone! Don't leave me!"

My voice echoes again and again in my ears, growing fainter as within me a terrible thirst grows. Water. I crave water, but there is no one to give me a drink. No one.

I am alone, and the sheer brutal horror of it overwhelms me more than the terrible thirst growing in my mouth and throat, and the throbbing pain of my self-inflicted injuries. My eyes strain against the complete and utter darkness, and I wonder if they are even open. The world inside my mind has dimmed, and it is only at greater and greater intervals that sheer terror arouses me from my stupor and makes me writhe in agony against the chains.

Dear God, I can't get out. *I can't get out. I CAN'T GET OUT!*

29

Initiation

I boarded the bus in Miami, resigned to a long and boring crosstown trip. The bus was a local and my stop practically the last one. I stared moodily out at the rainy city around me as a middle-aged man with a haggard face and a worn-out business suit plopped into the seat beside me and shoved a briefcase underneath it.

"Are you a student?" he asked me as the bus lurched into heavy rush-hour traffic.

"Yes," I said shortly, not wanting to talk. I had a lot on my mind. My girlfriend had broken up with me over lunch this afternoon, and I wanted to brood about it.

"I was in college once, a long time ago now," the man mused, leaning back against the seat and staring around at the crowd in the bus. It was a varied lot, from a mother of three to men in business attire to teenagers absorbed in their cell phones. "Used to belong to a fraternity. Do you belong to a fraternity?" he asked, voice and eyes suddenly sharp. The intensity with which he asked the question made me nervous.

"No, sir," I said. "I don't have time. I'm pre-med and have a lot of studying to do to get into grad school."

"Good," said the stranger, relaxing again. "Never join a fraternity, son. They're no good. My fraternity had a brutal initiation rite. They'd take candidates out to a ruin of a house outside town that they said was haunted. They'd tie the fellows up and leave them there all night with the ghosts. Nasty."

"If you believe in ghosts," I said dryly. I didn't. I am a man of science, and I believe what science can prove. That went for religion as well as ghosts. Still, if I had been a praying man, I would have started right about then. This fellow with his intense manner and too-bright eyes was making me nervous.

"Me, I made it through initiation all right. But a bloke who joined the next year didn't fare so well. All the creaking and moaning in that house, hour after hour, well it turned his brain. About two in the morning, he started screaming. He ripped out of the ropes tying him down as if they were made of spaghetti and turned on the two fellows who were tied up with him. He killed them both with the Swiss Army knife he kept in his pocket. Then he hung himself. It was a bloody mess, and I mean that literally, son."

He looked at me with his too-bright eyes, and I squirmed a bit, wondering if I should make an excuse and get off at the next stop. This guy was creeping me out.

"Happened on the third of December. I remember the date well," the stranger continued, turning his attention across the aisle to a pretty teenage girl who was rapidly texting on her phone. "Nobody in the fraternity could forget it. But it didn't end with the haunted house. No indeed. On December 3 the next year, one of the fraternity fellows who was responsible for the initiation of the crazy boy went crazy himself and shot his wife. It made the news. The next year, another one of that group flipped out and tried to run down his friends with his car. This also happened on December 3."

"That's terrible," I said, edging my body closer to the window. I was definitely getting off at the next stop—and wished the bus driver would hurry up and get us there.

"A year passed without incident," the man went on, turning his bright gaze away from the girl to study the mother and her three children. "Eight out of the ten or so boys who participated in the fatal initiation all graduated from college that year. Then one of them popped up on the news when he killed himself and his family on December 3."

Hurry up, bus driver, I thought, pushing my foot against the floor as if it were the accelerator. *Hurry up!*

"The next year, another former frat brother went crazy and drove his car off a bridge," the stranger continued, fiddling restlessly with the buttons on his worn gray business suit, his too-bright eyes resting on a red-haired businessman speaking animatedly into a cell phone. "And the following year one of the graduated frat brothers who joined the Army tried to shoot up the men serving in his platoon. Both events happened on December 3."

"Not good," I said at random, barely registering what I said, I was so jittery.

"Next year it was arson. Then murder again. Then it was suicide. And last year a former frat brother bombed a building in Chicago. All the tragedies happened on December 3, the same day the initiate went crazy all those years ago. It was like some kind of curse was killing off the men responsible for his death," the stranger said. "There's only one man left of that group now. Only one."

We were approaching the next bus stop, and not a minute too soon to my mind. As the bus slowed, a woman leaned forward

from the seat behind us and said, "Excuse me, sir," to the stranger riding beside me. "Do you happen to know the date?" She waved her checkbook at him in silent explanation for the question.

"Why yes, ma'am, I do," he said as I grabbed my backpack from underneath my seat and prepared to rise. "It's December 3."

He smiled as he said it. Then he reached into the inside pocket of his jacket and pulled out a gun.

30

Shattered

My identical twin sister and I turned sixteen the winter our parents took us snowmobiling in Yellowstone. Our dad was an outdoors nut, so we'd practically been raised in tents. When West Yellowstone and some of the other gateway towns started featuring winter snowmobiling treks into the park, Dad was quick to take advantage.

There was an unspoken reason why Dad dragged us out of school and took us to Yellowstone. He was trying to save my twin sister, Jamie. I only hoped it wasn't too late.

What can I tell you about me and Jamie? We were both green-eyed blondes with masses of straight hair and freckled faces. Folks had trouble telling us apart when we were little, until they got to know us. Personality-wise, we were opposites. Jamie wore her hair in long braids and was into dolls and clothes and makeup. Her room was white and frilly, and she had more nail polish than the local drug store. Me, I was the tomboy. My hair was shoulder-length and tangled, and my room was decorated with plants and horse posters and baseball memorabilia. One of my life's goals was to pitch for a professional women's league. I practiced pitching all the time, summer and winter. I was pretty deadly with a snowball, if I say so myself.

Jamie and I were close despite our differences. We were the kind of twins that the science books talked about. I felt Jamie break her arm in fifth grade, and she knew I'd been in a car accident in seventh. We both felt our grandmother die in eighth grade.

When we entered high school, things changed. Jamie started hanging out with a couple of girls who were into the occult. Not good earth magic or Native American medicine. Nope. These girls used Ouija boards and called on nasty spirits and did lots of terrible things I didn't want to know about. It seemed harmless enough when we were freshmen. But as the girls' powers grew, they turned more and more toward the dark arts, and they took Jamie with them.

By the time we entered our junior year, Jamie's sunny nature had turned dark and sullen. She painted her room black and raised black widow spiders as pets. And she hung a spell mirror framed with occult symbols over her dresser. I hated that mirror. The symbols around its frame writhed whenever I looked at them. Not that I saw much of it.

Jamie shut me out of her life at the beginning of the school year. And not just me—she wouldn't speak to any of us, even at meals. She hitched rides to school with her friends and didn't come home until late. Our parents' scolding fell on deaf ears. Even her teachers commented on her changed behavior.

The sixth sense that exists between twins told me that Jamie was sinking into a dark abyss from which there was no rescue. If we didn't act quickly, she would be lost to us. Feeling disloyal, I cornered Dad just before Christmas and told him everything I knew. He'd guessed some of it, but there was enough that he didn't know to make him appear rather green by the time I'd finished.

Two weeks later, our family flew to Salt Lake City and drove to West Yellowstone for a "fun family vacation" on snowmobiles. Jamie and I shared the room next door to our parents. Jamie hated sharing with me, but she wasn't given a choice. She chose the bed closest to the door and started unpacking her clothes. From the bottom of the suitcase she picked up a large, bubble-wrapped object. It was the spell mirror from her room. I bit my tongue hard to keep from shouting at her as Jamie unwrapped it lovingly and placed it on top of the dresser beside my signed baseball, which I always carried with me. Why had she brought that horrible thing?

I put my clothes away and suggested we explore the town. To my surprise, Jamie agreed. The next hour felt like old times. We poked our noses into all the shops, laughed over the funny postcards, and bought silly trinkets for one another. Our cheeks were red with cold when we got back to the hotel. Jamie lingered in the lobby, chatting with a member of the hotel staff while I rushed upstairs to heat some water in our electric coffeemaker. We'd bought packets of gourmet hot cocoa from the local grocery, and I couldn't wait to give it a try.

I was pouring a mug for Jamie when she burst into the room. She was smiling, but it wasn't her nice smile. It was the triumphant look she wore after she performed some particularly unpleasant ritual in the backwoods with her friends. "It's just as I thought. This hotel is haunted," Jamie exclaimed. "Where's my Ouija board? I must contact the spirit."

"You left your Ouija board at home," I said snappishly, handing her the mug of cocoa. She thrust it aside without drinking and sat on her bed, face dark as a thundercloud. She started cursing Mom and Dad for bringing us to Yellowstone.

Then she glared at me and cursed me too. I bolted from the room in tears and went to find Mom and Dad.

We were up early the next morning and suited up for the cold ride through Yellowstone National Park. I'd been snowmobiling before, but it was Jamie's first time. She spent the morning complaining about the noise and the smell and the way the machine handled. She was too hot, she was too cold, she hated everyone and everything. I blocked out her complaints and tried to enjoy the cold fresh air on my face and the feeling of speed beneath me. The winter landscape was enthralling. Deep snow covered the ground. Pine trees loomed above the glimmering landscape. Mountains edged the huge Yellowstone caldera and the ice-encrusted lakes took my breath away. We saw otters playing at the edge of the Firehole River, and a herd of bison walked down the snow-packed surface of the road in front of us. It was amazing!

The snow had mostly melted around the hot springs in the Upper Geyser Basin, and elk were grazing among the clouds of steam. It was an enchanting wonderland. When we stopped to watch Old Faithful erupt, I thought my heart would burst.

Somewhere around Biscuit Basin, Jamie stopped complaining. There was amazement in her eyes as we watched the geyser erupt, and something else I hadn't seen in a long time. Joy. I glanced at my parents, hardly recognizable under all their snow gear. They saw it too. *Oh, please, God, help us,* I prayed. We weren't a religious family, but the simple prayer burst out of my heart. I hoped it would reach someone out there who could help my sister find her way back to us.

Over dinner, Jamie talked eagerly about all we'd seen and heard that day—the snow-encrusted bison, the lone coyote jumping headlong into a snowbank after mice. She was as eager as a kid at Christmas. But after dinner, her mood changed. I saw her talking to a local fellow who gesticulated wildly and pointed toward the roof. Jamie raced upstairs after this conversation, but I was waylaid by my dad, who wanted to play checkers. After soundly trouncing my sire three games in a row, I arrived in triumph at the door to my room and found it barred against me.

"Come on, Jamie, open up," I said, knocking loudly.

"I'm contacting the ghost," she said through the door. "Go away."

I went. Back in the lounge, I dropped disconsolately into a chair and stared blankly at the TV. The local fellow, who was working the desk that evening, came over and sat opposite me. "Boy, your sister is really into the occult," he said.

"Tell me about it," I replied despondently.

"She made me tell her every story I'd ever heard about ghosts and supernatural stuff in West Yellowstone," he continued. "Your sister was really taken with one of our local stories—it's just a rumor really—about a man who was shot by his wife when she caught him in bed with a prostitute. Nasty story, but that's the Wild West for you." He got up and stretched. "I'd better get back to the desk. Give a holler if you need anything."

I nodded my thanks and dragged myself upstairs, hoping that Jamie had finished whatever nasty occult thing she was trying. Apparently, she had. There was no barrier this time when I pushed the door open. Jamie was in bed pretending to be asleep. I saw the gleam of her eyes as I stumbled around the dark room, undressing and brushing my teeth, but she didn't speak and neither did I.

Once in bed, I cradled my signed baseball and thought about my sister. Jamie was going to get in trouble with the police if she kept walking her chosen path. And there were even worse fates than that for people who practiced black magic. But I didn't know how to stop my sister, and neither did Dad and Mom. It would take some kind of miracle, and miracles were in short supply around here.

I was awakened in the night by a wicked breeze that painfully ripped the covers off my bed. My eyes sprang open in shock, heart pounding so hard against my ribs that I thought it would leap out of my chest. An eerie light glowed from the spell mirror above the dresser. I shrieked in fear when I saw a twisted face glaring out of the glass. Tangled hair writhed around an inhuman, red-eyed face that was the source of the strange light. I looked toward Jamie's bed and yelped again. Jamie, still encased in her covers, was floating three feet above her bed! The green light emanating from the mirror surrounded her body like a net. Down our sisterly sixth sense, I could hear Jamie screaming, though no sound came from her open lips. Her eyes bulged with terror, and one hand stretched pleadingly from her covers. In my head, I heard her cry, "Save me, Jessie. Save me!"

The cold wind whirled around the room, throwing park brochures every which way, banging the closet doors, rattling the hangers. I did the only thing I could think of. I grabbed my baseball, took aim, and threw my fastball at the abomination in the mirror. The ball hit the mirror with a resounding crack, and the glass shattered. The face vanished, and with it the green light and occult wind. Jamie landed on her bed with a thump that rattled the windows. For a moment, there was stunned silence.

Then Jamie started crying like a baby, and I jumped on the bed to take her in my arms.

Our parents started pounding on the adjoining door, and I got up to let them in. Jamie couldn't talk, so I told them what had happened. Mom burst into tears and hugged us both tightly. Dad was furious and frightened. He alternated between glaring at my twin and hugging her. Finally, he got up and started straightening the room. When he got to the glass-covered dresser, he stopped and stared at the remains of the spell mirror. Occult symbols writhed around the frame, and a few sharp pieces of glass clung to the edges like angry teeth. My baseball sat in the center of the mess, signature upward.

"I'll clean that up, Dad," I said firmly.

He nodded warily and picked up my bedcovers instead.

Mom and Dad took Jamie with them when they went back to their hotel room. I stayed behind to clean up the mess. I wrapped the mirror in a spare blanket without touching it and then broke it into tiny pieces. Then I found a dustpan and brush from the housekeeping closet down the hall and swept up the worst of the glass. Early the next morning, I threw the remains of the mirror away in four different dumpsters, hoping to break whatever spells still lingered by separating the pieces.

Jamie rushed to greet me with a bear hug when I came down to breakfast. When I looked into her eyes, I saw that my identical twin was back, safe and sound. The terror of the previous night had turned Jamie away from the occult forever.

I was exhausted but exhilarated that day as we explored the Canyon region on our snowmobiles, and I slept dreamlessly that night. When we left West Yellowstone at the end of the week, it was *Jamie* who begged Dad for a return trip.

As I buckled my seat belt in preparation for the flight, my foot nudged my backpack where my baseball lay. I closed my eyes and saw again a twisted green face throwing a net of power over my sister. *Oh, Jamie, that was much too close.*

Jamie bumped my elbow. I opened my eyes, and she pointed toward a cute guy across the aisle. I smiled at my twin. All was well.

31

Rubberoo

"Oh, Etienne, I almost forgot. We will be having a guest for dinner," Margaret said, looking up from her knitting. She was seated by the fire, which made a soft golden halo around her blond hair. In the dancing firelight, her face looked guileless and sweet.

Etienne looked up from his newspaper and frowned at his wife of twenty-five years. She knew he did not like surprises. She smiled at him warmly, and he relaxed a little, basking in her obvious adoration. And why shouldn't she adore him? He was an important attorney, a rich man, and he was thinking of running for mayor. He, in turn, was proud of his lovely wife. He had worked very hard to win her hand, and he deserved to bask now in her love.

"Who are we having to dinner, my dear?" he asked.

"An old friend of yours from Montreal," Margaret said with a happy smile. "Jean-Claude Dubois!"

Etienne started imperceptibly at the name and his eyes narrowed. But Margaret babbled on in sunny innocence: "I met him in front of the mercantile this afternoon. He had just arrived in town and had no fixed engagements, so I invited him to take dinner with us. He hasn't changed a bit since the last time I saw him. Remember? When he came with you to my coming-out dance?"

Oh, yes. Etienne remembered that day very well. Very well indeed. It was the day her former betrothed, Lucas, had been savagely killed by a rogue wolf on his way to the coming-out ball. Margaret and Lucas had planned to announce their engagement at the party. It has been a sad day for Margaret. And a happy one for Etienne. He remembered being impressed when Jean-Claude, his "friend" from Montreal, had arrived on time for the party, not a hair out of place or a wrinkle in his suit to declare what his business had been out there on a dark, empty road only a few minutes before the first dance was announced.

Before he could utter a word, the butler appeared in the doorway, announcing their guest. Etienne and Margaret rose as a suave, dark-haired man strolled into the room and bowed elegantly to them both. Margaret hurried forward, hands outstretched, and Jean-Claude kissed them one at a time before turning and offering Etienne a firm handshake.

"Jean-Claude," Etienne said, waving him to a seat. "How interesting to see you again. May I offer you a drink?"

Jean-Claude smoothly accepted and sat down on the settee beside Margaret.

"What brings you to Montana, *mon ami?*" Etienne asked, handing him a sherry and pouring another for his wife.

"I have family business in Butte with the copper kings," Jean-Claude said, shipping his sherry. "And other business takes me to British Columbia when I am done in Montana."

Etienne's glass shook a little as he recalled just what Jean-Claude's family business was. Assassinating. They were all assassins, and such was their skill and so unusual their gifts that no one in the United States or Canada would ever be able to convict them even if they could catch them in the act.

"Will you be staying long in town?" he asked, taking his former seat across from the settee.

"This is a mere stopover on my way to Butte," Jean-Claude purred gently. "It was an unsought pleasure to meet your charming wife outside the mercantile. I had no idea you were still living in Montana. Indeed, I had not realized you had wed one another until the lovely Madam Baptiste told me her married name."

He smiled suavely at Margaret, who pinked happily, threw her husband a loving glance, and took a sip of her sherry.

"I will never forget your kindness to me at my coming-out party," Margaret said shyly. "Do you remember, Etienne? That strange old railroad man accosted me in the garden, shouting out about rubberoos and waving his whiskey bottle around? If Jean-Claude hadn't stopped him, I don't know what might have happened!"

"I was happy to be of service to such a lovely lady," Jean-Claude said, placing a hand over his heart and bowing. Etienne frowned at such flamboyant behavior, but Margaret seemed to be enjoying it.

The butler appeared in the doorway and announced dinner. They all rose, and Jean-Claude took Margaret's arm and escorted her through to the dining parlor. Over dinner, they discussed politics, the settlement of the Montana territory, and the latest news from Montreal, where both Jean-Claude and Etienne had grown up. Etienne relaxed a little as the meal progressed. It was silly to be on edge. The contract that had originally brought the assassin to this town was finished long ago, on the night of the coming-out party, and no one had been the wiser. Jean-Claude's visit to town twenty-five years later was a coincidence, nothing more.

As they were eating dessert, Jean-Claude inquired after any children they might have. Etienne glared at him. How dare he bring up such a painful topic? Etienne had cast his only child out six months ago, unbeknownst to his mother. The cover story he'd told his wife was that the boy wanted to see the world before settling down to a career, and so he had started off on a grand tour of the United States with his father's blessing. But the truth was that Etienne had sent the defiant child away with barely a cent in his pocket to survive as best he could on his own. And he'd intercepted the letter his son had written to his mother, so Margaret never knew of the breach. He wanted Margaret to forget they ever had such a disobedient son, and the boy's sudden death had come as something of a relief. Now here was Jean-Claude, bringing up a subject that could only cause his wife more pain.

Before Etienne could interject, Margaret answered the assassin: "We had one son. Jonathan. He was making a grand tour of America, but he died in a freak accident while visiting one of the mines in Butte earlier this year." Her lovely blue eyes filled with tears at the memory.

"Madame, I grieve with you," Jean-Claude said, reaching over to take Margaret's hand.

Etienne was furious. If looks could kill, Jean-Claude would have dropped dead in his seat. *Take your hands off my wife,* he wanted to scream at the assassin. But politeness held his tongue. After all, the uncomfortable meal was almost over, the assassin would be gone forever, and he and Margaret would go back to their peaceful existence.

They lingered long over dessert and still longer in the parlor. Etienne grew sullen and impatient, but neither Jean-Claude nor Margaret seemed to notice. They talked and laughed together until the hour grew late, and the assassin finally rose to take his leave.

"No, Madame, stay in your comfortable seat by the warm fire," Jean-Claude said to Margaret. "*Mon ami* Etienne will see me safely on my way. And God bless you, Madame."

Margaret smiled at the assassin who—had she but known it—had killed her betrothed, and bade him a fond farewell. And then Etienne and Jean-Claude were out in the hallway. The assassin said: "*Mon ami,* walk with me to the gate, *s'il vous plait.*"

Etienne glanced nervously about, but the butler was nowhere to be seen. Reluctantly, he agreed. The two men shrugged on overcoats and scarves and walked out into the chilly, wind-swept night. Snow was deeply packed on either side of the shoveled brick walkway, and it mounded up so high near the street that the wrought-iron fence around the property was barely visible. The two men paused at the fence, and Jean-Claude said softly: "So it worked, *mon ami.* You hired me to kill Margaret's betrothed on the very night of her coming-out dance, and then you stepped into his shoes. I ask you now: Was it worth it? *Non,* you do not have to answer. One look at the lovely face of your wife says that it was. But what is the story with your son, I wonder?"

Etienne glared at him in the dim light reflected off the snow. "The boy was a disaster. Always in trouble. Always making up to his mother. Spending money recklessly. Drinking. Defying me. Me, his father! So I sent him away. And he got himself killed in a cave-in in the mines. That is all."

"So abrupt you are, *mon ami,*" Jean-Claude said lightly. "Do you not like talking to me? After all, we are old friends! And like all old friends, we share an old, old secret. Come, walk me to my hotel."

Etienne shivered then and hung back. "I'd rather not," he said. "Margaret will miss me."

"She will know where you have gone," Jean-Claude said, taking his arm in a grip of steel and pulling him through the gate onto the sidewalk. "Come, Etienne, how can a powerful man such as yourself be nervous walking with me? After all, I am only a . . . what was it the old railroad man called me? Ah, yes. I am only a rubberoo! Besides, I kill only by contract. What have you to fear from me?"

That was true, Etienne remembered. The assassin did have a code of honor—howbeit a strange one. He fell into step beside Jean-Claude Dubois, feeling relieved. Around them, the gas lamps made puddles of light on the icy streets. The wind was so cold it bit right through Etienne's coat and made him shudder. The assassin seemed to feel nothing.

"I made just the one mistake that night so long ago," Jean-Claude mused as they walked the midnight streets, through the whistling, jostling wind. "I let myself be seen by that drunken old railroad conductor as I was changing form. The stink of a passing steam train masked his scent from me. Before I could do anything about him, young Lucas was in sight and I had a paid contract to perform. By the time the boy was dead, the old man had disappeared into the station. It was sheer bad luck that the man knew Margaret and came to warn her about me. Fortunately, she did not understand him, and I was able to silence him permanently later that evening."

Etienne was mesmerized by the assassin's voice. The world had narrowed into an icy dream lit by the occasional street lamp. But the lights were getting fewer and farther apart, and suddenly Etienne realized that they were not heading toward the hotel at all. They were walking along a vacant side street that bordered the railroad tracks. It was the same side street where Lucas's savaged body had been discovered twenty-five years ago.

"Silenced him permanently?" he asked, shaking with cold and sudden fear. "I thought you only killed for money."

"Oh, I didn't kill the railroad conductor," Jean-Claude purred. "No, I paid him many pieces of gold to forget what he'd seen. And so he left town and started life over again in Butte." Jean-Claude paused and placed a hand on Etienne's arm.

Jean-Claude swung the suddenly trembling attorney to face him, and in the snow-filled night, the assassin's eyes glowed red. "Where, twenty-five years later, he met Jonathan, your despised and rejected son. He told the boy all about the rubberoo who had been hired to kill his mother's fiancé so that you could marry her."

Jean-Claude's voice was changing. It had grown deeper, and there was the growl of a wolf in it. Etienne felt the nails on the hand clutching his arm grow longer and sharper, cutting through the material of his coat.

"It was your son's wish that his despised father should face the same fate as Lucas. As he lay broken and perishing from his wounds in the charity hospital in Butte, Jonathan Baptiste begged the old railroad conductor to put out a contract on his father, Etienne Baptiste, and to pay the assassin who killed Lucas to fulfill it. I have in my pocket a letter from your son to his mother, telling her the whole story, which I mean to deliver to Margaret in the morning. And who knows? Maybe it is my turn to comfort the grieving widow!" The last word ended in a growl as Jean-Claude transformed from a suavely handsome man into a huge, gray wolf. *Loup garou.* Rubberoo. The perfect assassin.

With the last ounce of his humanity, Jean-Claude howled one word: "Run!"

And Etienne ran, stumbling and sliding, down an icy street where a young man named Lucas—handsome, laughing, and very much in love—had come face to face with a *loup garou* twenty-five years before. As then, so now—neither man stood a chance.

32

Jack O'Lantern

I thought I'd do some hunting in the marshlands on my day off. Much to my disgust, I didn't shoot a thing all day, and come sundown I was simmering with frustration. I'd wandered pretty deep into the bogs and swamps, and before I knew it dark was falling and I was a long, long walk from where I'd stashed my car. Worse still, I was a bit turned around. I was pretty sure I knew the way back, but what with the dusky twilight and the rising mist, I figured I had better hightail it out of there mighty quick.

At first, the walking wasn't too bad. I could still see the thin game trail I'd been following along the wobbly ground and through the treacherous tufts of grass. But the light was fading, and I hadn't brought a flashlight. Stupid of me. I clutched my rifle closer and kept moving forward slowly as the mist began to billow in strange shapes, swirling in a manner calculated to convert the greatest skeptic into a believer in ghosts.

I gulped a bit and kept going, until I almost fell headlong into a deep pool that loomed out of nowhere in the mist-shrouded darkness. I groped my way backward and sat down on a rotting log. It was no use going on tonight. If I did, I was sure to injure myself or fall into a pool of water and drown.

I shivered, already feeling the damp deep in my bones. It would be chilly tonight, but not cold enough to kill me,

I figured—for which I was grateful. What a stupid mess to have gotten into, I fumed, trying to make myself comfortable on the ground beside the log. Around me, I could hear the soft whirring and croaking and singing of the night creatures, and the wind soughed through the tall grasses and trees. The mist was so heavy now I couldn't see my hand until it was right in front of my nose.

And then the first light appeared, off to my right. I was startled. Was there another hunter out here? Someone with a flashlight who could get me out of this pickle?

I jumped up and shouted: "Hello there!"

My voice reverberated in the foggy air, but there was no response. I sat down again, watching for another light. Nothing.

I sighed and lay down beside the log, determined to get some sleep. And then the light appeared again, off to my left this time. It winked on and off. On and off. Then disappeared. That was when I realized what it was. It was the Jack O'Lantern. A will-o'-the-wisp. These fairy lights, common to marshlands around the world, were said by some to belong to evil spirits who tried to lure the unwary to their doom. This was nonsense, of course. Science said the lights were caused by marsh gases.

I relaxed, grinning to myself as I recalled the quaint piece of folklore attached to the marsh lights. According to my great-uncle, Jack was a nasty fellow who beat his wife and kids and was an all-around bad chap. When Jack's body finally got so wore out that he died, his spirit went straight to the gates of heaven, but Saint Peter refused to let such a wretched fellow in, and Jack was forced to go down to hell. But the Devil barred the door as soon as he saw Jack coming and wouldn't let him in to hell either. "Go away and don't come back," the Devil told Jack. "Go back where you came from."

"How am I supposed to get back in the dark?" Jack grumbled. "Give me a lantern."

The Devil threw a chunk of molten fire out to Jack, who took it for his lantern and went back to earth, where he wanders forever through the swamps and marshlands of the earth, a bitter spirit whose only delight was in luring the unwary to their doom with his lamp.

"Is that you, Jack O'Lantern?" I called jovially the next time I saw the light.

"Jack, (jack, jack)," a voice whispered back at me from the fog. I was seriously spooked. I clutched my gun to my chest, the hairs on my arms standing on end. Had that been an echo of my voice, or was someone out here with me?

"Who's there?" I shouted, trying to sound brave and menacing. I waved my gun around. "Show yourself."

"Jack, (jack, jack)," the voice hissed from a completely different section of the swamp. A light blinked on and then off. On and then off.

Shudders ran up my spine at the sound of that ghastly voice coming from nowhere. I huddled up against the log, wanting something firm at my back. Suddenly, the story of the Jack O'Lantern didn't seem so funny. After all, this was a man who had outwitted the Devil, and whose bitterness at being cast out of both heaven and hell caused him to lure the unwary to their deaths. Nonsense and hokum, of course. But it didn't seem like it here in the chill dark with the wind whispering through the grass and the fog obscuring everything from view except a strange, blinking light that wouldn't stay put.

My heart was pounding so hard it made my chest hurt. I strained my ears in the silence that fell over the swamp. I couldn't hear anything; no croaking frogs, no buzzing insects, no swish of owl wings. The silence was uncanny.

"Jack, (jack, jack)," the voice hissed, from somewhere to my left this time. The light blinked on, off, on . . . I counted ten heartbeats this time before it went out. The voice sounded closer. I held very still, my instincts screaming at me to hold my breath and not move until the menace had passed. Time enough tomorrow to laugh at my foolishness if this was just some hunter's prank. For now, best to stay safe, huddled with my back against the rotting log, the smell of the swamp stinging my nose.

The voice came again, far off to the right.

"Jack, (jack, jack)," it hissed. The light came on, off, on . . . off. It's moving away, I thought, relaxing just a bit. Feeling safer.

There was a long, long, long silence. Nothing stirred, not the wind in the grass, not the frogs or turtles in the water, not the crickets or night insects. Not even a bat on the wing.

"Jack, (jack, jack)," the voice hissed softly, right into my ear. And I looked up into the glowing red eyes and twisted face of the Jack O'Lantern.

I screamed and lashed out at it with my gun, and ran a few steps. I tripped and fell over, knocking my head on a sharp stone. For a moment I saw stars, and I felt blood pouring from my scalp. But the Jack O'Lantern was right behind me, and my only thought was to get away. I rolled and fell into the deep pool that had almost trapped me before. I plunged underneath the water, flailing desperately against ropelike grasses that tried to keep me down. My head finally burst out of the water, and I gasped desperately for air, treading water as best I could with my trembling limbs and aching head. I heard the creature laugh in the mist.

"Jack, (jack, jack)," the voice hissed delightedly, and the light blinked on, off, on right over my head, blinding my dazed eyes as horror flowed through me and froze my limbs so I could no longer swim. For a long moment, the grotesque face and red eyes of the Jack O'Lantern loomed out of the mist before my petrified gaze.

My head started to swim with pain and my cut bled more freely. The evil face above me, lit by its bright light, whirled around and around, growing dimmer as my eyes started to glaze. I was vaguely aware that I should keep swimming, keep trying to make my way to the edge of the pool, but the effort was too much for my suddenly heavy limbs. I barely noticed myself plunging down and down into the watery depths of the pool, too stunned by my injury to fight my way to the surface a second time.

Then there was only darkness, and silence, and a voice hissing in cold triumph: "Jack, (jack, jack)."

33

Don't Turn on the Light

She commandeered the small study room in the basement of her dormitory as soon as she realized she would have to pull an all-nighter in order to prepare for tomorrow's final exam in history. Her roommate, Jenna, liked to get to bed early, so she packed up everything she thought she would need and went downstairs to study . . . and study . . . and study some more.

Around midnight she ordered pizza and wings (thank goodness for all night cafés!) and munched away until close to two o'clock, when she realized that she'd left one of the textbooks she needed upstairs on her bed. She did a bit of creative cursing and for a moment contemplated leaving it there and just making do with the books she already had. But she knew that her professor had relied heavily on the information in that particular text in the midterm exam. With a dramatic sigh, she rose, stretched out the kinks in her back, and climbed the stairs slowly to her third-floor dorm room.

The lights were dim in the long hallway, and the old boards creaked under her weary tread. She'd have to walk more softly than that if she wasn't to wake Jenna, who was a light sleeper. She reached her room and turned the handle as softly as she could, pushing the door open just enough to slip inside, so that the hall lights wouldn't wake her roommate.

The room was filled with a strange, metallic smell that was new. She frowned a bit, her arms breaking out into chills. She was a bit frightened, though she could not fathom why. There was almost a feeling of malice in the room, as if a malevolent gaze were fixed upon her. Which was nonsense, of course. She obviously needed to get some sleep after finals were over, if this was the sort of trick her mind was starting to play on her.

She could hear Jenna breathing on the far side of the room— a heavy sound, almost as if she had been running. Jenna must have picked up a cold during the last tense week before finals. No wonder her roommate had wanted to go to bed early.

She crept along the wall until she reached her bed, groping among the covers for the stray history textbook. In the silence, she could hear a steady drip-drip-drip sound. She sighed silently. It must be the bathroom sink leaking again. Facilities had come to fix it just last week, but apparently they'd done a shoddy job. She'd have to call them again in the morning.

Her fingers closed on the textbook. She picked it up softly and withdrew from the room as silently as she could. There was no change in Jenna's heavy breathing, so she must not have awakened her. Good. Her roommate needed the rest to recover from her cold.

Relieved to be out of the room, she hurried back downstairs and collapsed into an overstuffed chair to peruse her book and take some more notes. The tedious hours ticked by. Around six o'clock, as it began to grow light outside, she decided that enough was enough. If she slipped upstairs now, she could get a couple hours' sleep before her nine o'clock exam. Collecting her books and papers, she packed up her bag and trudged slowly up the stairs to her room, exhausted almost beyond bearing.

The first of the sun's rays were beaming through the windows as she slowly slid the door open, hoping not to awaken Jenna. Her nose was met by an earthy, metallic smell a second before her eyes registered the scene in her dorm room. Jenna was spread-eagled on top of her bed against the far wall, her throat cut from ear to ear and her nightdress stained with blood. There was blood everywhere, spattered on the wall, saturating the bedclothes, and in a huge, congealing pool on the floor under the bed. As she gazed at the room in shock, two drops of blood fell from the saturated blanket with a drip-drip noise that sounded like a leaky faucet.

Vaguely, as if from a distance, she became aware of a horrible screeching sound. Scream after scream ripped through the building, as regular as clockwork. Dimly, she realized that she was the one wailing in terror, but she couldn't stop herself any more than she could cease wringing her hands. All along the hallway, she could hear voices exclaiming in fright, doors banging open, footsteps running down the passage.

Within moments, she was standing in the middle of a crowd in the doorway. Several other girls started to scream too, and people milled about in fright, exclaiming in horror at the scene before them. She felt her best friend—who stayed in a room a few doors down—grip her arm with a shaking hand. Her friend pointed a trembling finger toward the wall over her bed on the clean side of the room. She turned her head slowly to look, feeling old—very old.

Then her eyes widened in shock at what she saw on the wall. For a moment her heart seemed to stop in sheer terror. Then she fainted, hitting the floor with an audible thud.

On the wall above her bed, written in her roommate's blood, were the following words: "Aren't you glad you didn't turn on the light?"

34

Wendigo

The first sign of trouble came when Father tried to hire a native guide to take us deep into the northern woods of Wisconsin Territory the year after the Civil War ended to do some game hunting. It was just the three of us—Father, Jonathan, and me, Richard, the younger son. We lived in Chicago, and this trip was one of our very first ventures into the wilds of the American Frontier. It was by way of being a celebratory trip, since Jonathan had been taken into Father's very successful law practice as a junior member, and I had just graduated from a rather posh boarding school and been accepted into university.

I was just a gangling thing in those days, all long arms, long legs, awkward wrists, and floppy hair, who didn't look too promising. Nobody would have guessed, seeing me then, that I would top six-foot-six in my bare feet and have the brawny build of a lumberjack by the time I finished growing. In spite of my unprepossessing appearance and awkward ways back then, Father still graciously asked me to accompany him and Jonathan on the hunting trip.

Mother waved us off from our fancy Chicago home with tears in her eyes, fearful of what might happen to us in the terrible dark woods of the North Country. She'd heard stories all her life of fierce wolves and hungry bears, as well as dark spirits that would possess a man. Father just laughed at her. We would have a whole slew of native guides to accompany us on our trek to Lake Superior, and we would return triumphant, with more deer and bear meat than the family could eat in a year. But Mother wasn't so sure. She had a bad feeling about the trip, and she was frightened she would lose a member of her family to the evil denizens of the North County.

The first part of our trip was easy—sailing up the coast to the settlement. Folks there assured us that we would have no trouble hiring a few native tribesmen to guide us on our trip. And it was true that each man that Father approached listened to him eagerly for the first few minutes. Then his face would freeze partway through Father's speech, his mind pulling away from the conversation even though physically he did not move. And each conversation ended with a sharp negative shake of the head and with each potential guide walking away.

"What are you saying to them, Father?" asked Jonathan in that half-jovial, half-superior tone that I hated. Don't get me wrong, I do love my brother. But he was already as cynical a creature as ever walked the Earth, and vain to boot—though frankly, with his too-short frame, popped-out fish eyes, and slicked-back curly dark hair that perpetually shed white flakes of dandruff onto his shoulders, he really had no excuse for vanity.

"I don't understand it," Father said slowly. "Every time I tell the guides that we want to hunt up near Lake Superior, they break off negotiations. Tell me that the hunting is no good there and just walk away."

"The hunting, she *is* no good near the lake this year," a deep voice rumbled from behind us. A massive Potawatomi tribesman stepped out of the shadowy corner of the inn where we had repaired to eat our dinner and figure out what to do. "You should hunt somewhere else this season."

But Father had turned stubborn. First Mother and now this! He wanted to hunt up by Lake Superior. Two of his partners had gone hunting up there last season and had raved about it ever since. This was Father's first chance to go, and he was going to take it, even if it meant finding our way north without a guide.

The Potawatomi listened to his ranting in grave silence, dark eyes hooded against us. Now and then he asked a question or uttered a short sentence, and I was impressed by his clarity of thought, deftness of speech, and superior intelligence. If this man ever studied law, Father and Jonathan wouldn't stand a chance against him in court. But in this day and age, native tribesmen did not attend the white man's university or argue in his courts.

The Potawatomi's eyes were suddenly upon me, and we studied each other intently for a moment as Father raged, egged on unsubtly by Jonathan. Some sort of silent message passed between me and the tribesman, an acknowledgement of Father's stubbornness and Jonathan's vanity and the foolish pride of both that was sending us into danger. The fact was that nothing either of us said would change their minds. That moment of understanding sealed a lifelong friendship between me and the Potawatomi, who told us to call him Hawk.

The upshot of our conversation was that Hawk hired on to guide us north to hunt along the shores of Lake Superior. He brought along two other men to carry our equipment and keep camp for us: one was a French-Canadian trapper called Jean-Claude, and the other a wiry little Irish chap who gave his name as O'Toole. Nothing else. Just O'Toole. Together, the six of us headed north in the chill of autumn as the foliage grew brilliant and the birds began winging their way south. Jonathan tried to get Hawk to tell us why the other tribesmen were reluctant to make a potentially lucrative journey to the North Country, but Hawk wasn't talking.

We reached the shores of Lake Superior after a week of travel, canoeing the rivers and portaging across land. We had seen no one along the way. No lumber scouts. No settlers. No tribesmen. It was as if everyone in the North Country had fled the vicinity. The thought made me go cold. *Fled from what?* I wondered.

Hawk set up camp in a small clearing on the lakeshore, and soon we were gathered around the fire, eating beans and planning our first big hunt. Father and Jonathan talked excitedly about some bear tracks they had seen not far from our campsite and discussed various tracking methods with Jean-Claude. O'Toole— the expedition cook—hummed an Irish jig under his breath as he made another pot of coffee. The hunting talk didn't interest him. His duty was merely to stay in camp, catch fish, and prepare food and coffee at a moment's notice when we returned from a hard day's hunt.

On the far side of the fire, Hawk sat like a stone, dark eyes unfathomable. I watched the huge tribesman, who appeared to be sniffing the air, like a rabbit trying to scent the presence of a predator. The thought made me shiver. I accepted a mug of coffee from O'Toole and took a seat beside our guide.

"My mother says that dark spirits haunt the North Woods," I said softly, under cover of the lively conversation between my Father and Jean-Claude.

"Your mother is a wise woman," said Hawk, his tone equally low.

"Is something here with us?" I asked, my voice calm. In front of me, I watched the mug of coffee in my hands begin to tremble.

"I do not know," Hawk said reluctantly. "There have been rumors that something has come down from the far north. The elders of many tribes have seen it approaching in their dreams."

He broke off, staring into the fire.

"I myself have seen it," he said at last, his voice barely audible. "In a vision last summer."

I started, the hot coffee spilling out over my hand. I ignored the stinging sensation and whispered: "What have you seen?"

Hawk closed his eyes briefly, and his face grew grim.

"Wendigo," he whispered and then rose abruptly and walked off into the darkness.

Seeing his retreat, Jonathan smirked from the other side of the fire and said: "Don't scare off our native guide, little brother, unless you learned how to track bear at your boarding school."

"Knock it off, Jonathan," I said, rising and wiping my wet hand on my breeches. "I'm going to bed."

I crawled into the tent and settled down among the balsam boughs laid ready for the night, my mind churning. *Wendigo,* Hawk had said. What was a Wendigo? I'd never heard the term before, but the tone in which it was uttered had filled me with a nameless dread, and I was uncomfortably aware of being very far from civilization up here in the bleak splendor of the remote North Woods. I felt small and insignificant amid the beautiful, merciless forest with its massive trees and huge wild beasts. I stayed awake for a long time, trembling under the covers. It was only the familiar sound of my Father's bass voice singing some of the old French-Canadian *voyageur* songs with Jean-Claude that finally calmed my fears and lulled me to sleep.

I was awakened during the night by a loud sound in the tent. I froze, my heart pounding loudly against my rib cage, and held my breath, trying to identify the sound. Then my Father let out a second loud snore, and I let out my breath in a sigh of relief. I nudged him a little, and he turned over and settled down again, breathing softly now. Then I lay on my back, staring uneasily up at the dark roof of the tent, unable to get back to sleep. The night was unusually quiet. There was no sound save the soft whisper of the breeze. No night-owls called, no insects buzzed, no creatures stirred the underbrush. Within the primeval forest surrounding us was the silence of death.

As I lay there, I became aware of a sickly, almost sweet smell, like that of rotten fruit. I stiffened, remembering the way that Hawk had been sniffing the air. I drew the scent into my nose, body tense with fear, but already the smell was fading . . . fading . . . gone. After four or five minutes, I heard the tentative hooting of an owl followed by the croak of a frog, and then the rustle of little creatures in the underbrush. I relaxed and went back to sleep.

We woke early, ready to track bear in the dim light of dawn. We found the fire burnt down to coals, the food still tied up high in a tree, and O'Toole gone. Vanished into thin air. At first, Father thought the Irishman was playing a joke on us. All his gear was still in the tent he shared with Jean-Claude, so he couldn't have gone far. We called and searched the surrounding forest. It was Hawk's keen eyes that spotted the barely perceptible footprints leading toward water's edge—and not back again.

For a moment, the only sound was the wash of little waves along the rocky lake shore. Then Father said: "Do you think he drowned himself? Why would he do that?"

Hawk didn't answer. He was looking at the grass, at the rocks, at the dirt. I wondered what his dark eyes saw there. I couldn't even see the cook's footprints when they were pointed out to me. Whatever Hawk saw on the ground made his mouth go grim, and the shadow of a known horror passed over his face. "We must leave here at once," he said suddenly, straightening to his massive height and staring down at my father. "He was not drowned. He was taken."

It was then I remembered the strange silence in the night and the sickeningly sweet odor I had smelled. I envisioned the cook stepping out of his tent into that silence to answer the call of nature. And being taken by . . . what? That was the question Father was asking. What had taken the cook? A bear? A cougar?

"Wendigo," said Hawk grimly and began packing up our gear.

When he heard the word *Wendigo,* Jean-Claude gasped and crossed himself. Glancing toward him, I saw that the tough old *voyageur* was shaken to the core. He peered this way and that into the woods, his brown eyes searching for something that obviously terrified him, breath coming in short, sharp gasps, face as pale as snow.

Then he too leapt forward and rapidly began dismantling the tent.

"Stop, man, stop!" roared my Father. "Why must we leave? What is this Wendigo? I paid good money for this trip. And I'm not leaving until we find O'Toole!"

I shivered with nerves. The French-Canadian's terror was catching. Suddenly, I passionately wanted out of this place. Jean-Claude turned a face of livid terror toward Father. "You won't find O'Toole," he said fiercely. "Not if the Wendigo got him. You can stay here if you want. I'm leaving."

"We're all leaving," said Hawk, looming up behind Jonathan and making him start with fright. "Right now."

And we left, our gear mashed into packs and canoes any which way. Father and Jonathan were dancing with rage and irritation, but they followed the tall tribesman and the French-Canadian because they had no choice. We could never find our way alone in this vast, untamed wilderness.

We portaged with the canoes more than two miles before striking the river. Just before we pushed off, Hawk spotted something in the brush. He stalked forward, disappeared into the trees, and returned with the torn body of O'Toole. The cook's head lolled on a broken neck, his ribs had been split apart, and his guts torn out. There were teeth marks covering his throat and one side of his broken body. It was obvious that he had been eaten by something big.

My Father's protests died away at the sight of the poor dead cook. We couldn't get him buried fast enough, and Father himself pushed off the canoes. It was only when we were rapidly traveling downstream, me and Jonathan and Jean-Claude in one boat and Hawk and Father in the other, that I ventured to ask Jean-Claude about the creature that had killed the cook.

"Yes, what *is* a Wendigo?" Jonathan added loudly. Too loudly. Jean-Claude glanced about wildly and hushed him. Jonathan repeated his question sotto voce. This time, the French-Canadian answered him.

"Cannibal," he whispered as we paddled at top speed down the river. "Dark spirit of the woods with a craving for human flesh. The more the Wendigo eats, the more it craves. It is tall and gray-green like a rotting corpse, all cracked skin and clotted blood and pus. You smell them first—the sickly sweet odor of decay—and if they catch you, they eat you, like poor O'Toole." I gasped aloud when he described the smell, and he gave me a sympathetic smile, misunderstanding my fear. I had smelled the Wendigo last night. It had passed right beside my tent!

"Sometimes," Jean-Claude continued over the splash of the river, "a Wendigo will call a man by name. When it calls, you must obey. The Wendigo will run with you across the treetops, across the sky at blinding speed until you bleed beneath the eyes and your feet burn away to stumps. Then it drops you to the ground like a bird dropping a fish on a rock. Any man that runs with a Wendigo, becomes a Wendigo himself."

Regrettably, Jonathan—the hard-headed attorney—laughed when he heard this. "That's just nonsense," he said derisively. "It's obvious that O'Toole was eaten by a bear. Wendigo. Ha! Just a rural myth."

Jean-Claude clammed up after that and spoke not a word to either of us until we beached the canoes at dusk. Hawk wanted to keep going through the night, but Father insisted that we stop and rest. We had traveled many miles downriver during the day, and surely had left the beast that killed O'Toole far behind, Father argued. This would have been true enough if we were dealing with a living creature. But I wasn't as convinced as Jonathan was that we were. Wendigo—dark spirit of the North Country—the creature that my mother feared would kill her family. Was it only a myth? If not, then we were dealing with a creature that could fly through the air. To such a creature, what were a few miles?

I could see Hawk and Jean-Claude felt as I did. They left most of our belongings in the canoes, ready to launch out onto the river immediately if something happened. Then Jean-Claude set up two of the three tents while Hawk made a large fire and cooked a simple meal for us. Father and Jonathan—the two practical attorneys—sat on one side of the fire, talking in low tones about the superstitious nonsense that had ruined our hunting trip. I sat with Hawk and Jean-Claude on the other side. We ate in silence, listening to night settle over the forest around us. We were still five days from the nearest settlement, I thought, a tremor of fear shaking my body. Five days.

As soon as he finished eating, Jean-Claude fled into the tent to sleep, fear pulsing from his whipcord hard body. I am not sure what shelter a tent would provide from a determined Wendigo, but it seemed to offer comfort to the French-Canadian trapper. When he was gone, I said to Hawk: "Tell me about your vision. Did you see the Wendigo kill O'Toole?"

Hawk shook his dark head. "No, Richard," he said. "I saw myself . . ." he hesitated, staring into the fire.

"You saw yourself . . ." I prompted when the silence grew too long.

"I saw myself killing a Wendigo to save someone's life," he replied at length, avoiding my gaze. My eyes nearly popped out of my head.

"They can be killed?" I gasped. "How? I thought they were dark spirits?"

"A Wendigo has a heart made of ice and snow," said Hawk. "If you pierce that heart with an arrow of fire, the Wendigo is no more."

My eyes went to the bow and quiver of arrows that were always strapped to Hawk's side. I had wondered why he favored them over a gun. Now I knew.

We soon followed Jean-Claude's example and settled into the tents for the night. No one would be tempted to leave the shelter tonight for any reason. Not after what happened to O'Toole. Father placed himself in the center of the tent, between me and Jonathan, to protect us, I think. Anything coming through the door would get him first.

We lay awake a long time, pretending to sleep. I imagined Jean-Claude and Hawk lying awake in the next tent, listening . . . listening. Finally Jonathan started to snore, and Father after him. The familiar sound relaxed me, and I was nearly asleep when my nose was assailed by a sickeningly sweet scent. I sat bolt upright in terror. Wendigo! I wanted to shout for Hawk. But in that moment, a violent movement shook the tent. Father woke with a startled shout, and Jonathan rolled over, trembling with shock. From somewhere outside came a thunderous voice. It was close to the tent, but came from overhead rather than beside us. The volume of sound was immense and wild, full of an abominable power that was as sickly sweet as the smell of the demon. It called a man's name.

"Jon-a-thannnnnn."

And Jonathan was on his feet, leaping past Father, bumping into the tent pole, then plunging through the canvas door. He was running so fast his body seemed to blur in the dim firelight. As he ran, he was joined by an immensely tall gray-green figure. They disappeared into the trees before Father and I could draw a breath.

I think I screamed. I know Father did. We bumped into each other twice before we managed to scramble from the tent. "Jonathan," Father bellowed. "Johnny! Come back, son! Come back!"

He ran toward the woods in the direction taken by his elder son, but Hawk caught him and pulled him back.

"There's nothing you can do," the Potawatomi said. "The Wendigo has taken him."

"Let me go! I must find my son," screamed Father. It took all of the massive tribesman's strength to hold him back.

"What can you do in the dark, *mon ami*?" asked Jean-Claude, who stood trembling beside the fire, his face as white as a ghost. "At least wait until morning to look for him."

"Jonathan just panicked when the wind struck our tent," Father said defiantly. "That's all. There is no such thing as a Wendigo." He stared from one face to the other, and the grave compassion he saw there broke his defiance. "He will come back to camp. You'll see," he continued almost pleadingly. "And I'm staying right here until he returns. I will not leave here without my son!"

"We did not ask you to leave," said Hawk, laying a massive hand on Father's shoulder.

And then, from somewhere high above us, we heard a terrible cry. "Oh! Oh! My feet of fire! My burning feet of fire!" It was Jonathan's voice. Father gasped and dropped to his knees, as somewhere above the trees, Jonathan shrieked: "Oh! Oh! This height and fiery speed!"

A terrible rush of wind whipped the treetops, as if a storm were approaching. Then all was silence, and the stench of decay slowly faded from the riverbank. Father, his face gray with pain, looked up into Hawk's dark eyes. "I will not leave without my son," he repeated. The Potawatomi nodded his understanding, his eyes brimming with sorrow.

We sat by the fire, silently waiting through the long hours for dawn to come. None of us spoke. What could we say? We had all heard that horrified wail. But there was nothing we could do to help Jonathan during the long darkness of night.

I dozed a couple of times, leaning against my grief-stricken Father for comfort. Toward dawn, I was awakened by the sound of a rushing wind. Something dropped heavily through the trees beside the river. In the dim gray light, I felt Father stiffen beside me and saw Hawk leapt to his feet, bow in one hand and arrow in the other. The tip of the arrow was wrapped in cloth, and he pushed it into the fire as I sat up, rubbing my eyes.

Then I saw him. Jonathan came lurching toward us through the half-light, his step faltering, uncertain. At least, I think it was Jonathan, though it seemed a ghastly caricature of the brother I had known all my life. The face was twisted, features drawn about into strange and terrible proportions, skin loose and hanging, as though Jonathan had been subjected to extraordinary air pressures and tensions. The skin below his eyes was red with blood, and his feet were blackened stumps. My nose caught the penetrating odor of rotten fruit as my brother lurched toward the clearing, his eyes fixed on Father.

There was something about the look in his eyes . . .

I didn't think; I just reacted, shoving myself in front of Father as Jonathan suddenly sprang forward with supernatural speed, his mouth a gaping black hole as he screamed in hunger and fury. There were claws at the ends of his hands, curved and vicious, and his eyes burned as he slashed out at me, intent on the kill. Then a fiery arrow winged its way over my shoulder from Hawk's bow. It caught Jonathan in the chest, penetrating his icy heart, stopping him a mere two feet from my body. He fell to the ground, momentum sliding him forward until he reached my feet. He screamed in agony, and gray-green smoke billowed out of his mouth and rose to the treetops.

Behind me, Hawk sent another flaming arrow up toward the swirling gray-green mist that was forming into a tall man-shaped figure that looked like a rotting corpse, all cracked skin and clotted blood and pus. The Wendigo rose with a terrific rushing noise that whipped the trees with hurricane force.

But the flaming arrow rose faster, smashing right through the center of the Wendigo. It screamed and exploded into flames. At my feet, Jonathan's body also burst into flames. Jean-Claude and Father pulled me backward, away from the danger, as my brother and the Wendigo burned to death before my eyes.

We carried what was left of Jonathan back to the settlement wrapped in a deerskin that the trapper gave us from his pack. Father wanted to bury him in the family plot in Chicago. Although we never spoke of it, I realized that in his vision, Hawk had seen himself shooting Jonathan to save my life. That was why he had accompanied us to the North Country when no other tribesman would go. Jean-Claude left us as soon as we reached the settlement, glad to be rid of us and the terrible memory of that aborted hunting trip. But the Potawatomi tribesman accompanied us to our ship and bade us farewell. Father tried to press money on him in thanks for saving my life, but Hawk would not accept it. It was enough for him to know that he was sending two of Mother's menfolk back home to her, when she could so easily have lost us all.

Father never went hunting again. He lost his heart for it after our terrible trip. But not me. Every year, on the anniversary of Jonathan's death, Hawk and I take a hunting trip up north, and I visit the small cross we had erected on the riverbank where Jonathan died and Hawk defeated the Wendigo.

35

Bloody Mary

I finished pounding the nail into the horseshoe and carefully set the horse's hoof down onto the floor. The mare shifted her weight gratefully back onto all four feet and sighed deeply. I patted her flank, then put my tools down and led her into the small stall I kept next to the smithy for the use of my customers. She settled down quickly and began pulling at the hay in the rack.

"Papa," I heard a small voice call from behind me. I turned and smiled when I saw my only daughter, my sweet little Emily. With her cornflower blue eyes and long golden braids, she was the image of her mother. Emily had a deep basket hanging from her little arm. Even from here, I could smell roast chicken and sage-and-onion stuffing. My favorite.

"Mama asked me to bring you lunch, since you have such a busy schedule today," Emily said. She carried the basket into the smithy and set it onto a low table. "She sent extra so I could have lunch with you," she added with a grin that revealed a missing front tooth. I grinned back and bowed her into a chair.

We sat munching the good food and talking about which animals I had seen today and who needed what metalwork done around town. Thump, thump, thump. Emily's small feet bounced against the leg of the chair as we talked together. Suddenly the thumping stopped, and Emily's blue eyes grew large. She was staring out into the yard, and I saw her tremble. I turned at once, wanting to see what had upset her.

An old crone with a cruel, wrinkled face and long, straggly white hair stood in the yard, leaning heavily on a cane. It was Bloody Mary. Or rather, it was Frau Gansmueller, I should have said. Bloody Mary was a nickname the children had given the old woman long ago. They thought she was a witch and were frightened by her.

Frau Gansmueller lived deep in the forest in a tiny cottage and sold herbal remedies for a living. None of the good folk living in town dared to cross the old crone for fear that their cows would go dry, their food stores rot away before winter, their children take sick of fever, or any number of terrible things that an angry witch could do to her neighbors.

I stepped hastily into the yard and sketched a bow to the old woman. "How may I be of service, Frau Gansmueller?" I asked quickly. Bloody Mary glared at me with narrow, coal-black eyes.

"I've come for an andiron, Herr Smith," she said in her soft, sibilant voice. I repressed a shiver at the soft hissing tone. Her voice sounded like that of a talking snake.

"Fine, fine," I stammered. I hurried inside, motioned to Emily to stay where she was, and brought out a new andiron for the old crone. I handed it to her, naming a sum half of what it was worth. I wasn't taking any chances on upsetting the old witch. She examined it critically before putting it into her basket next to the small mirror she always carried. The she counted out the money into my hand.

As she turned to leave, Bloody Mary stopped suddenly, glancing back into the smithy. "What a pretty little girl you have, Herr Smith," she said, offering Emily a crooked smile and stroking the small mirror in her basket. Emily turned white with fear and smiled back.

"Thank you, Frau Gansmueller," I said as politely as I could. She hobbled away then, and I watched her until she disappeared around a bend in the road. A moment later, a small hand crept into mine, and Emily said, "I do not like her, Papa."

"Neither do I, child," I said. Then a stab of fear went through my heart. What would Bloody Mary do to Emily if she ever heard the child saying such things about her? I added, "But we must always be polite to her, Emily, and never speak unkindly about her. Promise me that you will always be polite and kind."

Emily looked deeply into my eyes and nodded solemnly. "I promise, Papa," she said, and I knew she would keep her word. We finished our meal in silence, then Emily took the basket home to her mama.

It was about a week after the incident at the smithy that the first little girl went missing from our town. Little Rosa, the daughter of the shoemaker, disappeared from her home in the middle of the night. She was just a wee mite of a girl who rarely ever left her yard. A search party was formed. We scoured the woods, the local buildings, and all the houses and barns, but there was no sign of the missing girl. Her mother sat and rocked in a corner all day, clutching her daughter's favorite doll and saying nothing. No one could comfort her.

Then the buxom twelve-year-old daughter of Franklin Taylor went for a walk in the woods with a few friends and did not come home. Her girlfriends looked everywhere but could not find her. Another search party was formed, and we examined every tree, every meadow, every stream, to no avail. A few brave souls even went to Bloody Mary's cottage in the woods to see if the witch had taken the girl, but she denied any knowledge of the disappearance.

Next it was Theresa, the brown-eyed, eight-year-old daughter of the basketmaker who went to fetch groceries from the mercantile and did not return. Again we searched, and again the girl remained missing. Everyone in town was frantic with fear. The young girls were instructed to walk in pairs and never to go out without letting their parents know about it. Of course, Bloody Mary was at the back of everyone's mind. Who else but a witch could make three young girls disappear so completely? But there was no proof, and no one dared to say anything.

During the hunt for young Theresa, Bloody Mary had insisted that the girl's father come into her house and search it, so that no suspicion should attach itself to her. The cottage was completely normal save for a fancy mirror on the kitchen wall next to the fireplace, a strange luxury for a poor woman's house. Stranger still was the way the mirror sometimes reflected things that weren't there. The basketmaker glimpsed his house in the village within the glass as he turned away from his examination of the fireplace chimney, but when he walked over to look in the mirror, it reflected only his face and the room behind it. Not surprisingly, the basketmaker found nothing else in the cottage or grounds of Bloody Mary to connect her with his daughter's disappearance.

My wife was keeping Emily in the house all the time now. Only the boys went to the schoolhouse each day, while my wife tutored Emily at home. Sometimes, as I worked at the lathe or hammered hot horseshoes, I remembered Bloody Mary looking into the smithy at Emily and telling me what a pretty child she was. In those moments, I would shiver uncontrollably, unable to warm myself in spite of the heat pouring off the hot smithy fire.

"Herr Smith," a sibilant voice calling from the smithy doorway broke into my thoughts. I knew that voice. It was Bloody Mary. I turned to look at the crone and bit my lip to keep from exclaiming aloud in amazement. Her haggard appearance had changed dramatically. She looked younger and much more attractive.

"How may I be of service, Frau Gansmueller?" I asked, laying down my hammer and tongs.

"I need some new pothooks," Bloody Mary said, her black eyes snapping at me with a malicious amusement that made my hands shake with fear. I drew in a deep breath before I fetched some pothooks for her. Again, I named a low price, and again she examined them carefully before paying me.

"Say good day from me to your mistress and your pretty young daughter," Bloody Mary said, fingering the mirror in her basket thoughtfully. Then she gave me a wicked smile and turned away with a rather flirtatious flick of her long skirts. I swallowed hard as I watched her leave. Her reference to Emily frightened me badly.

As soon as I could, I closed the shop and hurried home. To my relief, I found Emily studying her books in the corner, her blond head bent industriously over her work. My wife looked up from her cooking in surprise at my early arrival. I took her aside and told her about Bloody Mary's visit. She gasped, and her body started trembling uncontrollably. I took her into my arms, and we clung together for a long time. Then we discussed the matter and decided that the child would have to go and stay with her grandmother until the crisis had passed. Until arrangements could be made, one of us would have to be with her at every moment of the day. With this decided, we went and broke the news to Emily and her brothers.

I lay awake late into the night, praying for the safety of my little girl. I had barely dozed off before I was awakened by my wife. She had a sore tooth and was finding it hard to lie on her right side. She motioned me back to sleep and went downstairs to find the herbal remedy given to her by the apothecary.

I was awakened for the second time by soft strains of music that seemed to be coming from everywhere and nowhere at the same time. Even as I listened, the eerie, luring melody faded away. And then I heard my wife screaming.

I jumped out of bed and ran downstairs. My wife was racing out the front door, her blue eyes fixed on a small, barefooted figure clad in a white nightdress that was walking toward the edge of town. It was Emily! I leaped passed my wife and ran to intercept my daughter. Emily was in a trance, a happy smile on her face, her eyes glazed. She must be hearing the same music that had awakened me.

I caught her in my arms, but she pulled away immediately and continued walking toward the edge of town and the dark woods beyond. I was shocked. Emily was a tiny girl, but she had thrust my work-hardened blacksmith's body away as if I were a stripling. I ran forward and grabbed hold of her again, bracing my body as she struggled against me. My wife wrapped her arms around my waist, holding on tightly and screaming for help.

Her desperate cries woke our neighbors, and they came to assist us in our struggle. Lights went on everywhere as the townsfolk realized that another child was in trouble. Suddenly, a sharp-eyed lad gave a shout and pointed toward a strange light at the edge of the woods.

Leaving my wife and the other women to restrain Emily, I led the men toward the mysterious light. As we entered the field just outside the woods, we saw Bloody Mary standing beside a large oak tree, holding her small mirror in one hand and a magic wand in the other. The wand was pointed toward my house, and reflected in the mirror was the beautiful young face of my daughter. Bloody Mary was glowing with an unearthly radiance as she set her evil spell upon Emily.

Many of the men who had responded to my wife's screams had the forethought to bring guns and pitchforks. One of them thrust a gun into my hand as we ran toward the witch. "It has silver bullets," he shouted to me. I nodded grimly. Silver bullets were the only kind that could kill a witch.

When she heard the commotion, Bloody Mary broke off her spell and fled back into the woods. I stopped, took aim with the gun, and shot at her. The bullet hit Bloody Mary in the hip, and she fell to the ground. Immediately, angry townsmen swarmed upon her, pulling her to her feet and carrying her back into the field. Grimly, I picked up the wand and the mirror that had fallen into the dirt and leaves when I shot their owner.

The judge, who had been the first neighbor to arrive on the scene when we tried to restrain the entranced Emily, quickly pronounced Bloody Mary guilty of witchcraft, kidnapping, and the murder of the three missing girls. He sentenced her to death at the stake, and the townsmen immediately built a huge bonfire, right there in the field. They tied the witch and her magic wand to the wood and set it ablaze. I smashed the magic hand mirror myself.

As she burned, Bloody Mary glared at us through the flames. Staring straight into my eyes, she screamed a curse against all of us. "If anyone," she cried, "mentions my name aloud before a mirror, I will send my spirit to them and will revenge myself upon them in payment for my death!" The witch pointed her hand toward the shards of glass at my feet as she spoke. For a moment they glowed blue, then faded again into darkness.

Many who heard the curse shuddered and stepped back from the fire, but I stood as still as stone and watched as the evil woman paid for her black deeds. When she was dead, I led the villagers to her house in the woods, where we smashed her other magic mirror. With the destruction of the mirror, the concealment spell on the cottage lifted, and we soon found the unmarked graves of the little girls the evil witch had murdered and buried underneath the woodpile. According to the records she kept, she had created a spell that used their blood to make her young again.

So the lives of the other young girls in town were spared, and my Emily was safe at last. My daughter grew into a beautiful young woman who married the minister's son and had three children of her own. But Bloody Mary's curse also lived, if only in rumor. Tales have been told of young people who were foolish enough to chant Bloody Mary's name before a darkened mirror, and so summoned the vengeful spirit of the witch. It is said that the witch tore the poor victims' bodies to pieces and ripped their souls from their mutilated flesh, trapping them forever in burning torment inside the mirror with her. Having seen the witch at work, I find I cannot discount the tales, though I myself have never tried it.

PART THREE

S. E. Schlosser's Favorite Classic Horror Stories

36

The Masque of the Red Death

BY EDGAR ALLAN POE

The "Red Death" had long devastated the country. No pestilence had ever been so fatal, or so hideous. Blood was its Avatar and its seal—the redness and the horror of blood. There were sharp pains and sudden dizziness, and then profuse bleeding at the pores, with dissolution. The scarlet stains upon the body and especially upon the face of the victim, were the pest ban which shut him out from the aid and from the sympathy of his fellow-men. And the whole seizure, progress and termination of the disease, were the incidents of half an hour.

But the Prince Prospero was happy and dauntless and sagacious. When his dominions were half depopulated, he summoned to his presence a thousand hale and light-hearted friends from among the knights and dames of his court, and with these retired to the deep seclusion of one of his castellated abbeys. This was an extensive and magnificent structure, the creation of the prince's own eccentric yet august taste. A strong and lofty wall girdled it in. This wall had gates of iron.

The courtiers, having entered, brought furnaces and massy hammers and welded the bolts. They resolved to leave means neither of ingress nor egress to the sudden impulses of despair or of frenzy from within. The abbey was amply provisioned. With such precautions the courtiers might bid defiance to contagion. The external world could take care of itself. In the meantime it was folly to grieve, or to think. The prince had provided all the appliances of pleasure. There were buffoons, there were improvisatori, there were ballet-dancers, there were musicians, there was beauty, there was wine. All these and security were within. Without was the Red Death.

It was towards the close of the fifth or sixth month of his seclusion, and while the pestilence raged most furiously abroad, that the Prince Prospero entertained his thousand friends at a masked ball of the most unusual magnificence.

It was a voluptuous scene, that masquerade. But first let me tell of the rooms in which it was held. These were seven—an imperial suite. In many palaces, however, such suites form a long and straight vista, while the folding doors slide back nearly to the walls on either hand, so that the view of the whole extent is scarcely impeded. Here the case was very different, as might have been expected from the duke's love of the bizarre. The apartments were so irregularly disposed that the vision embraced but little more than one at a time. There was a sharp turn at every twenty or thirty yards, and at each turn a novel effect. To the right and left, in the middle of each wall, a tall and narrow Gothic window looked out upon a closed corridor which pursued the windings of the suite. These windows were of stained glass whose colour varied in accordance with the prevailing hue of the decorations of the chamber into which it opened. That at the eastern extremity was hung, for example in blue—and vividly blue were its windows. The second chamber was purple in its ornaments and tapestries, and here the panes were purple. The third was green throughout, and so were the casements. The fourth was furnished and lighted with orange—the fifth with white—the sixth with violet. The seventh apartment was closely shrouded in black velvet tapestries that hung all over the ceiling and down the walls, falling in heavy folds upon a carpet of the same material and hue. But in this chamber only, the colour of the windows failed to correspond with the decorations. The panes here were scarlet—a deep blood colour.

Now in no one of the seven apartments was there any lamp or candelabrum, amid the profusion of golden ornaments that lay scattered to and fro or depended from the roof. There was no light of any kind emanating from lamp or candle within the suite of chambers. But in the corridors that followed the suite, there stood, opposite to each window, a heavy tripod, bearing a brazier of fire, that projected its rays through the tinted glass and so glaringly illumined the room. And thus were produced a multitude of gaudy and fantastic appearances. But in the western or black chamber the effect of the fire-light that streamed upon the dark hangings through the blood-tinted panes, was ghastly in the extreme, and produced so wild a look upon the countenances of those who entered, that there were few of the company bold enough to set foot within its precincts at all.

It was in this apartment, also, that there stood against the western wall, a gigantic clock of ebony. Its pendulum swung to and fro with a dull, heavy, monotonous clang; and when the minute-hand made the circuit of the face, and the hour was to be stricken, there came from the brazen lungs of the clock a sound which was clear and loud and deep and exceedingly musical, but of so peculiar a note and emphasis that, at each lapse of an hour, the musicians of the orchestra were constrained to pause, momentarily, in their performance, to harken to the sound; and thus, the waltzers perforce ceased their evolutions; and there was a brief disconcert of the whole gay company; and, while the chimes of the clock yet rang, it was observed that the giddiest grew pale, and the more aged and sedate passed their hands over their brows as if in confused revery or meditation. But when the echoes had fully ceased, a light laughter at once pervaded the assembly; the musicians looked at each other and smiled as if at their own nervousness and folly, and made whispering vows, each to the other, that the next chiming of the clock should produce in them no similar emotion; and then, after the lapse of sixty minutes, (which embrace three thousand and six hundred seconds of the time that flies,) there came yet another chiming of the clock, and then were the same disconcert and tremulousness and meditation as before.

But, in spite of these things, it was a gay and magnificent revel. The tastes of the duke were peculiar. He had a fine eye for colours and effects. He disregarded the decora of mere fashion. His plans were bold and fiery, and his conceptions glowed with barbaric lustre. There are some who would have thought him mad. His followers felt that he was not. It was necessary to hear and see and touch him to be sure that he was not.

He had directed, in great part, the movable embellishments of the seven chambers, upon occasion of this great fête; and it was his own guiding taste which had given character to the masqueraders. Be sure they were grotesque. There were much glare and glitter and piquancy and phantasm—much of what has been since seen in "Hernani". There were arabesque figures with unsuited limbs and appointments. There were delirious fancies such as the madman fashions. There were much of the beautiful, much of the wanton, much of the bizarre, something of the terrible, and not a little of that which might have excited disgust.

To and fro in the seven chambers there stalked, in fact, a multitude of dreams. And these—the dreams—writhed in and about taking hue from the rooms, and causing the wild music of the orchestra to seem as the echo of their steps. And, anon, there strikes the ebony clock which stands in the hall of the velvet. And then, for a moment, all is still, and all is silent save the voice of the clock. The dreams are stiff-frozen as they stand. But the echoes of the chime die away—they have endured but an instant—and a light, half-subdued laughter floats after them as they depart.

And now again the music swells, and the dreams live, and writhe to and fro more merrily than ever, taking hue from the many tinted windows through which stream the rays from the tripods. But to the chamber which lies most westwardly of the seven, there are now none of the maskers who venture; for the night is waning away; and there flows a ruddier light through the blood-coloured panes; and the blackness of the sable drapery appalls; and to him whose foot falls upon the sable carpet, there comes from the near clock of ebony a muffled peal more solemnly emphatic than any which reaches their ears who indulged in the more remote gaieties of the other apartments.

But these other apartments were densely crowded, and in them beat feverishly the heart of life. And the revel went whirlingly on, until at length there commenced the sounding of midnight upon the clock. And then the music ceased, as I have told; and the evolutions of the waltzers were quieted; and there was an uneasy cessation of all things as before. But now there were twelve strokes to be sounded by the bell of the clock; and thus it happened, perhaps, that more of thought crept, with more of time, into the meditations of the thoughtful among those who revelled. And thus too, it happened, perhaps, that before the last echoes of the last chime had utterly sunk into silence, there were many individuals in the crowd who had found leisure to become aware of the presence of a masked figure which had arrested the attention of no single individual before. And the rumour of this new presence having spread itself whisperingly around, there arose at length from the whole company a buzz, or murmur, expressive of disapprobation and surprise—then, finally, of terror, of horror, and of disgust.

In an assembly of phantasms such as I have painted, it may well be supposed that no ordinary appearance could have excited such sensation. In truth, the masquerade licence of the night was nearly unlimited; but the figure in question had out-Heroded Herod, and gone beyond the bounds of even the prince's indefinite decorum. There are chords in the hearts of the most reckless, which cannot be touched without emotion. Even with the utterly lost, to whom life and death are equally jests, there are matters of which no jest can be made. The whole company, indeed, seemed now deeply to feel that in the costume and bearing of the stranger neither wit nor propriety existed. The figure was tall and gaunt, and shrouded from head to foot in the habiliments of the grave. The mask which concealed the visage was made so nearly to resemble the countenance of a stiffened corpse that the closest scrutiny must have had difficulty in detecting the cheat. And yet all this might have been endured, if not approved, by the mad revelers around. But the mummer had gone so far as to assume the type of the Red Death. His vesture was dabbled in blood—and his broad brow, with all the features of the face, was besprinkled with the scarlet horror.

When the eyes of the Prince Prospero fell upon this spectral image (which, with a slow and solemn movement, as if more fully

to sustain its role, stalked to and fro among the waltzers) he was seen to be convulsed, in the first moment with a strong shudder either of terror or distaste; but, in the next, his brow reddened with rage.

"Who dares,"—he demanded hoarsely of the courtiers who stood near him—"who dares insult us with this blasphemous mockery? Seize him and unmask him—that we may know whom we have to hang, at sunrise, from the battlements!"

It was in the eastern or blue chamber in which stood the Prince Prospero as he uttered these words. They rang throughout the seven rooms loudly and clearly, for the prince was a bold and robust man, and the music had become hushed at the waving of his hand.

It was in the blue room where stood the prince, with a group of pale courtiers by his side. At first, as he spoke, there was a slight rushing movement of this group in the direction of the intruder, who at the moment was also near at hand, and now, with deliberate and stately step, made closer approach to the speaker. But from a certain nameless awe with which the mad assumptions of the mummer had inspired the whole party, there were found none who put forth hand to seize him; so that, unimpeded, he passed within a yard of the prince's person; and, while the vast assembly, as if with one impulse, shrank from the centres of the rooms to the walls, he made his way uninterruptedly, but with the same solemn and measured step which had distinguished him from the first, through the blue chamber to the purple—through the purple to the green—through the green to the orange—through this again to the white—and even thence to the violet, ere a decided movement had been made to arrest him.

It was then, however, that the Prince Prospero, maddening with rage and the shame of his own momentary cowardice, rushed hurriedly through the six chambers, while none followed him on account of a deadly terror that had seized upon all. He bore aloft a drawn dagger, and had approached, in rapid impetuosity, to within three or four feet of the retreating figure, when the latter, having attained the extremity of the velvet apartment, turned suddenly and confronted his pursuer. There was a sharp cry—and the dagger dropped gleaming upon the sable carpet, upon which, instantly afterwards, fell prostrate in death the Prince Prospero. Then, summoning the wild courage of despair, a throng of the revellers at once threw themselves into the black apartment, and, seizing the mummer, whose tall figure stood erect and motionless within the shadow of the ebony clock, gasped in unutterable horror at finding the grave cerements and corpse-like mask, which they handled with so violent a rudeness, untenanted by any tangible form.

And now was acknowledged the presence of the Red Death. He had come like a thief in the night. And one by one dropped the revellers in the blood-bedewed halls of their revel, and died each in the despairing posture of his fall. And the life of the ebony clock went out with that of the last of the gay. And the flames of the tripods expired. And Darkness and Decay and the Red Death held illimitable dominion over all.

37

The Trial for Murder

BY CHARLES DICKENS

I have always noticed a prevalent want of courage, even among persons of superior intelligence and culture, as to imparting their own psychological experiences when those have been of a strange sort. Almost all men are afraid that what they could relate in such wise would find no parallel or response in a listener's internal life, and might be suspected or laughed at. A truthful traveller, who should have seen some extraordinary creature in the likeness of a sea-serpent, would have no fear of mentioning it; but the same traveller, having had some singular presentiment, impulse, vagary of thought, vision (so-called), dream, or other remarkable mental impression, would hesitate considerably before he would own to it. To this reticence I attribute much of the obscurity in which such subjects are involved. We do not habitually communicate our experiences of these subjective things as we do our experiences of objective creation. The consequence is, that the general stock of experience in this regard appears exceptional, and really is so, in respect of being miserably imperfect.

In what I am going to relate, I have no intention of setting up, opposing, or supporting, any theory whatever. I know the history of the Bookseller of Berlin, I have studied the case of the wife of a late Astronomer Royal as related by Sir David

Brewster, and I have followed the minutest details of a much more remarkable case of Spectral Illusion occurring within my private circle of friends. It may be necessary to state as to this last, that the sufferer (a lady) was in no degree, however distant, related to me. A mistaken assumption on that head might suggest an explanation of a part of my own case—but only a part—which would be wholly without foundation. It cannot be referred to my inheritance of any developed peculiarity, nor had I ever before any at all similar experience, nor have I ever had any at all similar experience since.

It does not signify how many years ago, or how few, a certain murder was committed in England, which attracted great attention. We hear more than enough of murderers as they rise in succession to their atrocious eminence, and I would bury the memory of this particular brute, if I could, as his body was buried, in Newgate Jail. I purposely abstain from giving any direct clue to the criminal's individuality.

When the murder was first discovered, no suspicion fell—or I ought rather to say, for I cannot be too precise in my facts, it was nowhere publicly hinted that any suspicion fell—on the man who was afterwards brought to trial. As no reference was at that time made to him in the newspapers, it is obviously impossible that any description of him can at that time have been given in the newspapers. It is essential that this fact be remembered.

Unfolding at breakfast my morning paper, containing the account of that first discovery, I found it to be deeply interesting, and I read it with close attention. I read it twice, if not three times. The discovery had been made in a bedroom, and, when I laid down the paper, I was aware of a flash—rush—flow—I do not know what to call it—no word I can find is satisfactorily descriptive—in which I seemed to see that bedroom passing through my room, like a picture impossibly painted on a running river. Though almost instantaneous in its passing, it was perfectly clear; so clear that I distinctly, and with a sense of relief, observed the absence of the dead body from the bed.

It was in no romantic place that I had this curious sensation, but in chambers in Piccadilly, very near to the corner of St. James's Street. It was entirely new to me. I was in my easy-chair at the moment, and the sensation was accompanied with a peculiar shiver which started the chair from its position. (But it is to be noted that the chair ran easily on castors.) I went to one of the windows (there are two in the room, and the room is on the second floor) to refresh my eyes with the moving objects down in Piccadilly. It was a bright autumn morning, and the street was sparkling and cheerful. The wind was high. As I looked out, it brought down from the Park a quantity of fallen leaves, which a gust took, and whirled into a spiral pillar. As the pillar fell and the leaves dispersed, I saw two men on the opposite side of the way, going from West to East. They were one behind the other. The foremost man often looked back over his shoulder. The second man followed him, at a distance of some thirty paces, with his right hand menacingly raised.

First, the singularity and steadiness of this threatening gesture in so public a thoroughfare attracted my attention; and next, the more remarkable circumstance that nobody heeded it. Both men threaded their way among the other passengers with a smoothness hardly consistent even with the action of walking on a pavement; and no single creature, that I could see, gave them place, touched them, or looked after them. In passing before my windows, they both stared up at me. I saw their two faces very distinctly, and I knew that I could recognise them anywhere. Not that I had consciously noticed anything very remarkable in either face, except that the man who went first had an unusually lowering appearance, and that the face of the man who followed him was of the colour of impure wax.

I am a bachelor, and my valet and his wife constitute my whole establishment. My occupation is in a certain Branch Bank, and I wish that my duties as head of a Department were as light as they are popularly supposed to be. They kept me in town that autumn, when I stood in need of change. I was not ill, but I was not well. My reader is to make the most that can be reasonably made of my feeling jaded, having a depressing sense upon me of a monotonous life, and being "slightly dyspeptic." I am assured by my renowned doctor that my real state of health at that time justifies no stronger description, and I quote his own from his written answer to my request for it.

As the circumstances of the murder, gradually unravelling, took stronger and stronger possession of the public mind, I kept them away from mine by knowing as little about them as was possible in the midst of the universal excitement. But I knew that a verdict of Wilful Murder had been found against the suspected murderer, and that he had been committed to Newgate for trial. I also knew that his trial had been postponed over one Sessions of the Central Criminal Court, on the ground of general prejudice and want of time for the preparation of the defence. I may further have known, but I believe I did not, when, or about when, the Sessions to which his trial stood postponed would come on.

My sitting-room, bedroom, and dressing-room, are all on one floor. With the last, there is no communication but through the bedroom. True, there is a door in it, once communicating

with the staircase; but a part of the fitting of my bath has been—
and had then been for some years—fixed across it. At the same
period, and as a part of the same arrangement—the door had
been nailed up and canvased over.

I was standing in my bedroom late one night, giving some
directions to my servant before he went to bed. My face was
towards the only available door of communication with the
dressing-room, and it was closed. My servant's back was towards
that door. While I was speaking to him, I saw it open, and a man
look in, who very earnestly and mysteriously beckoned to me.
That man was the man who had gone second of the two along
Piccadilly, and whose face was of the colour of impure wax.

The figure, having beckoned, drew back, and closed the
door. With no longer pause than was made by my crossing the
bedroom, I opened the dressing-room door, and looked in. I had
a lighted candle already in my hand. I felt no inward expectation of
seeing the figure in the dressing-room, and I did not see it there.

Conscious that my servant stood amazed, I turned round to
him, and said: "Derrick, could you believe that in my cool senses
I fancied I saw a —" As I there laid my hand upon his breast, with
a sudden start he trembled violently, and said, "O Lord, yes, sir!
A dead man beckoning!"

Now I do not believe that this John Derrick, my trusty and
attached servant for more than twenty years, had any impression
whatever of having seen any such figure, until I touched him. The
change in him was so startling, when I touched him, that I fully
believe he derived his impression in some occult manner from me
at that instant.

I bade John Derrick bring some brandy, and I gave him a
dram, and was glad to take one myself. Of what had preceded that

night's phenomenon, I told him not a single word. Reflecting on it, I was absolutely certain that I had never seen that face before, except on the one occasion in Piccadilly. Comparing its expression when beckoning at the door with its expression when it had stared up at me as I stood at my window, I came to the conclusion that on the first occasion it had sought to fasten itself upon my memory, and that on the second occasion it had made sure of being immediately remembered.

I was not very comfortable that night, though I felt a certainty, difficult to explain, that the figure would not return. At daylight I fell into a heavy sleep, from which I was awakened by John Derrick's coming to my bedside with a paper in his hand.

This paper, it appeared, had been the subject of an altercation at the door between its bearer and my servant. It was a summons to me to serve upon a Jury at the forthcoming Sessions of the Central Criminal Court at the Old Bailey. I had never before been summoned on such a Jury, as John Derrick well knew. He believed—I am not certain at this hour whether with reason or otherwise—that that class of Jurors were customarily chosen on a lower qualification than mine, and he had at first refused to accept the summons. The man who served it had taken the matter very coolly. He had said that my attendance or non-attendance was nothing to him; there the summons was; and I should deal with it at my own peril, and not at his.

For a day or two I was undecided whether to respond to this call, or take no notice of it. I was not conscious of the slightest mysterious bias, influence, or attraction, one way or other. Of that I am as strictly sure as of every other statement that I make here. Ultimately I decided, as a break in the monotony of my life, that I would go.

The appointed morning was a raw morning in the month of November. There was a dense brown fog in Piccadilly, and it became positively black and in the last degree oppressive East of Temple Bar. I found the passages and staircases of the Court House flaringly lighted with gas, and the Court itself similarly illuminated. I think that, until I was conducted by officers into the Old Court and saw its crowded state, I did not know that the Murderer was to be tried that day. I think that, until I was so helped into the Old Court with considerable difficulty, I did not know into which of the two Courts sitting my summons would take me. But this must not be received as a positive assertion, for I am not completely satisfied in my mind on either point.

I took my seat in the place appropriated to Jurors in waiting, and I looked about the Court as well as I could through the cloud of fog and breath that was heavy in it. I noticed the black vapour hanging like a murky curtain outside the great windows, and I noticed the stifled sound of wheels on the straw or tan that was littered in the street; also, the hum of the people gathered there, which a shrill whistle, or a louder song or hail than the rest, occasionally pierced. Soon afterwards the Judges, two in number, entered, and took their seats. The buzz in the Court was awfully hushed. The direction was given to put the Murderer to the bar. He appeared there. And in that same instant I recognised in him the first of the two men who had gone down Piccadilly.

If my name had been called then, I doubt if I could have answered to it audibly. But it was called about sixth or eighth in the panel, and I was by that time able to say, "Here!" Now, observe. As I stepped into the box, the prisoner, who had been looking on attentively, but with no sign of concern, became violently agitated, and beckoned to his attorney. The prisoner's wish to challenge me was so manifest, that it occasioned a pause, during which the attorney, with his hand upon the dock, whispered with his client, and shook his head. I afterwards had it from that gentleman, that the prisoner's first affrighted words to him were, "At all hazards, challenge that man!" But that, as he would give no reason for it, and admitted that he had not even known my name until he heard it called and I appeared, it was not done.

Both on the ground already explained, that I wish to avoid reviving the unwholesome memory of that Murderer, and also because a detailed account of his long trial is by no means indispensable to my narrative, I shall confine myself closely to such incidents in the ten days and nights during which we, the Jury, were kept together, as directly bear on my own curious personal experience. It is in that, and not in the Murderer, that I seek to interest my reader. It is to that, and not to a page of the Newgate Calendar, that I beg attention.

I was chosen Foreman of the Jury. On the second morning of the trial, after evidence had been taken for two hours (I heard the church clocks strike), happening to cast my eyes over my brother jurymen, I found an inexplicable difficulty in counting them. I counted them several times, yet always with the same difficulty. In short, I made them one too many.

I touched the brother jurymen whose place was next me, and I whispered to him, "Oblige me by counting us." He looked surprised by the request, but turned his head and counted. "Why," says he, suddenly, "we are Thirt—; but no, it's not possible. No. We are twelve."

According to my counting that day, we were always right in detail, but in the gross we were always one too many. There was no appearance—no figure—to account for it; but I had now an inward foreshadowing of the figure that was surely coming.

The Jury were housed at the London Tavern. We all slept in one large room on separate tables, and we were constantly in the charge and under the eye of the officer sworn to hold us in safe-keeping. I see no reason for suppressing the real name of that officer. He was intelligent, highly polite, and obliging, and (I was glad to hear) much respected in the City. He had an agreeable presence, good eyes, enviable black whiskers, and a fine sonorous voice. His name was Mr. Harker.

When we turned into our twelve beds at night, Mr. Harker's bed was drawn across the door. On the night of the second day, not being disposed to lie down, and seeing Mr. Harker sitting on his bed, I went and sat beside him, and offered him a pinch of snuff. As Mr. Harker's hand touched mine in taking it from my box, a peculiar shiver crossed him, and he said, "Who is this?"

Following Mr. Harker's eyes, and looking along the room, I saw again the figure I expected—the second of the two men who had gone down Piccadilly. I rose, and advanced a few steps; then stopped, and looked round at Mr. Harker. He was quite unconcerned, laughed, and said in a pleasant way, "I thought for a moment we had a thirteenth juryman, without a bed. But I see it is the moonlight."

Making no revelation to Mr. Harker, but inviting him to take a walk with me to the end of the room, I watched what the figure did. It stood for a few moments by the bedside of each of my eleven brother jurymen, close to the pillow. It always went to the right-hand side of the bed, and always passed out crossing the foot of the next bed. It seemed, from the action of the head, merely to look down pensively at each recumbent figure. It took no notice of me, or of my bed, which was that nearest to Mr. Harker's. It seemed to go out where the moonlight came in, through a high window, as by an aërial flight of stairs.

Next morning at breakfast, it appeared that everybody present had dreamed of the murdered man last night, except myself and Mr. Harker. I now felt as convinced that the second man who had gone down Piccadilly was the murdered man (so to speak), as if it had been borne into my comprehension by his immediate testimony. But even this took place, and in a manner for which I was not at all prepared.

On the fifth day of the trial, when the case for the prosecution was drawing to a close, a miniature of the murdered man, missing from his bedroom upon the discovery of the deed, and afterwards found in a hiding-place where the Murderer had been seen digging, was put in evidence. Having been identified by the witness under examination, it was handed up to the Bench, and thence handed down to be inspected by the Jury. As an officer in a black gown was making his way with it across to me, the figure of the second man who had gone down Piccadilly impetuously started from the crowd, caught the miniature from the officer, and gave it to me with his own hands, at the same time saying, in a low and hollow tone—before I saw the miniature, which was in a locket—"_I was younger then_, _and my face was not then drained of blood_." It also came between me and the brother juryman to whom I would have given the miniature, and between him and the brother juryman to whom he would have given it, and so passed it on through the whole of our number, and back into my possession. Not one of them, however, detected this.

At table, and generally when we were shut up together in Mr. Harker's custody, we had from the first naturally discussed the day's proceedings a good deal. On that fifth day, the case for the prosecution being closed, and we having that side of the question in a completed shape before us, our discussion was more animated and serious. Among our number was a vestryman—the densest idiot I have ever seen at large—who met the plainest evidence with the most preposterous objections, and who was sided with by two flabby parochial parasites; all the three impanelled from a district so delivered over to Fever that they ought to have been upon their own trial for five hundred Murders. When these mischievous blockheads were at their loudest, which was towards midnight, while some of us were already preparing for bed, I again saw the murdered man. He stood grimly behind them, beckoning to me. On my going towards them, and striking into the conversation, he immediately retired. This was the beginning of a separate series of appearances, confined to that long room in which we were confined. Whenever a knot of my brother jurymen laid their heads together, I saw the head of the murdered man among theirs. Whenever their comparison of notes was going against him, he would solemnly and irresistibly beckon to me.

It will be borne in mind that down to the production of the miniature, on the fifth day of the trial, I had never seen the Appearance in Court. Three changes occurred now that we entered on the case for the defence. Two of them I will mention together, first. The figure was now in Court continually, and it never there addressed itself to me, but always to the person who was speaking at the time. For instance: the throat of the murdered man had been cut straight across. In the opening speech for the defence, it was suggested that the deceased might have cut his own throat. At that very moment, the figure, with its throat in the dreadful condition referred to (this it had concealed before), stood at the speaker's elbow, motioning across and across its windpipe, now with the right hand, now with the left, vigorously suggesting to the speaker himself the impossibility of such a wound having been self-inflicted by either hand. For another instance: a witness to character, a woman, deposed to the prisoner's being the most amiable of mankind. The figure at that instant stood on the floor before her, looking her full in the face, and pointing out the prisoner's evil countenance with an extended arm and an outstretched finger.

The third change now to be added impressed me strongly as the most marked and striking of all. I do not theorise upon it; I accurately state it, and there leave it. Although the Appearance was not itself perceived by those whom it addressed, its coming close to such persons was invariably attended by some trepidation or disturbance on their part. It seemed to me as if it were prevented, by laws to which I was not amenable, from fully revealing itself to others, and yet as if it could invisibly, dumbly, and darkly overshadow their minds. When the leading counsel for the defence suggested that hypothesis of suicide, and the figure stood at the learned gentleman's elbow, frightfully sawing at its severed throat, it is undeniable that the counsel faltered in his speech, lost for a few seconds the thread of his ingenious discourse, wiped his forehead with his handkerchief, and turned extremely pale. When the witness to character was confronted by the Appearance, her eyes most certainly did follow the direction of its pointed finger, and rest in great hesitation and trouble upon the prisoner's face. Two additional illustrations will suffice. On the eighth day of the trial, after the pause which was every day made early in the afternoon for a few minutes' rest and refreshment, I came back into Court with the rest of the Jury some little time before the return of the Judges. Standing up in the box and looking about me, I thought the figure was not there, until, chancing to raise my eyes to the gallery, I saw it bending forward, and leaning over a very decent woman, as if to assure itself whether the Judges had resumed their seats or not. Immediately afterwards, that woman screamed, fainted, and was carried out. So with the venerable, sagacious, and patient Judge who conducted the trial. When the case was over, and he settled himself and his papers to sum up, the murdered man, entering by the Judges' door, advanced to his Lordship's desk, and looked eagerly over his shoulder at the pages of his notes which he was turning. A change came over his Lordship's face; his hand stopped; the peculiar shiver, that I knew so well, passed over him; he faltered, "Excuse me, gentlemen, for a few moments. I am somewhat oppressed by the vitiated air;" and did not recover until he had drunk a glass of water.

Through all the monotony of six of those interminable ten days—the same Judges and others on the bench, the same Murderer in the dock, the same lawyers at the table, the same tones of question and answer rising to the roof of the court, the same scratching of the Judge's pen, the same ushers going in and out, the same lights kindled at the same hour when there had been any natural light of day, the same foggy curtain outside the great windows when it was foggy, the same rain pattering and dripping when it was rainy, the same footmarks of turnkeys and prisoner day after day on the same sawdust, the same keys locking and unlocking the same heavy doors—through all the wearisome monotony which made me feel as if I had been Foreman of the Jury for a vast period of time, and Piccadilly had flourished coevally with Babylon, the murdered man never lost one trace of his distinctness in my eyes, nor was he at any moment less distinct than anybody else. I must not omit, as a matter of fact, that I never once saw the Appearance which I call by the name of the murdered man look at the Murderer. Again and again I wondered, "Why does he not?" But he never did.

Nor did he look at me, after the production of the miniature, until the last closing minutes of the trial arrived. We retired to consider, at seven minutes before ten at night. The idiotic vestryman and his two parochial parasites gave us so much trouble that we twice returned into Court to beg to have certain extracts from the Judge's notes re-read. Nine of us had not the smallest doubt about those passages, neither, I believe, had any one in the Court; the dunder-headed triumvirate, having no idea but obstruction, disputed them for that very reason. At length we prevailed, and finally the Jury returned into Court at ten minutes past twelve.

The murdered man at that time stood directly opposite the Jury-box, on the other side of the Court. As I took my place, his eyes rested on me with great attention; he seemed satisfied, and slowly shook a great gray veil, which he carried on his arm for the first time, over his head and whole form. As I gave in our verdict, "Guilty," the veil collapsed, all was gone, and his place was empty.

The Murderer, being asked by the Judge, according to usage, whether he had anything to say before sentence of Death should be passed upon him, indistinctly muttered something which was described in the leading newspapers of the following day as "a few rambling, incoherent, and half-audible words, in which he was understood to complain that he had not had a fair trial, because the Foreman of the Jury was prepossessed against him."

The remarkable declaration that he really made was this: "My Lord, I knew I was a doomed man, when the Foreman of my Jury came into the box. My Lord, I knew he would never let me off, because, before I was taken, he somehow got to my bedside in the night, woke me, and put a rope round my neck."

38

Dracula's Guest

BY BRAM STOKER

When we started for our drive the sun was shining brightly on Munich, and the air was full of the joyousness of early summer. Just as we were about to depart, Herr Delbrück (the maître d'hôtel of the Quatre Saisons, where I was staying) came down, bareheaded, to the carriage and, after wishing me a pleasant drive, said to the coachman, still holding his hand on the handle of the carriage door:

"Remember you are back by nightfall. The sky looks bright but there is a shiver in the north wind that says there may be a sudden storm. But I am sure you will not be late." Here he smiled, and added, "for you know what night it is."

Johann answered with an emphatic, "Ja, mein Herr," and, touching his hat, drove off quickly. When we had cleared the town, I said, after signalling to him to stop: "Tell me, Johann, what is tonight?"

He crossed himself, as he answered laconically: "Walpurgis Nacht." Then he took out his watch, a great, old-fashioned German silver thing as big as a turnip, and looked at it, with his eyebrows gathered together and a little impatient shrug of his shoulders. I realized that this was his way of respectfully protesting against the unnecessary delay, and sank back in the carriage,

merely motioning him to proceed. He started off rapidly, as if to make up for lost time. Every now and then the horses seemed to throw up their heads and sniffed the air suspiciously. On such occasions I often looked round in alarm. The road was pretty bleak, for we were traversing a sort of high, wind-swept plateau.

As we drove, I saw a road that looked but little used, and which seemed to dip through a little, winding valley. It looked so inviting that, even at the risk of offending him, I called Johann to stop—and when he had pulled up, I told him I would like to drive down that road. He made all sorts of excuses, and frequently crossed himself as he spoke. This somewhat piqued my curiosity, so I asked him various questions. He answered fencingly, and repeatedly looked at his watch in protest. Finally I said: "Well, Johann, I want to go down this road. I shall not ask you to come unless you like; but tell me why you do not like to go, that is all I ask." For answer he seemed to throw himself off the box, so quickly did he reach the ground. Then he stretched out his hands appealingly to me, and implored me not to go. There was just enough of English mixed with the German for me to understand the drift of his talk. He seemed always just about to tell me something—the very idea of which evidently frightened him; but each time he pulled himself up, saying, as he crossed himself: "Walpurgis Nacht!"

I tried to argue with him, but it was difficult to argue with a man when I did not know his language. The advantage certainly rested with him, for although he began to speak in English, of a very crude and broken kind, he always got excited and broke into his native tongue—and every time he did so, he looked at his watch. Then the horses became restless and sniffed the air. At this he grew very pale, and, looking around in a frightened way, he suddenly jumped forward, took them by the bridles and led them on some twenty feet. I followed, and asked why he had done this. For answer he crossed himself, pointed to the spot we had left and drew his carriage in the direction of the other road, indicating a cross, and said, first in German, then in English: "Buried him— him what killed themselves."

I remembered the old custom of burying suicides at cross-roads: "Ah! I see, a suicide. How interesting!" But for the life of me I could not make out why the horses were frightened.

Whilst we were talking, we heard a sort of sound between a yelp and a bark. It was far away; but the horses got very restless, and it took Johann all his time to quiet them. He was pale, and said, "It sounds like a wolf—but yet there are no wolves here now."

"No?" I said, questioning him; "isn't it long since the wolves were so near the city?"

"Long, long," he answered, "in the spring and summer; but with the snow the wolves have been here not so long."

Whilst he was petting the horses and trying to quiet them, dark clouds drifted rapidly across the sky. The sunshine passed away, and a breath of cold wind seemed to drift past us. It was only a breath, however, and more in the nature of a warning than a fact, for the sun came out brightly again. Johann looked under his lifted hand at the horizon and said: "The storm of snow, he comes before long time." Then he looked at his watch again, and, straightway holding his reins firmly—for the horses were still pawing the ground restlessly and shaking their heads—he climbed to his box as though the time had come for proceeding on our journey.

I felt a little obstinate and did not at once get into the carriage. "Tell me," I said, "about this place where the road leads," and I pointed down.

Again he crossed himself and mumbled a prayer, before he answered, "It is unholy."

"What is unholy?" I enquired.

"The village."

"Then there is a village?"

"No, no. No one lives there hundreds of years."

My curiosity was piqued, "But you said there was a village."

"There was."

"Where is it now?"

Whereupon he burst out into a long story in German and English, so mixed up that I could not quite understand exactly what he said, but roughly I gathered that long ago, hundreds of years, men had died there and been buried in their graves; and sounds were heard under the clay, and when the graves were opened, men and women were found rosy with life, and their mouths red with blood. And so, in haste to save their lives (aye, and their souls!—and here he crossed himself) those who were left fled away to other places, where the living lived, and the dead were dead and not—not something. He was evidently afraid to speak the last words. As he proceeded with his narration, he grew more and more excited. It seemed as if his imagination had got hold of him, and he ended in a perfect paroxysm of fear— white-faced, perspiring, trembling and looking round him, as if expecting that some dreadful presence would manifest itself there in the bright sunshine on the open plain.

Finally, in an agony of desperation, he cried: "Walpurgis Nacht!" and pointed to the carriage for me to get in.

All my English blood rose at this, and, standing back, I said: "You are afraid, Johann—you are afraid. Go home; I shall return alone; the walk will do me good."

The carriage door was open. I took from the seat my oak walking-stick—which I always carry on my holiday excursions—and closed the door, pointing back to Munich, and said, "Go home, Johann—Walpurgis Nacht doesn't concern Englishmen."

The horses were now more restive than ever, and Johann was trying to hold them in, while excitedly imploring me not to do anything so foolish. I pitied the poor fellow, he was deeply in earnest; but all the same I could not help laughing. His English was quite gone now. In his anxiety he had forgotten that his only means of making me understand was to talk my language, so he jabbered away in his native German. It began to be a little tedious. After giving the direction, "Home!" I turned to go down the cross-road into the valley. With a despairing gesture, Johann turned his horses towards Munich. I leaned on my stick and looked after him. He went slowly along the road for a while: then there came over the crest of the hill a man tall and thin. I could see so much in the distance. When he drew near the horses, they began to jump and kick about, then to scream with terror. Johann could not hold them in; they bolted down the road, running away madly. I watched them out of sight, then looked for the stranger, but I found that he, too, was gone.

With a light heart I turned down the side road through the deepening valley to which Johann had objected. There was not the slightest reason, that I could see, for his objection; and I daresay I tramped for a couple of hours without thinking of time or distance, and certainly without seeing a person or a house. So far as the place was concerned, it was desolation itself. But I did not notice this particularly till, on turning a bend in the road, I came upon a scattered fringe of wood; then I recognised that I had been impressed unconsciously by the desolation of the region through which I had passed.

I sat down to rest myself, and began to look around. It struck me that it was considerably colder than it had been at the commencement of my walk—a sort of sighing sound seemed to be around me, with, now and then, high overhead, a sort of muffled roar. Looking upwards I noticed that great thick clouds were drifting rapidly across the sky from North to South at a great height. There were signs of coming storm in some lofty stratum of the air. I was a little chilly, and, thinking that it was the sitting still after the exercise of walking, I resumed my journey.

The ground I passed over was now much more picturesque. There were no striking objects that the eye might single out; but in all there was a charm of beauty. I took little heed of time and it was only when the deepening twilight forced itself upon me that I began to think of how I should find my way home. The brightness of the day had gone. The air was cold, and the drifting of clouds high overhead was more marked. They were accompanied by a sort of far-away rushing sound, through which seemed to come at intervals that mysterious cry which the driver had said came from a wolf. For a while I hesitated. I had said I would see the deserted village, so on I went, and presently came on a wide stretch of open country, shut in by hills all around. Their sides were covered with trees which spread down to the plain, dotting, in clumps, the gentler slopes and hollows which showed here and there. I followed with my eye the winding of the road, and saw that it curved close to one of the densest of these clumps and was lost behind it.

As I looked there came a cold shiver in the air, and the snow began to fall. I thought of the miles and miles of bleak country I had passed, and then hurried on to seek the shelter of the wood in front. Darker and darker grew the sky, and faster and heavier fell the snow, till the earth before and around me was a glistening white carpet the further edge of which was lost in misty vagueness. The road was here but crude, and when on the level its boundaries were not so marked, as when it passed through the cuttings; and in a little while I found that I must have strayed from it, for I missed underfoot the hard surface, and my feet sank deeper in the grass and moss. Then the wind grew stronger and blew with ever increasing force, till I was fain to run before it. The air became icy-cold, and in spite of my exercise I began to suffer. The snow was now falling so thickly and whirling around me in such rapid eddies that I could hardly keep my eyes open. Every now and then the heavens were torn asunder by vivid lightning, and in the flashes I could see ahead of me a great mass of trees, chiefly yew and cypress all heavily coated with snow.

I was soon amongst the shelter of the trees, and there, in comparative silence, I could hear the rush of the wind high overhead. Presently the blackness of the storm had become merged in the darkness of the night. By-and-by the storm seemed to be passing away: it now only came in fierce puffs or blasts. At such moments the weird sound of the wolf appeared to be echoed by many similar sounds around me.

Now and again, through the black mass of drifting cloud, came a straggling ray of moonlight, which lit up the expanse, and showed me that I was at the edge of a dense mass of cypress and yew trees. As the snow had ceased to fall, I walked out from the shelter and began to investigate more closely. It appeared to me that, amongst so many old foundations as I had passed, there might be still standing a house in which, though in ruins, I could find some sort of shelter for a while. As I skirted the edge of the copse, I found that a low wall encircled it, and following this I presently found an opening. Here the cypresses formed an alley leading up to a square mass of some kind of building. Just as I caught sight of this, however, the drifting clouds obscured the moon, and I passed up the path in darkness. The wind must have grown colder, for I felt myself shiver as I walked; but there was hope of shelter, and I groped my way blindly on.

I stopped, for there was a sudden stillness. The storm had passed; and, perhaps in sympathy with nature's silence, my heart seemed to cease to beat. But this was only momentarily; for suddenly the moonlight broke through the clouds, showing me that I was in a graveyard, and that the square object before me was a great massive tomb of marble, as white as the snow that lay on and all around it. With the moonlight there came a fierce sigh of the storm, which appeared to resume its course with a long, low howl, as of many dogs or wolves. I was awed and shocked, and felt the cold perceptibly grow upon me till it seemed to grip me by the heart. Then while the flood of moonlight still fell on the marble tomb, the storm gave further evidence of renewing, as though it was returning on its track. Impelled by some sort of fascination, I approached the sepulchre to see what it was, and why such a thing stood alone in such a place. I walked around it, and read, over the Doric door, in German:

COUNTESS DOLINGEN OF GRATZ
IN STYRIA
SOUGHT AND FOUND DEATH
1801

On the top of the tomb, seemingly driven through the solid marble—for the structure was composed of a few vast blocks of stone—was a great iron spike or stake. On going to the back I saw, graven in great Russian letters: "The dead travel fast."

There was something so weird and uncanny about the whole thing that it gave me a turn and made me feel quite faint. I began to wish, for the first time, that I had taken Johann's advice. Here a thought struck me, which came under almost mysterious circumstances and with a terrible shock. This was Walpurgis Night!

Walpurgis Night, when, according to the belief of millions of people, the devil was abroad—when the graves were opened and the dead came forth and walked. When all evil things of earth and air and water held revel. This very place the driver had specially shunned. This was the depopulated village of centuries ago. This was where the suicide lay; and this was the place where I was alone—unmanned, shivering with cold in a shroud of snow with a wild storm gathering again upon me! It took all my philosophy, all the religion I had been taught, all my courage, not to collapse in a paroxysm of fright.

And now a perfect tornado burst upon me. The ground shook as though thousands of horses thundered across it; and this time the storm bore on its icy wings, not snow, but great hailstones which drove with such violence that they might have come from the thongs of Balearic slingers—hailstones that beat down leaf and branch and made the shelter of the cypresses of no more avail than though their stems were standing-corn. At the first I had rushed to the nearest tree; but I was soon fain to leave it and seek the only spot that seemed to afford refuge, the deep Doric doorway of the marble tomb. There, crouching against the massive bronze door,

I gained a certain amount of protection from the beating of the hailstones, for now they only drove against me as they ricocheted from the ground and the side of the marble.

As I leaned against the door, it moved slightly and opened inwards. The shelter of even a tomb was welcome in that pitiless tempest, and I was about to enter it when there came a flash of forked-lightning that lit up the whole expanse of the heavens. In the instant, as I am a living man, I saw, as my eyes were turned into the darkness of the tomb, a beautiful woman, with rounded cheeks and red lips, seemingly sleeping on a bier.

As the thunder broke overhead, I was grasped as by the hand of a giant and hurled out into the storm. The whole thing was so sudden that, before I could realise the shock, moral as well as physical, I found the hailstones beating me down. At the same time I had a strange, dominating feeling that I was not alone. I looked towards the tomb. Just then there came another blinding flash, which seemed to strike the iron stake that surmounted the tomb and to pour through to the earth, blasting and crumbling the marble, as in a burst of flame. The dead woman rose for a moment of agony, while she was lapped in the flame, and her bitter scream of pain was drowned in the thunder crash. The last thing I heard was this mingling of dreadful sound, as again I was seized in the giant-grasp and dragged away, while the hailstones beat on me, and the air around seemed reverberant with the howling of wolves. The last sight that I remembered was a vague, white, moving mass, as if all the graves around me had sent out the phantoms of their sheeted-dead, and that they were closing in on me through the white cloudiness of the driving hail.

Gradually there came a sort of vague beginning of consciousness; then a sense of weariness that was dreadful. For a time I remembered nothing; but slowly my senses returned. My feet seemed positively racked with pain, yet I could not move them. They seemed to be numbed. There was an icy feeling at the back of my neck and all down my spine, and my ears, like my feet, were dead, yet in torment; but there was in my breast a sense of warmth which was, by comparison, delicious. It was as a nightmare—a physical nightmare, if one may use such an expression; for some heavy weight on my chest made it difficult for me to breathe.

This period of semi-lethargy seemed to remain a long time, and as it faded away I must have slept or swooned. Then came a sort of loathing, like the first stage of sea-sickness, and a wild desire to be free from something—I knew not what. A vast stillness enveloped me, as though all the world were asleep or dead—only broken by the low panting as of some animal close to me. I felt a warm rasping at my throat, then came a consciousness of the awful truth, which chilled me to the heart and sent the blood surging up through my brain. Some great animal was lying on me and now licking my throat. I feared to stir, for some instinct of prudence bade me lie still; but the brute seemed to realise that there was now some change in me, for it raised its head. Through my eyelashes I saw above me the two great flaming eyes of a gigantic wolf. Its sharp white teeth gleamed in the gaping red mouth, and I could feel its hot breath fierce and acrid upon me.

For another spell of time I remembered no more. Then I became conscious of a low growl, followed by a yelp, renewed again and again. Then, seemingly very far away, I heard a "Holloa! holloa!" as of many voices calling in unison. Cautiously I raised my head and looked in the direction whence the sound came;

but the cemetery blocked my view. The wolf still continued to yelp in a strange way, and a red glare began to move round the grove of cypresses, as though following the sound. As the voices drew closer, the wolf yelped faster and louder. I feared to make either sound or motion. Nearer came the red glow, over the white pall which stretched into the darkness around me. Then all at once from beyond the trees there came at a trot a troop of horsemen bearing torches. The wolf rose from my breast and made for the cemetery. I saw one of the horsemen (soldiers by their caps and their long military cloaks) raise his carbine and take aim. A companion knocked up his arm, and I heard the ball whizz over my head. He had evidently taken my body for that of the wolf. Another sighted the animal as it slunk away, and a shot followed. Then, at a gallop, the troop rode forward—some towards me, others following the wolf as it disappeared amongst the snow-clad cypresses.

As they drew nearer I tried to move, but was powerless, although I could see and hear all that went on around me. Two or three of the soldiers jumped from their horses and knelt beside me. One of them raised my head, and placed his hand over my heart.

"Good news, comrades!" he cried. "His heart still beats!"

Then some brandy was poured down my throat; it put vigour into me, and I was able to open my eyes fully and look around. Lights and shadows were moving among the trees, and I heard men call to one another. They drew together, uttering frightened exclamations; and the lights flashed as the others came pouring out of the cemetery pell-mell, like men possessed. When the further ones came close to us, those who were around me asked them eagerly:

"Well, have you found him?"

The reply rang out hurriedly: "No! no! Come away quick—quick! This is no place to stay, and on this of all nights!"

"What was it?" was the question, asked in all manner of keys. The answer came variously and all indefinitely as though the men were moved by some common impulse to speak, yet were restrained by some common fear from giving their thoughts.

"It—it—indeed!" gibbered one, whose wits had plainly given out for the moment.

"A wolf—and yet not a wolf!" another put in shudderingly.

"No use trying for him without the sacred bullet," a third remarked in a more ordinary manner.

"Serve us right for coming out on this night! Truly we have earned our thousand marks!" were the ejaculations of a fourth.

"There was blood on the broken marble," another said after a pause—"the lightning never brought that there. And for him—is he safe? Look at his throat! See, comrades, the wolf has been lying on him and keeping his blood warm."

The officer looked at my throat and replied: "He is all right; the skin is not pierced. What does it all mean? We should never have found him but for the yelping of the wolf."

"What became of it?" asked the man who was holding up my head, and who seemed the least panic-stricken of the party, for his hands were steady and without tremor. On his sleeve was the chevron of a petty officer.

"It went to its home," answered the man, whose long face was pallid, and who actually shook with terror as he glanced around him fearfully.

"There are graves enough there in which it may lie. Come, comrades—come quickly! Let us leave this cursed spot."

The officer raised me to a sitting posture, as he uttered a word of command; then several men placed me upon a horse. He sprang to the saddle behind me, took me in his arms, gave the word to advance; and, turning our faces away from the cypresses, we rode away in swift, military order.

As yet my tongue refused its office, and I was perforce silent. I must have fallen asleep; for the next thing I remembered was finding myself standing up, supported by a soldier on each side of me. It was almost broad daylight, and to the north a red streak of sunlight was reflected, like a path of blood, over the waste of snow. The officer was telling the men to say nothing of what they had seen, except that they found an English stranger, guarded by a large dog.

"Dog! that was no dog," cut in the man who had exhibited such fear. "I think I know a wolf when I see one."

The young officer answered calmly: "I said a dog."

"Dog!" reiterated the other ironically. It was evident that his courage was rising with the sun; and, pointing to me, he said, "Look at his throat. Is that the work of a dog, master?" Instinctively I raised my hand to my throat, and as I touched it I cried out in pain. The men crowded round to look, some stooping down from their saddles; and again there came the calm voice of the young officer: "A dog, as I said. If aught else were said we should only be laughed at."

I was then mounted behind a trooper, and we rode on into the suburbs of Munich. Here we came across a stray carriage, into which I was lifted, and it was driven off to the Quatre Saisons—the young officer accompanying me, whilst a trooper followed with his horse, and the others rode off to their barracks.

When we arrived, Herr Delbrück rushed so quickly down the steps to meet me that it was apparent he had been watching within. Taking me by both hands he solicitously led me in. The officer saluted me and was turning to withdraw, when I recognised his purpose, and insisted that he should come to my rooms. Over a glass of wine I warmly thanked him and his brave comrades for saving me. He replied simply that he was more than glad, and that Herr Delbrück had at the first taken steps to make all the searching party pleased; at which ambiguous utterance the maître d'hôtel smiled, while the officer pleaded duty and withdrew.

"But Herr Delbrück," I enquired, "how and why was it that the soldiers searched for me?"

He shrugged his shoulders, as if in depreciation of his own deed, as he replied:

"I was so fortunate as to obtain leave from the commander of the regiment in which I served, to ask for volunteers."

"But how did you know I was lost?" I asked.

"The driver came hither with the remains of his carriage, which had been upset when the horses ran away."

"But surely you would not send a search-party of soldiers merely on this account?"

"Oh, no!" he answered; "but even before the coachman arrived, I had this telegram from the Boyar whose guest you are," and he took from his pocket a telegram which he handed to me, and I read:

Bistritz.

Be careful of my guest—his safety is most precious to me. Should aught happen to him, or if he be missed, spare nothing to find him and ensure his safety. He is English and therefore adventurous.

There are often dangers from snow and wolves and night. Lose not a moment if you suspect harm to him. I answer your zeal with my fortune. —Dracula.

As I held the telegram in my hand, the room seemed to whirl around me; and, if the attentive maître d'hôtel had not caught me, I think I should have fallen. There was something so strange in all this, something so weird and impossible to imagine, that there grew on me a sense of my being in some way the sport of opposite forces—the mere vague idea of which seemed in a way to paralyse me. I was certainly under some form of mysterious protection. From a distant country had come, in the very nick of time, a message that took me out of the danger of the snow-sleep and the jaws of the wolf.

39

The Robber Bridegroom

BY JACOB AND WILHELM GRIMM

There was once on a time a miller who had a beautiful daughter, and as she was grown up, he wished that she was provided for and well married. He thought, "If any good suitor comes and asks for her, I will give her to him."

Not long afterwards, a suitor came who appeared to be very rich, and as the miller had no fault to find with him, he promised his daughter to him. The maiden, however, did not like him quite so much as a girl should like the man to whom she is engaged, and had no confidence in him. Whenever she saw or thought of him, she felt a secret horror.

Once he said to her, "Thou art my betrothed, and yet thou hast never once paid me a visit."

The maiden replied, "I know not where thy house is."

Then said the bridegroom, "My house is out there in the dark forest."

She tried to excuse herself and said she could not find the way there.

The bridegroom said, "Next Sunday thou must come out there to me; I have already invited the guests, and I will strew ashes in order that thou mayst find thy way through the forest."

When Sunday came, and the maiden had to set out on her way, she became very uneasy, she herself knew not exactly why, and to mark her way she filled both her pockets full of peas and lentils. Ashes were strewn at the entrance of the forest, and these she followed, but at every step she threw a couple of peas on the ground.

She walked almost the whole day until she reached the middle of the forest, where it was the darkest, and there stood a solitary house, which she did not like, for it looked so dark and dismal. She went inside it, but no one was within, and the most absolute stillness reigned.

Suddenly a voice cried, *"Turn back, turn back, young maiden dear, 'Tis a murderer's house you enter here."*

The maiden looked up, and saw that the voice came from a bird, which was hanging in a cage on the wall. Again it cried, *"Turn back, turn back, young maiden dear, 'Tis a murderer's house you enter here."*

Then the young maiden went on farther from one room to another, and walked through the whole house, but it was entirely empty and not one human being was to be found. At last she came to the cellar, and there sat an extremely aged woman, whose head shook constantly.

"Can you not tell me," said the maiden, "if my betrothed lives here?"

"Alas, poor child," replied the old woman, "whither hast thou come? Thou art in a murderer's den. Thou thinkest thou art a bride soon to be married, but thou wilt keep thy wedding with death. Look, I have been forced to put a great kettle on there, with water in it, and when they have thee in their power, they will

cut thee to pieces without mercy, will cook thee, and eat thee, for they are eaters of human flesh. If I do not have compassion on thee, and save thee, thou art lost."

Thereupon the old woman led her behind a great hogshead where she could not be seen. "Be as still as a mouse," said she, "do not make a sound, or move, or all will be over with thee. At night, when the robbers are asleep, we will escape; I have long waited for an opportunity."

Hardly was this done, than the godless crew came home. They dragged with them another young girl. They were drunk, and paid no heed to her screams and lamentations. They gave her wine to drink, three glasses full, one glass of white wine, one glass of red, and a glass of yellow, and with this her heart burst in twain. Thereupon they tore off her delicate raiment, laid her on a table, cut her beautiful body in pieces and strewed salt thereon.

The poor bride behind the cask trembled and shook, for she saw right well what fate the robbers had destined for her. One of them noticed a gold ring on the little finger of the murdered girl, and as it would not come off at once, he took an axe and cut the finger off, but it sprang up in the air, away over the cask and fell straight into the bride's bosom. The robber took a candle and wanted to look for it, but could not find it. Then another of them said, "Hast thou looked behind the great hogshead?" But the old woman cried, "Come and get something to eat, and leave off looking till the morning, the finger won't run away from you."

Then the robbers said, "The old woman is right," and gave up their search, and sat down to eat, and the old woman poured a sleeping-draught in their wine, so that they soon lay down in the cellar, and slept and snored. When the bride heard that, she came out from behind the hogshead, and had to step over the sleepers, for they lay in rows on the ground, and great was her terror lest she should waken one of them. But God helped her, and she got safely over.

The old woman went up with her, opened the doors, and they hurried out of the murderers' den with all the speed in their power. The wind had blown away the strewn ashes, but the peas and lentils had sprouted and grown up, and showed them the way in the moonlight. They walked the whole night, until in the morning they arrived at the mill, and then the maiden told her father everything exactly as it had happened.

When the day came when the wedding was to be celebrated, the bridegroom appeared, and the Miller had invited all his relations and friends. As they sat at table, each was bidden to relate something. The bride sat still, and said nothing.

Then said the bridegroom to the bride, "Come, my darling, dost thou know nothing? Relate something to us like the rest."

She replied, "Then I will relate a dream. I was walking alone through a wood, and at last I came to a house, in which no living soul was, but on the wall there was a bird in a cage which cried, *"Turn back, turn back, young maiden dear, 'Tis a murderer's house you enter here."* And this it cried once more.

-My darling, I only dreamt this.-

Then I went through all the rooms, and they were all empty, and there was something so horrible about them! At last I went down into the cellar, and there sat a very very old woman, whose head shook; I asked her, 'Does my bridegroom live in this house? She answered, 'Alas poor child, thou hast got into a murderer's den, thy bridegroom does live here, but he will hew thee in pieces, and kill thee, and then he will cook thee, and eat thee.'

-My darling, I only dreamt this.-

But the old woman hid me behind a great hogshead, and, scarcely was I hidden, when the robbers came home, dragging a maiden with them, to whom they gave three kinds of wine to drink, white, red, and yellow, with which her heart broke in twain.

-My darling, I only dreamt this.-

Thereupon they pulled off her pretty clothes, and hewed her fair body in pieces on a table, and sprinkled them with salt.

-My darling, I only dreamt this.-

And one of the robbers saw that there was still a ring on her little finger, and as it was hard to draw off, he took an axe and cut it off, but the finger sprang up in the air, and sprang behind the great hogshead, and fell in my bosom. And there is the finger with the ring!"

And with these words she drew it forth, and showed it to those present.

The robber, who had during this story become as pale as ashes, leapt up and wanted to escape, but the guests held him fast, and delivered him over to justice. Then he and his whole troop were executed for their infamous deeds.

40

The Legend of Sleepy Hollow

BY WASHINGTON IRVING

FOUND AMONG THE PAPERS OF THE LATE DIEDRICH
KNICKERBOCKER.

> *A pleasing land of drowsy head it was,*
> *Of dreams that wave before the half-shut eye;*
> *And of gay castles in the clouds that pass,*
> *Forever flushing round a summer sky.*
> CASTLE OF INDOLENCE.

In the bosom of one of those spacious coves which indent the
eastern shore of the Hudson, at that broad expansion of the river
denominated by the ancient Dutch navigators the Tappan Zee,
and where they always prudently shortened sail and implored the
protection of St. Nicholas when they crossed, there lies a small
market town or rural port, which by some is called Greensburgh,
but which is more generally and properly known by the name
of Tarry Town. This name was given, we are told, in former
days, by the good housewives of the adjacent country, from
the inveterate propensity of their husbands to linger about the
village tavern on market days. Be that as it may, I do not vouch
for the fact, but merely advert to it, for the sake of being precise
and authentic.

Not far from this village, perhaps about two miles, there is a little valley or rather lap of land among high hills, which is one of the quietest places in the whole world. A small brook glides through it, with just murmur enough to lull one to repose; and the occasional whistle of a quail or tapping of a woodpecker is almost the only sound that ever breaks in upon the uniform tranquillity.

I recollect that, when a stripling, my first exploit in squirrel-shooting was in a grove of tall walnut-trees that shades one side of the valley. I had wandered into it at noontime, when all nature is peculiarly quiet, and was startled by the roar of my own gun, as it broke the Sabbath stillness around and was prolonged and reverberated by the angry echoes. If ever I should wish for a retreat whither I might steal from the world and its distractions, and dream quietly away the remnant of a troubled life, I know of none more promising than this little valley.

From the listless repose of the place, and the peculiar character of its inhabitants, who are descendants from the original Dutch settlers, this sequestered glen has long been known by the name of SLEEPY HOLLOW, and its rustic lads are called the Sleepy Hollow Boys throughout all the neighboring country. A drowsy, dreamy influence seems to hang over the land, and to pervade the very atmosphere. Some say that the place was bewitched by a High German doctor, during the early days of the settlement; others, that an old Indian chief, the prophet or wizard of his tribe, held his powwows there before the country was discovered by Master Hendrick Hudson. Certain it is, the place still continues under the sway of some witching power, that holds a spell over the minds of the good people, causing them to walk in a continual reverie. They are given to all kinds of marvellous beliefs, are subject to trances and visions, and frequently see strange sights, and hear music and voices in the air. The whole neighborhood abounds with local tales, haunted spots, and twilight superstitions; stars shoot and meteors glare oftener across the valley than in any other part of the country, and the nightmare, with her whole ninefold, seems to make it the favorite scene of her gambols.

The dominant spirit, however, that haunts this enchanted region, and seems to be commander-in-chief of all the powers of the air, is the apparition of a figure on horseback, without a head.

It is said by some to be the ghost of a Hessian trooper, whose head had been carried away by a cannon-ball, in some nameless battle during the Revolutionary War, and who is ever and anon seen by the country folk hurrying along in the gloom of night, as if on the wings of the wind. His haunts are not confined to the valley, but extend at times to the adjacent roads, and especially to the vicinity of a church at no great distance. Indeed, certain of the most authentic historians of those parts, who have been careful in collecting and collating the floating facts concerning this spectre, allege that the body of the trooper having been buried in the churchyard, the ghost rides forth to the scene of battle in nightly quest of his head, and that the rushing speed with which he sometimes passes along the Hollow, like a midnight blast, is owing to his being belated, and in a hurry to get back to the churchyard before daybreak.

Such is the general purport of this legendary superstition, which has furnished materials for many a wild story in that region of shadows; and the spectre is known at all the country firesides, by the name of the Headless Horseman of Sleepy Hollow.

It is remarkable that the visionary propensity I have mentioned is not confined to the native inhabitants of the valley,

THE FRENCH PAYMASTER

but is unconsciously imbibed by every one who resides there for a time. However wide awake they may have been before they entered that sleepy region, they are sure, in a little time, to inhale the witching influence of the air, and begin to grow imaginative, to dream dreams, and see apparitions.

I mention this peaceful spot with all possible laud, for it is in such little retired Dutch valleys, found here and there embosomed in the great State of New York, that population, manners, and customs remain fixed, while the great torrent of migration and improvement, which is making such incessant changes in other parts of this restless country, sweeps by them unobserved. They are like those little nooks of still water, which border a rapid stream, where we may see the straw and bubble riding quietly at anchor, or slowly revolving in their mimic harbor, undisturbed by the rush of the passing current. Though many years have elapsed since I trod the drowsy shades of Sleepy Hollow, yet I question whether I should not still find the same trees and the same families vegetating in its sheltered bosom.

In this by-place of nature there abode, in a remote period of American history, that is to say, some thirty years since, a worthy wight of the name of Ichabod Crane, who sojourned, or, as he expressed it, "tarried," in Sleepy Hollow, for the purpose of instructing the children of the vicinity. He was a native of Connecticut, a State which supplies the Union with pioneers for the mind as well as for the forest, and sends forth yearly its legions of frontier woodmen and country schoolmasters.

The cognomen of Crane was not inapplicable to his person. He was tall, but exceedingly lank, with narrow shoulders, long arms and legs, hands that dangled a mile out of his sleeves, feet that might have served for shovels, and his whole frame most loosely hung together. His head was small, and flat at top, with huge ears, large green glassy eyes, and a long snipe nose, so that it looked like a weather-cock perched upon his spindle neck to tell which way the wind blew. To see him striding along the profile of a hill on a windy day, with his clothes bagging and fluttering about him, one might have mistaken him for the genius of famine descending upon the earth, or some scarecrow eloped from a cornfield.

His schoolhouse was a low building of one large room, rudely constructed of logs; the windows partly glazed, and partly patched with leaves of old copybooks. It was most ingeniously secured at vacant hours, by a withe twisted in the handle of the door, and stakes set against the window shutters; so that though a thief might get in with perfect ease, he would find some embarrassment in getting out—an idea most probably borrowed by the architect, Yost Van Houten, from the mystery of an eelpot. The schoolhouse stood in a rather lonely but pleasant situation, just at the foot of a woody hill, with a brook running close by, and a formidable birch-tree growing at one end of it. From hence the low murmur of his pupils' voices, conning over their lessons, might be heard in a drowsy summer's day, like the hum of a beehive; interrupted now and then by the authoritative voice of the master, in the tone of menace or command as he urged some tardy loiterer along the flowery path of knowledge.

When school hours were over, he was even the companion and playmate of the larger boys; and on holiday afternoons would convoy some of the smaller ones home, who happened to have pretty sisters, or good housewives for mothers, noted for the comforts of the cupboard. Indeed, it behooved him to keep on good terms with his pupils. The revenue arising from his school

was small, and would have been scarcely sufficient to furnish him
with daily bread, for he was a huge feeder, and, though lank,
had the dilating powers of an anaconda; but to help out his
maintenance, he was, according to country custom in those parts,
boarded and lodged at the houses of the farmers whose children
he instructed. With these he lived successively a week at a time,
thus going the rounds of the neighborhood, with all his worldly
effects tied up in a cotton handkerchief.

That all this might not be too onerous on the purses of his
rustic patrons, who are apt to consider the costs of schooling
a grievous burden, and schoolmasters as mere drones, he had
various ways of rendering himself both useful and agreeable. He
assisted the farmers occasionally in the lighter labors of their farms,
helped to make hay, mended the fences, took the horses to water,
drove the cows from pasture, and cut wood for the winter fire. He
laid aside, too, all the dominant dignity and absolute sway with
which he lorded it in his little empire, the school, and became
wonderfully gentle and ingratiating. He found favor in the eyes
of the mothers by petting the children, particularly the youngest;
and like the lion bold, which whilom so magnanimously the lamb
did hold, he would sit with a child on one knee, and rock a cradle
with his foot for whole hours together.

In addition to his other vocations, he was the singing-master
of the neighborhood, and picked up many bright shillings by
instructing the young folks in psalmody. It was a matter of no little
vanity to him on Sundays, to take his station in front of the church
gallery, with a band of chosen singers; where, in his own mind,
he completely carried away the palm from the parson. Certain it
is, his voice resounded far above all the rest of the congregation;
and there are peculiar quavers still to be heard in that church, and

which may even be heard half a mile off, quite to the opposite side of the millpond, on a still Sunday morning, which are said to be legitimately descended from the nose of Ichabod Crane. Thus, by divers little makeshifts, in that ingenious way which is commonly denominated "by hook and by crook," the worthy pedagogue got on tolerably enough, and was thought, by all who understood nothing of the labor of headwork, to have a wonderfully easy life of it.

The schoolmaster is generally a man of some importance in the female circle of a rural neighborhood; being considered a kind of idle, gentlemanlike personage, of vastly superior taste and accomplishments to the rough country swains, and, indeed, inferior in learning only to the parson. His appearance, therefore, is apt to occasion some little stir at the tea-table of a farmhouse, and the addition of a supernumerary dish of cakes or sweetmeats, or, peradventure, the parade of a silver teapot. Our man of letters, therefore, was peculiarly happy in the smiles of all the country damsels. How he would figure among them in the churchyard, between services on Sundays; gathering grapes for them from the wild vines that overran the surrounding trees; reciting for their amusement all the epitaphs on the tombstones; or sauntering, with a whole bevy of them, along the banks of the adjacent millpond; while the more bashful country bumpkins hung sheepishly back, envying his superior elegance and address.

From his half-itinerant life, also, he was a kind of travelling gazette, carrying the whole budget of local gossip from house to house, so that his appearance was always greeted with satisfaction. He was, moreover, esteemed by the women as a man of great erudition, for he had read several books quite through, and was a perfect master of Cotton Mather's "History of New England

Witchcraft," in which, by the way, he most firmly and potently believed.

He was, in fact, an odd mixture of small shrewdness and simple credulity. His appetite for the marvellous, and his powers of digesting it, were equally extraordinary; and both had been increased by his residence in this spell-bound region. No tale was too gross or monstrous for his capacious swallow. It was often his delight, after his school was dismissed in the afternoon, to stretch himself on the rich bed of clover bordering the little brook that whimpered by his schoolhouse, and there con over old Mather's direful tales, until the gathering dusk of evening made the printed page a mere mist before his eyes. Then, as he wended his way by swamp and stream and awful woodland, to the farmhouse where he happened to be quartered, every sound of nature, at that witching hour, fluttered his excited imagination, the moan of the whip-poor-will from the hillside, the boding cry of the tree toad, that harbinger of storm, the dreary hooting of the screech owl, or the sudden rustling in the thicket of birds frightened from their roost. The fireflies, too, which sparkled most vividly in the darkest places, now and then startled him, as one of uncommon brightness would stream across his path; and if, by chance, a huge blockhead of a beetle came winging his blundering flight against him, the poor varlet was ready to give up the ghost, with the idea that he was struck with a witch's token. His only resource on such occasions, either to drown thought or drive away evil spirits, was to sing psalm tunes and the good people of Sleepy Hollow, as they sat by their doors of an evening, were often filled with awe at hearing his nasal melody, "in linked sweetness long drawn out," floating from the distant hill, or along the dusky road.

Another of his sources of fearful pleasure was to pass long winter evenings with the old Dutch wives, as they sat spinning by the fire, with a row of apples roasting and spluttering along the hearth, and listen to their marvellous tales of ghosts and goblins, and haunted fields, and haunted brooks, and haunted bridges, and haunted houses, and particularly of the headless horseman, or Galloping Hessian of the Hollow, as they sometimes called him. He would delight them equally by his anecdotes of witchcraft, and of the direful omens and portentous sights and sounds in the air, which prevailed in the earlier times of Connecticut; and would frighten them woefully with speculations upon comets and shooting stars; and with the alarming fact that the world did absolutely turn round, and that they were half the time topsy-turvy!

But if there was a pleasure in all this, while snugly cuddling in the chimney corner of a chamber that was all of a ruddy glow from the crackling wood fire, and where, of course, no spectre dared to show its face, it was dearly purchased by the terrors of his subsequent walk homewards. What fearful shapes and shadows beset his path, amidst the dim and ghastly glare of a snowy night! With what wistful look did he eye every trembling ray of light streaming across the waste fields from some distant window! How often was he appalled by some shrub covered with snow, which, like a sheeted spectre, beset his very path! How often did he shrink with curdling awe at the sound of his own steps on the frosty crust beneath his feet; and dread to look over his shoulder, lest he should behold some uncouth being tramping close behind him! And how often was he thrown into complete dismay by some rushing blast, howling among the trees, in the idea that it was the Galloping Hessian on one of his nightly scourings!

All these, however, were mere terrors of the night, phantoms of the mind that walk in darkness; and though he had seen many spectres in his time, and been more than once beset by Satan in divers shapes, in his lonely perambulations, yet daylight put an end to all these evils; and he would have passed a pleasant life of it, in despite of the Devil and all his works, if his path had not been crossed by a being that causes more perplexity to mortal man than ghosts, goblins, and the whole race of witches put together, and that was—a woman.

Among the musical disciples who assembled, one evening in each week, to receive his instructions in psalmody, was Katrina Van Tassel, the daughter and only child of a substantial Dutch farmer. She was a blooming lass of fresh eighteen; plump as a partridge; ripe and melting and rosy-cheeked as one of her father's peaches, and universally famed, not merely for her beauty, but her vast expectations. She was withal a little of a coquette, as might be perceived even in her dress, which was a mixture of ancient and modern fashions, as most suited to set off her charms. She wore the ornaments of pure yellow gold, which her great-great-grandmother had brought over from Saardam; the tempting stomacher of the olden time, and withal a provokingly short petticoat, to display the prettiest foot and ankle in the country round.

Ichabod Crane had a soft and foolish heart towards the sex; and it is not to be wondered at that so tempting a morsel soon found favor in his eyes, more especially after he had visited her in her paternal mansion. Old Baltus Van Tassel was a perfect picture of a thriving, contented, liberal-hearted farmer. He seldom, it is true, sent either his eyes or his thoughts beyond the boundaries of his own farm; but within those everything was snug, happy and well-conditioned. He was satisfied with his wealth, but not proud of it; and piqued himself upon the hearty abundance, rather than the style in which he lived. His stronghold was situated on the banks of the Hudson, in one of those green, sheltered, fertile nooks in which the Dutch farmers are so fond of nestling. A great elm tree spread its broad branches over it, at the foot of which bubbled up a spring of the softest and sweetest water, in a little well formed of a barrel; and then stole sparkling away through the grass, to a neighboring brook, that babbled along among alders and dwarf willows. Hard by the farmhouse was a vast barn, that might have served for a church; every window and crevice of which seemed bursting forth with the treasures of the farm; the flail was busily resounding within it from morning to night; swallows and martins skimmed twittering about the eaves; and rows of pigeons, some with one eye turned up, as if watching the weather, some with their heads under their wings or buried in their bosoms, and others swelling, and cooing, and bowing about their dames, were enjoying the sunshine on the roof. Sleek unwieldy porkers were grunting in the repose and abundance of their pens, from whence sallied forth, now and then, troops of sucking pigs, as if to snuff the air. A stately squadron of snowy geese were riding in an adjoining pond, convoying whole fleets of ducks; regiments of turkeys were gobbling through the farmyard, and Guinea fowls fretting about it, like ill-tempered housewives, with their peevish, discontented cry. Before the barn door strutted the gallant cock, that pattern of a husband, a warrior and a fine gentleman, clapping his burnished wings and crowing in the pride and gladness of his heart—sometimes tearing up the earth with his feet, and then generously calling his ever-hungry family of wives and children to enjoy the rich morsel which he had discovered.

The pedagogue's mouth watered as he looked upon this sumptuous promise of luxurious winter fare. In his devouring mind's eye, he pictured to himself every roasting-pig running about with a pudding in his belly, and an apple in his mouth; the pigeons were snugly put to bed in a comfortable pie, and tucked in with a coverlet of crust; the geese were swimming in their own gravy; and the ducks pairing cosily in dishes, like snug married couples, with a decent competency of onion sauce. In the porkers he saw carved out the future sleek side of bacon, and juicy relishing ham; not a turkey but he beheld daintily trussed up, with its gizzard under its wing, and, peradventure, a necklace of savory sausages; and even bright chanticleer himself lay sprawling on his back, in a side dish, with uplifted claws, as if craving that quarter which his chivalrous spirit disdained to ask while living.

As the enraptured Ichabod fancied all this, and as he rolled his great green eyes over the fat meadow lands, the rich fields of wheat, of rye, of buckwheat, and Indian corn, and the orchards burdened with ruddy fruit, which surrounded the warm tenement of Van Tassel, his heart yearned after the damsel who was to inherit these domains, and his imagination expanded with the idea, how they might be readily turned into cash, and the money invested in immense tracts of wild land, and shingle palaces in the wilderness. Nay, his busy fancy already realized his hopes, and presented to him the blooming Katrina, with a whole family of children, mounted on the top of a wagon loaded with household trumpery, with pots and kettles dangling beneath; and he beheld himself bestriding a pacing mare, with a colt at her heels, setting out for Kentucky, Tennessee—or the Lord knows where!

When he entered the house, the conquest of his heart was complete. It was one of those spacious farmhouses, with high-ridged but lowly sloping roofs, built in the style handed down from the first Dutch settlers; the low projecting eaves forming a piazza along the front, capable of being closed up in bad weather. Under this were hung flails, harness, various utensils of husbandry, and nets for fishing in the neighboring river. Benches were built along the sides for summer use; and a great spinning-wheel at one end, and a churn at the other, showed the various uses to which this important porch might be devoted. From this piazza the wondering Ichabod entered the hall, which formed the centre of the mansion, and the place of usual residence. Here rows of resplendent pewter, ranged on a long dresser, dazzled his eyes. In one corner stood a huge bag of wool, ready to be spun; in another, a quantity of linsey-woolsey just from the loom; ears of Indian corn, and strings of dried apples and peaches, hung in gay festoons along the walls, mingled with the gaud of red peppers; and a door left ajar gave him a peep into the best parlor, where the claw-footed chairs and dark mahogany tables shone like mirrors; andirons, with their accompanying shovel and tongs, glistened from their covert of asparagus tops; mock-oranges and conch-shells decorated the mantelpiece; strings of various-colored birds eggs were suspended above it; a great ostrich egg was hung from the centre of the room, and a corner cupboard, knowingly left open, displayed immense treasures of old silver and well-mended china.

From the moment Ichabod laid his eyes upon these regions of delight, the peace of his mind was at an end, and his only study was how to gain the affections of the peerless daughter of Van Tassel. In this enterprise, however, he had more real difficulties than generally fell to the lot of a knight-errant of yore, who seldom had anything but giants, enchanters, fiery dragons, and such like easily conquered adversaries, to contend with and had to make his way merely through gates of iron and brass, and walls of adamant to the castle keep, where the lady of his heart was confined; all which he achieved as easily as a man would carve his way to the centre of a Christmas pie; and then the lady gave him her hand as a matter of course. Ichabod, on the contrary, had to win his way to the heart of a country coquette, beset with a labyrinth of whims and caprices, which were forever presenting new difficulties and impediments; and he had to encounter a host of fearful adversaries of real flesh and blood, the numerous rustic admirers, who beset every portal to her heart, keeping a watchful and angry eye upon each other, but ready to fly out in the common cause against any new competitor.

Among these, the most formidable was a burly, roaring, roystering blade, of the name of Abraham, or, according to the Dutch abbreviation, Brom Van Brunt, the hero of the country round, which rang with his feats of strength and hardihood. He was broad-shouldered and double-jointed, with short curly black hair, and a bluff but not unpleasant countenance, having a mingled air of fun and arrogance. From his Herculean frame and great powers of limb he had received the nickname of BROM BONES, by which he was universally known. He was famed for great knowledge and skill in horsemanship, being as dexterous on horseback as a Tartar. He was foremost at all races and cock fights; and, with the ascendancy which bodily strength always acquires in rustic life, was the umpire in all disputes, setting his hat on one side, and giving his decisions with an air and tone that admitted of no gainsay or appeal. He was always ready for either a fight or a frolic; but had more mischief than ill-will in his composition; and with all his overbearing roughness, there was a strong dash of waggish good humor at bottom. He had three or four boon companions, who regarded him as their model, and at the head of whom he scoured the country, attending every scene of feud or merriment for miles round. In cold weather he was distinguished by a fur cap, surmounted with a flaunting fox's tail; and when the folks at a country gathering descried this well-known crest at a distance, whisking about among a squad of hard riders, they always stood by for a squall. Sometimes his crew would be heard dashing along past the farmhouses at midnight, with whoop and halloo, like a troop of Don Cossacks; and the old dames, startled out of their sleep, would listen for a moment till the hurry-scurry had clattered by, and then exclaim, "Ay, there goes Brom Bones and his gang!" The neighbors looked upon him with a mixture of awe, admiration, and good-will; and, when any madcap prank or rustic brawl occurred in the vicinity, always shook their heads, and warranted Brom Bones was at the bottom of it.

This rantipole hero had for some time singled out the blooming Katrina for the object of his uncouth gallantries, and though his amorous toyings were something like the gentle caresses and endearments of a bear, yet it was whispered that she did not altogether discourage his hopes. Certain it is, his advances were signals for rival candidates to retire, who felt no inclination to cross a lion in his amours; insomuch, that when his horse was seen tied to Van Tassel's paling, on a Sunday night, a sure sign that his master was courting, or, as it is termed, "sparking," within, all other suitors passed by in despair, and carried the war into other quarters.

Such was the formidable rival with whom Ichabod Crane had to contend, and, considering all things, a stouter man than he would have shrunk from the competition, and a wiser man would have despaired. He had, however, a happy mixture of pliability and perseverance in his nature; he was in form and spirit like a supple-jack—yielding, but tough; though he bent, he never broke; and though he bowed beneath the slightest pressure, yet, the moment it was away—jerk!—he was as erect, and carried his head as high as ever.

To have taken the field openly against his rival would have been madness; for he was not a man to be thwarted in his amours, any more than that stormy lover, Achilles. Ichabod, therefore, made his advances in a quiet and gently insinuating manner. Under cover of his character of singing-master, he made frequent visits at the farmhouse; not that he had anything to apprehend from the meddlesome interference of parents, which is so often a stumbling-block in the path of lovers. Balt Van Tassel was an easy indulgent soul; he loved his daughter better even than his pipe, and, like a reasonable man and an excellent father, let her have her way in everything. His notable little wife, too, had enough to do to attend to her housekeeping and manage her poultry; for, as she sagely observed, ducks and geese are foolish things, and must be looked after, but girls can take care of themselves. Thus, while the busy dame bustled about the house, or plied her spinning-wheel at one end of the piazza, honest Balt would sit smoking his evening pipe at the other, watching the achievements of a little wooden warrior, who, armed with a sword in each hand, was most valiantly fighting the wind on the pinnacle of the barn. In the mean time, Ichabod would carry on his suit with the daughter by the side of the spring under the great elm, or sauntering along in the twilight, that hour so favorable to the lover's eloquence.

I profess not to know how women's hearts are wooed and won. To me they have always been matters of riddle and admiration. Some seem to have but one vulnerable point, or door of access; while others have a thousand avenues, and may be captured in a thousand different ways. It is a great triumph of skill to gain the former, but a still greater proof of generalship to maintain possession of the latter, for man must battle for his fortress at every door and window. He who wins a thousand common hearts is therefore entitled to some renown; but he who keeps undisputed sway over the heart of a coquette is indeed a hero. Certain it is, this was not the case with the redoubtable Brom Bones; and from the moment Ichabod Crane made his advances, the interests of the former evidently declined: his horse was no longer seen tied to the palings on Sunday nights, and a deadly feud gradually arose between him and the preceptor of Sleepy Hollow.

Brom, who had a degree of rough chivalry in his nature, would fain have carried matters to open warfare and have settled their pretensions to the lady, according to the mode of those most concise and simple reasoners, the knights-errant of yore—by single combat; but Ichabod was too conscious of the superior might of his adversary to enter the lists against him; he had overheard a boast of Bones, that he would "double the schoolmaster up, and lay him on a shelf of his own schoolhouse;" and he was too wary to give him an opportunity. There was something extremely provoking in this obstinately pacific system; it left Brom no alternative but to draw upon the funds of rustic waggery in his disposition, and to play off boorish practical jokes upon his rival. Ichabod became the object of whimsical persecution to Bones and his gang of rough riders. They harried his hitherto peaceful domains; smoked out his singing school by stopping up the chimney; broke into the schoolhouse at night, in spite of its formidable fastenings of with and window stakes, and turned everything topsy-turvy, so that the poor schoolmaster began to think all the witches in the country held their meetings there. But what was still more annoying, Brom took all opportunities of turning him into ridicule in presence of his mistress, and had a scoundrel dog whom he taught to whine in the most ludicrous manner, and introduced as a rival of Ichabod's, to instruct her in psalmody.

In this way matters went on for some time, without producing any material effect on the relative situations of the contending powers. On a fine autumnal afternoon, Ichabod, in pensive mood, sat enthroned on the lofty stool from whence he usually watched all the concerns of his little literary realm. In his hand he swayed a ferule, that sceptre of despotic power; the birch of justice reposed on three nails behind the throne, a constant terror to evil doers, while on the desk before him might be seen sundry contraband articles and prohibited weapons, detected upon the persons of idle urchins, such as half-munched apples, popguns, whirligigs, fly-cages, and whole legions of rampant little paper gamecocks. Apparently there had been some appalling act of justice recently inflicted, for his scholars were all busily intent upon their books, or slyly whispering behind them with one eye kept upon the master; and a kind of buzzing stillness reigned throughout the schoolroom. It was suddenly interrupted by the appearance of a man in tow-cloth jacket and trowsers, a round-crowned fragment of a hat, like the cap of Mercury, and mounted on the back of a ragged, wild, half-broken colt, which he managed with a rope by way of halter. He came clattering up to the school door with an invitation to Ichabod to attend a merry-making or "quilting frolic," to be held that evening at Mynheer Van Tassel's; and having delivered his message, he dashed over the brook and was seen scampering away up the hollow, full of the importance and hurry of his mission.

All was now bustle and hubbub in the late quiet schoolroom. The scholars were hurried through their lessons without stopping at trifles. Books were flung aside without being put away on the shelves, inkstands were overturned, benches thrown down, and the whole school was turned loose an hour before the usual time, bursting forth like a legion of young imps, yelping and racketing about the green in joy at their early emancipation.

The gallant Ichabod now spent at least an extra half hour at his toilet, brushing and furbishing up his best, and indeed only suit of rusty black, and arranging his locks by a bit of broken looking-glass that hung up in the schoolhouse. That he might make his appearance before his mistress in the true style of a cavalier, he borrowed a horse from the farmer with whom he was domiciliated, a choleric old Dutchman of the name of Hans Van Ripper, and, thus gallantly mounted, issued forth like a knight-errant in quest of adventures. But it is meet I should, in the true spirit of romantic story, give some account of the looks and equipments of my hero and his steed. The animal he bestrode was a broken-down plow-horse, that had outlived almost everything but its viciousness. He was gaunt and shagged, with a ewe neck, and a head like a hammer; his rusty mane and tail were tangled and knotted with burs; one eye had lost its pupil, and was glaring and spectral, but the other had the gleam of a genuine devil in it. Still, he must have had fire and mettle in his day, if we may judge from the name he bore of Gunpowder. He had, in fact, been a favorite steed of his master's, the choleric Van Ripper, who was a furious rider, and had infused, very probably, some of his own spirit into the animal; for, old and broken-down as he looked, there was more of the lurking devil in him than in any young filly in the country.

Ichabod was a suitable figure for such a steed. He rode with short stirrups, which brought his knees nearly up to the pommel of the saddle; his sharp elbows stuck out like grasshoppers'; he carried his whip perpendicularly in his hand, like a sceptre, and as his horse jogged on, the motion of his arms was not unlike the flapping of a pair of wings. A small wool hat rested on the top of his nose, for so his scanty strip of forehead might be called, and the skirts of his black coat fluttered out almost to the horses tail. Such was the appearance of Ichabod and his steed as they shambled out of the gate of Hans Van Ripper, and it was altogether such an apparition as is seldom to be met with in broad daylight.

It was, as I have said, a fine autumnal day; the sky was clear and serene, and nature wore that rich and golden livery which we always associate with the idea of abundance. The forests had put on their sober brown and yellow, while some trees of the tenderer kind had been nipped by the frosts into brilliant dyes of orange, purple, and scarlet. Streaming files of wild ducks began to make their appearance high in the air; the bark of the squirrel might be heard from the groves of beech and hickory-nuts, and the pensive whistle of the quail at intervals from the neighboring stubble field.

The small birds were taking their farewell banquets. In the fullness of their revelry, they fluttered, chirping and frolicking from bush to bush, and tree to tree, capricious from the very profusion and variety around them. There was the honest cock robin, the favorite game of stripling sportsmen, with its loud querulous note; and the twittering blackbirds flying in sable clouds; and the golden-winged woodpecker with his crimson crest, his broad black gorget, and splendid plumage; and the cedar bird, with its red-tipt wings and yellow-tipt tail and its little monteiro cap of feathers; and the blue jay, that noisy coxcomb, in his gay light blue coat and white underclothes, screaming and chattering, nodding and bobbing and bowing, and pretending to be on good terms with every songster of the grove.

As Ichabod jogged slowly on his way, his eye, ever open to every symptom of culinary abundance, ranged with delight over the treasures of jolly autumn. On all sides he beheld vast store of apples; some hanging in oppressive opulence on the trees; some gathered into baskets and barrels for the market; others heaped up in rich piles for the cider-press. Farther on he beheld great fields of Indian corn, with its golden ears peeping from their leafy coverts, and holding out the promise of cakes and hasty-pudding; and the yellow pumpkins lying beneath them, turning up their fair round bellies to the sun, and giving ample prospects of the most luxurious of pies; and anon he passed the fragrant buckwheat fields breathing the odor of the beehive, and as he beheld them, soft anticipations stole over his mind of dainty slapjacks, well buttered, and garnished with honey or treacle, by the delicate little dimpled hand of Katrina Van Tassel.

Thus feeding his mind with many sweet thoughts and "sugared suppositions," he journeyed along the sides of a range of hills which look out upon some of the goodliest scenes of the mighty Hudson. The sun gradually wheeled his broad disk down in the west. The wide bosom of the Tappan Zee lay motionless and glassy, excepting that here and there a gentle undulation waved and prolonged the blue shadow of the distant mountain.

A few amber clouds floated in the sky, without a breath of air to move them. The horizon was of a fine golden tint, changing gradually into a pure apple green, and from that into the deep blue of the mid-heaven. A slanting ray lingered on the woody crests of the precipices that overhung some parts of the river, giving greater depth to the dark gray and purple of their rocky sides. A sloop was loitering in the distance, dropping slowly down with the tide, her sail hanging uselessly against the mast; and as the reflection of the sky gleamed along the still water, it seemed as if the vessel was suspended in the air.

It was toward evening that Ichabod arrived at the castle of the Heer Van Tassel, which he found thronged with the pride and flower of the adjacent country. Old farmers, a spare leathern-faced race, in homespun coats and breeches, blue stockings, huge shoes, and magnificent pewter buckles. Their brisk, withered little dames, in close-crimped caps, long-waisted short gowns, homespun petticoats, with scissors and pincushions, and gay calico pockets hanging on the outside. Buxom lasses, almost as antiquated as their mothers, excepting where a straw hat, a fine ribbon, or perhaps a white frock, gave symptoms of city innovation. The sons, in short square-skirted coats, with rows of stupendous brass buttons, and their hair generally queued in the fashion of the times, especially if they could procure an eel-skin for the purpose, it being esteemed throughout the country as a potent nourisher and strengthener of the hair.

Brom Bones, however, was the hero of the scene, having come to the gathering on his favorite steed Daredevil, a creature, like himself, full of mettle and mischief, and which no one but himself could manage. He was, in fact, noted for preferring vicious animals, given to all kinds of tricks which kept the rider in constant risk of his neck, for he held a tractable, well-broken horse as unworthy of a lad of spirit.

Fain would I pause to dwell upon the world of charms that burst upon the enraptured gaze of my hero, as he entered the state parlor of Van Tassel's mansion. Not those of the bevy of buxom lasses, with their luxurious display of red and white; but the ample charms of a genuine Dutch country tea-table, in the sumptuous time of autumn. Such heaped up platters of cakes of various and almost indescribable kinds, known only to experienced Dutch housewives! There was the doughty doughnut, the tender oly koek, and the crisp and crumbling cruller; sweet cakes and short cakes, ginger cakes and honey cakes, and the whole family of cakes. And then there were apple pies, and peach pies, and pumpkin pies; besides slices of ham and smoked beef; and moreover delectable dishes of preserved plums, and peaches, and pears, and quinces; not to mention broiled shad and roasted chickens; together with bowls of milk and cream, all mingled higgledy-piggledy, pretty much as I have enumerated them, with the motherly teapot sending up its clouds of vapor from the midst—Heaven bless the mark! I want breath and time to discuss this banquet as it deserves, and am too eager to get on with my story. Happily, Ichabod Crane was not in so great a hurry as his historian, but did ample justice to every dainty.

He was a kind and thankful creature, whose heart dilated in proportion as his skin was filled with good cheer, and whose spirits rose with eating, as some men's do with drink. He could not help, too, rolling his large eyes round him as he ate, and chuckling with the possibility that he might one day be lord of all this scene of almost unimaginable luxury and splendor.

Old Baltus Van Tassel moved about among his guests with a face dilated with content and good humor, round and jolly as the harvest moon. His hospitable attentions were brief, but expressive, being confined to a shake of the hand, a slap on the shoulder, a loud laugh, and a pressing invitation to "fall to, and help themselves."

And now the sound of the music from the common room, or hall, summoned to the dance. The musician was an old gray-headed man, who had been the itinerant orchestra of the neighborhood for more than half a century. His instrument was as old and battered as himself. The greater part of the time he scraped on two or three strings, accompanying every movement of the bow with a motion of the head; bowing almost to the ground, and stamping with his foot whenever a fresh couple were to start.

Ichabod prided himself upon his dancing as much as upon his vocal powers. Not a limb, not a fibre about him was idle; and to have seen his loosely hung frame in full motion, and clattering about the room, you would have thought St. Vitus himself, that blessed patron of the dance, was figuring before you in person. He was the admiration of everyone; who, having gathered from the farm and the neighborhood, stood forming a pyramid of shining faces at every door and window, gazing with delight at the scene. How could he be otherwise than animated and joyous? The lady of his heart was his partner in the dance, and smiling graciously in reply to all his amorous oglings; while Brom Bones, sorely smitten with love and jealousy, sat brooding by himself in one corner.

When the dance was at an end, Ichabod was attracted to a knot of the sager folks, who, with Old Van Tassel, sat smoking at one end of the piazza, gossiping over former times, and drawing out long stories about the war. This neighborhood, at the time of which I am speaking, was one of those highly favored places which abound with chronicle and great men. The British and American line had run near it during the war; it had, therefore, been the scene of marauding and infested with refugees, cowboys, and all kinds of border chivalry. Just sufficient time had elapsed to enable each storyteller to dress up his tale with a little becoming fiction, and, in the indistinctness of his recollection, to make himself the hero of every exploit.

There was the story of Doffue Martling, a large blue-bearded Dutchman, who had nearly taken a British frigate with an old iron nine-pounder from a mud breastwork, only that his gun burst at the sixth discharge. And there was an old gentleman who shall be nameless, being too rich a mynheer to be lightly mentioned, who, in the battle of White Plains, being an excellent master of defence, parried a musket-ball with a small sword, insomuch that he absolutely felt it whiz round the blade, and glance off at the hilt; in proof of which he was ready at any time to show the sword, with the hilt a little bent. There were several more that had been equally great in the field, not one of whom but was persuaded that he had a considerable hand in bringing the war to a happy termination.

But all these were nothing to the tales of ghosts and apparitions that succeeded. The neighborhood is rich in legendary treasures of the kind. Local tales and superstitions thrive best in these sheltered, long-settled retreats; but are trampled under foot by the shifting throng that forms the population of most of our country places. Besides, there is no encouragement for ghosts in most of our villages, for they have scarcely had time to finish their first nap and turn themselves in their graves, before their surviving friends have travelled away from the neighborhood; so that when they turn out at night to walk their rounds, they have no acquaintance left to call upon. This is perhaps the reason why we so seldom hear of ghosts except in our long-established Dutch communities.

The immediate cause, however, of the prevalence of supernatural stories in these parts, was doubtless owing to the vicinity of Sleepy Hollow. There was a contagion in the very air that blew from that haunted region; it breathed forth an atmosphere of dreams and fancies infecting all the land. Several of the Sleepy Hollow people were present at Van Tassel's, and, as usual, were doling out their wild and wonderful legends. Many dismal tales were told about funeral trains, and mourning cries and wailings heard and seen about the great tree where the unfortunate Major André was taken, and which stood in the neighborhood. Some mention was made also of the woman in white, that haunted the dark glen at Raven Rock, and was often heard to shriek on winter nights before a storm, having perished there in the snow. The chief part of the stories, however, turned upon the favorite spectre of Sleepy Hollow, the Headless Horseman, who had been heard several times of late, patrolling the country; and, it was said, tethered his horse nightly among the graves in the churchyard.

The sequestered situation of this church seems always to have made it a favorite haunt of troubled spirits. It stands on a knoll, surrounded by locust-trees and lofty elms, from among which its decent, whitewashed walls shine modestly forth, like Christian purity beaming through the shades of retirement. A gentle slope descends from it to a silver sheet of water, bordered by high trees, between which, peeps may be caught at the blue hills of the

Hudson. To look upon its grass-grown yard, where the sunbeams seem to sleep so quietly, one would think that there at least the dead might rest in peace. On one side of the church extends a wide woody dell, along which raves a large brook among broken rocks and trunks of fallen trees. Over a deep black part of the stream, not far from the church, was formerly thrown a wooden bridge; the road that led to it, and the bridge itself, were thickly shaded by overhanging trees, which cast a gloom about it, even in the daytime; but occasioned a fearful darkness at night. Such was one of the favorite haunts of the Headless Horseman, and the place where he was most frequently encountered. The tale was told of old Brouwer, a most heretical disbeliever in ghosts, how he met the Horseman returning from his foray into Sleepy Hollow, and was obliged to get up behind him; how they galloped over bush and brake, over hill and swamp, until they reached the bridge; when the Horseman suddenly turned into a skeleton, threw old Brouwer into the brook, and sprang away over the tree-tops with a clap of thunder.

This story was immediately matched by a thrice marvellous adventure of Brom Bones, who made light of the Galloping Hessian as an arrant jockey. He affirmed that on returning one night from the neighboring village of Sing Sing, he had been overtaken by this midnight trooper; that he had offered to race with him for a bowl of punch, and should have won it too, for Daredevil beat the goblin horse all hollow, but just as they came to the church bridge, the Hessian bolted, and vanished in a flash of fire.

All these tales, told in that drowsy undertone with which men talk in the dark, the countenances of the listeners only now and then receiving a casual gleam from the glare of a pipe, sank deep in the mind of Ichabod. He repaid them in kind with large extracts from his invaluable author, Cotton Mather, and added many marvellous events that had taken place in his native State of Connecticut, and fearful sights which he had seen in his nightly walks about Sleepy Hollow.

The revel now gradually broke up. The old farmers gathered together their families in their wagons, and were heard for some time rattling along the hollow roads, and over the distant hills. Some of the damsels mounted on pillions behind their favorite swains, and their light-hearted laughter, mingling with the clatter of hoofs, echoed along the silent woodlands, sounding fainter and fainter, until they gradually died away—and the late scene of noise and frolic was all silent and deserted. Ichabod only lingered behind, according to the custom of country lovers, to have a tête-à-tête with the heiress; fully convinced that he was now on the high road to success. What passed at this interview I will not pretend to say, for in fact I do not know. Something, however, I fear me, must have gone wrong, for he certainly sallied forth, after no very great interval, with an air quite desolate and chapfallen. Oh, these women! these women! Could that girl have been playing off any of her coquettish tricks? Was her encouragement of the poor pedagogue all a mere sham to secure her conquest of his rival?

Heaven only knows, not I! Let it suffice to say, Ichabod stole forth with the air of one who had been sacking a henroost, rather than a fair lady's heart. Without looking to the right or left to notice the scene of rural wealth, on which he had so often gloated, he went straight to the stable, and with several hearty cuffs and kicks roused his steed most uncourteously from the comfortable quarters in which he was soundly sleeping, dreaming of mountains of corn and oats, and whole valleys of timothy and clover.

It was the very witching time of night that Ichabod, heavy-hearted and crestfallen, pursued his travels homewards, along the sides of the lofty hills which rise above Tarry Town, and which he had traversed so cheerily in the afternoon. The hour was as dismal as himself. Far below him, the Tappan Zee spread its dusky and indistinct waste of waters, with here and there the tall mast of a sloop, riding quietly at anchor under the land. In the dead hush of midnight, he could even hear the barking of the watchdog from the opposite shore of the Hudson; but it was so vague and faint as only to give an idea of his distance from this faithful companion of man. Now and then, too, the long-drawn crowing of a cock, accidentally awakened, would sound far, far off, from some farmhouse away among the hills—but it was like a dreaming sound in his ear. No signs of life occurred near him, but occasionally the melancholy chirp of a cricket, or perhaps the guttural twang of a bullfrog from a neighboring marsh, as if sleeping uncomfortably and turning suddenly in his bed.

All the stories of ghosts and goblins that he had heard in the afternoon now came crowding upon his recollection. The night grew darker and darker; the stars seemed to sink deeper in the sky, and driving clouds occasionally hid them from his sight. He had never felt so lonely and dismal. He was, moreover, approaching the very place where many of the scenes of the ghost stories had been laid. In the centre of the road stood an enormous tulip-tree, which towered like a giant above all the other trees of the neighborhood, and formed a kind of landmark. Its limbs were gnarled and fantastic, large enough to form trunks for ordinary trees, twisting down almost to the earth, and rising again into the air. It was connected with the tragical story of the unfortunate André, who had been taken prisoner hard by; and was universally known by the name of Major André's tree. The common people regarded it with a mixture of respect and superstition, partly out of sympathy for the fate of its ill-starred namesake, and partly from the tales of strange sights, and doleful lamentations, told concerning it.

As Ichabod approached this fearful tree, he began to whistle; he thought his whistle was answered; it was but a blast sweeping sharply through the dry branches. As he approached a little nearer, he thought he saw something white, hanging in the midst of the tree: he paused and ceased whistling but, on looking more narrowly, perceived that it was a place where the tree had been scathed by lightning, and the white wood laid bare. Suddenly he heard a groan—his teeth chattered, and his knees smote against the saddle: it was but the rubbing of one huge bough upon another, as they were swayed about by the breeze. He passed the tree in safety, but new perils lay before him.

About two hundred yards from the tree, a small brook crossed the road, and ran into a marshy and thickly-wooded glen, known by the name of Wiley's Swamp. A few rough logs, laid side by side, served for a bridge over this stream. On that side of the road where the brook entered the wood, a group of oaks and chestnuts, matted thick with wild grape-vines, threw a cavernous gloom over it. To pass this bridge was the severest trial. It was at this identical spot that the unfortunate André was captured, and under the covert of those chestnuts and vines were the sturdy yeomen concealed who surprised him. This has ever since been considered a haunted stream, and fearful are the feelings of the schoolboy who has to pass it alone after dark.

As he approached the stream, his heart began to thump; he summoned up, however, all his resolution, gave his horse half a score of kicks in the ribs, and attempted to dash briskly across the bridge; but instead of starting forward, the perverse old animal made a lateral movement, and ran broadside against the fence. Ichabod, whose fears increased with the delay, jerked the reins on the other side, and kicked lustily with the contrary foot: it was all in vain; his steed started, it is true, but it was only to plunge to the opposite side of the road into a thicket of brambles and alder bushes. The schoolmaster now bestowed both whip and heel upon the starveling ribs of old Gunpowder, who dashed forward, snuffling and snorting, but came to a stand just by the bridge, with a suddenness that had nearly sent his rider sprawling over his head. Just at this moment, a plashy tramp by the side of the bridge caught the sensitive ear of Ichabod. In the dark shadow of the grove, on the margin of the brook, he beheld something huge, misshapen and towering. It stirred not, but seemed gathered up in the gloom, like some gigantic monster ready to spring upon the traveller.

The hair of the affrighted pedagogue rose upon his head with terror. What was to be done? To turn and fly was now too late; and besides, what chance was there of escaping ghost or goblin, if such it was, which could ride upon the wings of the wind? Summoning up, therefore, a show of courage, he demanded in stammering accents, "Who are you?" He received no reply. He repeated his demand in a still more agitated voice. Still, there was no answer. Once more he cudgelled the sides of the inflexible Gunpowder, and, shutting his eyes, broke forth with involuntary fervor into a psalm tune. Just then the shadowy object of alarm put itself in motion, and with a scramble and a bound stood at once in the middle of the road. Though the night was dark and dismal, yet the form of the unknown might now in some degree be ascertained. He appeared to be a horseman of large dimensions, and mounted on a black horse of powerful frame. He made no offer of molestation or sociability, but kept aloof on one side of the road, jogging along on the blind side of old Gunpowder, who had now got over his fright and waywardness.

Ichabod, who had no relish for this strange midnight companion, and bethought himself of the adventure of Brom Bones with the Galloping Hessian, now quickened his steed in hopes of leaving him behind. The stranger, however, quickened his horse to an equal pace. Ichabod pulled up, and fell into a walk, thinking to lag behind—the other did the same. His heart began to sink within him; he endeavored to resume his psalm tune, but his parched tongue clove to the roof of his mouth, and he could not utter a stave. There was something in the moody and dogged silence of this pertinacious companion that was mysterious and appalling. It was soon fearfully accounted for. On mounting a rising ground, which brought the figure of his fellow-traveller in relief against the sky, gigantic in height, and muffled in a cloak, Ichabod was horror-struck on perceiving that he was headless!— but his horror was still more increased on observing that the head, which should have rested on his shoulders, was carried before him on the pommel of his saddle! His terror rose to desperation; he rained a shower of kicks and blows upon Gunpowder, hoping by a sudden movement to give his companion the slip; but the spectre started full jump with him. Away, then, they dashed through thick and thin; stones flying and sparks flashing at every bound.

Ichabod's flimsy garments fluttered in the air, as he stretched his long lank body away over his horse's head, in the eagerness of his flight. They had now reached the road which turns off to Sleepy Hollow; but Gunpowder, who seemed possessed with a demon, instead of keeping up it, made an opposite turn, and plunged headlong downhill to the left. This road leads through a sandy hollow shaded by trees for about a quarter of a mile, where it crosses the bridge famous in goblin story; and just beyond swells the green knoll on which stands the whitewashed church.

As yet the panic of the steed had given his unskillful rider an apparent advantage in the chase, but just as he had got half way through the hollow, the girths of the saddle gave way, and he felt it slipping from under him. He seized it by the pommel, and endeavored to hold it firm, but in vain; and had just time to save himself by clasping old Gunpowder round the neck, when the saddle fell to the earth, and he heard it trampled under foot by his pursuer. For a moment the terror of Hans Van Ripper's wrath passed across his mind—for it was his Sunday saddle but this was no time for petty fears; the goblin was hard on his haunches; and (unskillful rider that he was!) he had much ado to maintain his seat; sometimes slipping on one side, sometimes on another, and sometimes jolted on the high ridge of his horse's backbone, with a violence that he verily feared would cleave him asunder.

An opening in the trees now cheered him with the hopes that the church bridge was at hand. The wavering reflection of a silver star in the bosom of the brook told him that he was not mistaken. He saw the walls of the church dimly glaring under the trees beyond. He recollected the place where Brom Bones's ghostly competitor had disappeared. "If I can but reach that bridge," thought Ichabod, "I am safe." Just then he heard the black steed panting and blowing close behind him; he even fancied that he felt his hot breath. Another convulsive kick in the ribs, and old Gunpowder sprang upon the bridge; he thundered over the resounding planks; he gained the opposite side; and now Ichabod cast a look behind to see if his pursuer should vanish, according to rule, in a flash of fire and brimstone. Just then he saw the goblin rising in his stirrups, and in the very act of hurling his head at him. Ichabod endeavored to dodge the horrible missile, but too late. It encountered his cranium with a tremendous crash,—he was tumbled headlong into the dust, and Gunpowder, the black steed, and the goblin rider, passed by like a whirlwind.

The next morning the old horse was found without his saddle, and with the bridle under his feet, soberly cropping the grass at his master's gate. Ichabod did not make his appearance at breakfast; dinner—hour came, but no Ichabod. The boys assembled at the schoolhouse, and strolled idly about the banks of the brook; but no schoolmaster. Hans Van Ripper now began to feel some uneasiness about the fate of poor Ichabod, and his saddle. An inquiry was set on foot, and after diligent investigation they came upon his traces. In one part of the road leading to the church was found the saddle trampled in the dirt; the tracks of horses' hoofs deeply dented in the road, and evidently at furious speed, were traced to the bridge, beyond which, on the bank of a broad part of the brook, where the water ran deep and black, was found the hat of the unfortunate Ichabod, and close beside it a shattered pumpkin.

The brook was searched, but the body of the schoolmaster was not to be discovered. Hans Van Ripper as executor of his estate, examined the bundle which contained all his worldly effects. They consisted of two shirts and a half; two stocks for the neck; a pair or two of worsted stockings; an old pair of corduroy small-clothes; a rusty razor; a book of psalm tunes full of dog's-ears; and a broken pitch-pipe. As to the books and furniture of the schoolhouse, they belonged to the community, excepting Cotton Mather's "History of Witchcraft," a "New England Almanac," and a book of dreams and fortune-telling; in which last was a sheet of foolscap much scribbled and blotted in several fruitless attempts to make a copy of verses in honor of the heiress of Van Tassel. These magic books and the poetic scrawl were forthwith consigned to the flames by Hans Van Ripper; who, from that time forward, determined to send his children no more to school, observing that he never knew any good come of this same reading and writing. Whatever money the schoolmaster possessed, and he had received his quarter's pay but a day or two before, he must have had about his person at the time of his disappearance.

The mysterious event caused much speculation at the church on the following Sunday. Knots of gazers and gossips were collected in the churchyard, at the bridge, and at the spot where the hat and pumpkin had been found. The stories of Brouwer, of Bones, and a whole budget of others were called to mind; and when they had diligently considered them all, and compared them with the symptoms of the present case, they shook their heads, and came to the conclusion that Ichabod had been carried off by the Galloping Hessian. As he was a bachelor, and in nobody's debt, nobody troubled his head any more about him; the school was removed to a different quarter of the hollow, and another pedagogue reigned in his stead.

It is true, an old farmer, who had been down to New York on a visit several years after, and from whom this account of the ghostly adventure was received, brought home the intelligence that Ichabod Crane was still alive; that he had left the neighborhood partly through fear of the goblin and Hans Van Ripper, and partly in mortification at having been suddenly dismissed by the heiress; that he had changed his quarters to a distant part of the country; had kept school and studied law at the same time; had been admitted to the bar; turned politician; electioneered; written for the newspapers; and finally had been made a justice of the Ten Pound Court. Brom Bones, too, who, shortly after his rival's disappearance conducted the blooming Katrina in triumph to the altar, was observed to look exceedingly knowing whenever the story of Ichabod was related, and always burst into a hearty laugh at the mention of the pumpkin; which led some to suspect that he knew more about the matter than he chose to tell.

The old country wives, however, who are the best judges of these matters, maintain to this day that Ichabod was spirited away by supernatural means; and it is a favorite story often told about the neighborhood round the winter evening fire. The bridge became more than ever an object of superstitious awe; and that may be the reason why the road has been altered of late years, so as to approach the church by the border of the millpond. The schoolhouse being deserted soon fell to decay, and was reported to be haunted by the ghost of the unfortunate pedagogue and the plowboy, loitering homeward of a still summer evening, has often fancied his voice at a distance, chanting a melancholy psalm tune among the tranquil solitudes of Sleepy Hollow.

POSTSCRIPT

FOUND IN THE HANDWRITING OF MR. KNICKERBOCKER

The preceding tale is given almost in the precise words in which I heard it related at a Corporation meeting at the ancient city of Manhattoes, at which were present many of its sagest and most illustrious burghers. The narrator was a pleasant, shabby, gentlemanly old fellow, in pepper-and-salt clothes, with a sadly humourous face, and one whom I strongly suspected of being poor—he made such efforts to be entertaining. When his story was concluded, there was much laughter and approbation, particularly from two or three deputy aldermen, who had been asleep the greater part of the time. There was, however, one tall, dry-looking old gentleman, with beetling eyebrows, who maintained a grave and rather severe face throughout, now and then folding his arms, inclining his head, and looking down upon the floor, as if turning a doubt over in his mind. He was one of your wary men, who never laugh but upon good grounds—when they have reason and law on their side. When the mirth of the rest of the company had subsided, and silence was restored, he leaned one arm on the elbow of his chair, and sticking the other akimbo, demanded, with a slight, but exceedingly sage motion of the head, and contraction of the brow, what was the moral of the story, and what it went to prove?

The storyteller, who was just putting a glass of wine to his lips, as a refreshment after his toils, paused for a moment, looked at his inquirer with an air of infinite deference, and, lowering the glass slowly to the table, observed that the story was intended most logically to prove—"That there is no situation in life but has its advantages and pleasures—provided we will but take a joke as we find it: That, therefore, he that runs races with goblin troopers is likely to have rough riding of it. Ergo, for a country schoolmaster to be refused the hand of a Dutch heiress is a certain step to high preferment in the state."

The cautious old gentleman knit his brows tenfold closer after this explanation, being sorely puzzled by the ratiocination of the syllogism, while, methought, the one in pepper-and-salt eyed him with something of a triumphant leer. At length he observed that all this was very well, but still he thought the story a little on the extravagant—there were one or two points on which he had his doubts.

"Faith, sir," replied the story-teller, "as to that matter, I don't believe one-half of it myself."

D. K.

Editorial Note

The stories in this collection were originally published in the following books and magazines. They are listed in order of appearance within the collection.

Part One: Ghost Stories Retold by S. E. Schlosser

1. **Dispatched**. S. E. Schlosser. *Spooky South Carolina*. Guilford, CT: Globe Pequot Press, 2011, p. 134.

2. **Bell Ringer**. S. E. Schlosser. *Spooky Georgia*. Guilford, CT: Globe Pequot Press, 2012, p. 48.

3. **Plucked**. S. E. Schlosser. *Spooky North Carolina*. Guilford, CT: Globe Pequot Press, 2009, p. 83.

4. The **Sausage Factory**. S. E. Schlosser. *Spooky New Orleans*. Guilford, CT: Globe Pequot Press, 2016, p. 41.

5. **Forty-Nine Beaus**. S. E. Schlosser. *Spooky New Orleans*. Guilford, CT: Globe Pequot Press, 2016, p. 135.

6. **The Mad Logger**. S. E. Schlosser. *Spooky Oregon*. Guilford, CT: Globe Pequot Press, 2009, p. 44.

7. **Sifty-Sifty-San**. S. E. Schlosser. *Spooky Texas*. Guilford, CT: Globe Pequot Press, 2008, p. 38.

8. **Get Out!** S. E. Schlosser. *Spooky Washington*. Guilford, CT: Globe Pequot Press, 2010, p. 74.

9. **One Last Head**. S. E. Schlosser. *Spooky Michigan*. Guilford, CT: Insiders' Guide, 2007, p. 74.

10. **The Miner**. S. E. Schlosser. *Spooky South Carolina*. Guilford, CT: Globe Pequot Press, 2011, p. 81.

11. **Heartbeat**. S. E. Schlosser. *Spooky Maryland*. Guilford, CT: Insiders' Guide, 2007, p. 138.

12. **Barn Dance**. S. E. Schlosser. *Spooky Wisconsin*. Guilford, CT: Globe Pequot Press, 2008, p. 75.

13. **Dark Presence**. S. E. Schlosser. *Spooky Yellowstone*. Guilford, CT: Globe Pequot Press, 2013, p. 88.

14. **Pray**. S. E. Schlosser. *Spooky Montana*. Guilford, CT: Globe Pequot Press, 2009, p. 70.

15. **I Know Moonrise**. S. E. Schlosser. *Spooky Georgia*. Guilford, CT: Globe Pequot Press, 2012, p. 74.

16. **The Handshake**. S. E. Schlosser. *Spooky North Carolina*. Guilford, CT: Globe Pequot Press, 2009, p. 45.

17. The **Wraith of the Creek**. S. E. Schlosser. *Spooky Michigan*. Guilford, CT: Insiders' Guide, 2007, p. 2.

18. **The Face**. S. E. Schlosser. *Spooky Indiana*. Guilford, CT: Globe Pequot Press, 2012, p. 56.

19. **Mary Whales**. Original title: **Bloody Mary Whales**. S. E. Schlosser. *Spooky Indiana*. Guilford, CT: Globe Pequot Press, 2012, p. 103.

Part Two: Dark Tales Retold by S. E. Schlosser

20. **Dance with the Devil**. Original title: **The Dance**. S. E. Schlosser. *Spooky Southwest*. Guilford, CT: Globe Pequot Press, 2004, p. 103.

21. **Morning Star**. S. E. Schlosser. *Spooky Pennsylvania*. Guilford, CT: Insiders' Guide, 2007, p. 125.

22. **Laughing Devil**. S. E. Schlosser. *Spooky Oregon*. Guilford, CT: Globe Pequot Press, 2009, p. 141.

23. **The New Neighbor**. S. E. Schlosser. *Spooky Oregon*. Guilford, CT: Globe Pequot Press, 2009, p. 178.

24. **White Wolf.** S. E. Schlosser. *Spooky Texas.* Guilford, CT: Globe Pequot Press, 2008, p. 74.

25. **Old Granny Tucker.** S. E. Schlosser. *Spooky Southwest.* Guilford, CT: Globe Pequot Press, 2004, p. 135.

26. **No Trespassing.** S. E. Schlosser. *Spooky Texas.* Guilford, CT: Globe Pequot Press, 2008, p. 128.

27. **Black Magic.** S. E. Schlosser. *Spooky Massachusetts.* Guilford, CT: Globe Pequot Press, 2008, p. 114.

28. The **Brick Wall.** S. E. Schlosser. *Spooky Massachusetts.* Guilford, CT: Globe Pequot Press, 2008, p. 134.

29. **Initiation.** S. E. Schlosser. *Spooky Florida.* Guilford, CT: Globe Pequot Press, 2010, p. 175.

30. **Shattered.** S. E. Schlosser. *Spooky Yellowstone.* Guilford, CT: Globe Pequot Press, 2013, p. 178.

31. **Rubberoo.** S. E. Schlosser. *Spooky Montana.* Guilford, CT: Globe Pequot Press, 2009, p. 128.

32. **Jack O'Lantern.** S. E. Schlosser. *Spooky Maryland.* Guilford, CT: Insiders' Guide, 2007, p. 145.

33. **Don't Turn on the Light.** S. E. Schlosser. *Spooky Maryland.* Guilford, CT: Insiders' Guide, 2007, p. 182.

34. Wendigo: Original title: **Deadly Hunter.** S. E. Schlosser. *Spooky Wisconsin.* Guilford, CT: Globe Pequot Press, 2008, p. 173.

35. **Bloody Mary.** S. E. Schlosser. *Spooky Pennsylvania.* Guilford, CT: Insiders' Guide, 2007, p. 98.

Part Three: S. E. Schlosser's Favorite Classic Horror Stories

36. **The Masque of the Red Death.** Poe, Edgar Allan, 1809–1849. *The Mask of the Red Death. A Fantasy.* (First printing). Philadelphia: Graham's Magazine, 1842, May (vol. XX, no. 5). Copyright

status/usage terms: Public domain in the USA. First published in 1842.

37. **The Trial for Murder**. Original title: **To Be Taken With a Grain of Salt**. Dickens, Charles, 1812-1870. *Charles Dickens's New Christmas story: Dr. Marigold's Prescriptions.* (First printing) New York: Harper & Brothers, Publishers, 1866. Copyright status/usage terms: Public domain in the USA. First published in 1866.

    Reprint version: Two Ghost Stories. I. The Trial for Murder. Dickens, Charles. *Christmas Stories. From "Household Words" and "All the Year Round."* London: Chapman & Hall, 1894. Copyright status/usage terms: Public domain in the USA.

38. **Dracula's Guest**. Stoker, Bram, 1847–1912. *Dracula's Guest and other Weird Tales.* (First printing) London: George Routledge & Sons, 1914. Copyright status/usage terms: Public domain in the USA. First published in 1914.

39. **The Robber Bridegroom**. Original: Grimm, Jacob, 1785–1863 und Grimm, Wilhelm, 1786–1859. *Kinder- und Hausmärchen.* Berlin: Realschulbuchhandlung, 1812 (vol. 1) und 1815 (vol. 2). Erstdruck (First printing). Copyright status/usage terms: Public domain in the USA. First published in 1812. **The Robber Bridegroom.** English translation: Grimm, Jacob, 1785–1863 and Grimm, Wilhelm, 1786–1859. Translator: Hunt, Alfred William, Mrs., 1831–1912. *Grimm's household tales with the author's notes.* London: G. Bell, 1884. Copyright status/usage terms: Public domain in the USA. Translation first published in 1884.

40. **The Legend of Sleepy Hollow**. Irving, Washington, 1783–1859. The *Sketch-Book of Geoffrey Crayon, Esq.* (First printing.) Paris: Baudry's European Library, 1836. Copyright status/usage terms: Public domain in the USA. First published in 1836.

About the Author

S. E. Schlosser has been telling stories since she was a child, when games of "let's pretend" quickly built themselves into full-length stories. She created and maintains the website AmericanFolklore .net, where she shares a wealth of stories from all fifty states, some dating back to the origins of America. She lives in Arizona.

About the Illustrator

Artist **Paul G. Hoffman** trained in painting and printmaking. His first extensive illustration work on assignment was in Egypt, drawing ancient wall reliefs for the University of Chicago. His work graces books of many genres—including children's titles, textbooks, short story collections, natural history volumes, and numerous cookbooks. For *Spookiest Campfire Stories*, he employed scratchboard technique and an active imagination.